SUCH A THING

The final part of The Long Lost Trilogy

PRAISE FOR CHRIS BRIDGE'S WRITING

'Suspenseful, poignant and funny.'
Helen Cadbury, author of *To Catch a Rabbit*

'This is an author who excels at hinting at the unsaid … whose contained and precise prose marches across the page.'
Anna Belfrage, review in *Historical Novel Society*

'The characterisation is skilfully done.'
Carole Bromley, author of *The Stonegate Devil*

'An exceptional debut … I await with anticipation how Chris Bridge follows this.'
John Fish, review in *The Last Word*

The Long Lost Trilogy

When Gary Goulden – entrepreneur, wealthy businessman and bully – dies, no one mourns him. His wife, Izzy, feels liberated, and is free to search for the child she gave up for adoption almost fifty years ago. His children emerge, blinking from under his shadow. They begin to rearrange their relationships with their mother, each other, their half-brother and themselves. Everything changes for each of them. THE LONG LOST TRILOGY – *Girl Without a Voice*, *Other Selves* and *Such a Thing* – explores sibling relationships against a background of the key issues facing Britain: fundamentalism, populism, and the battle between purity and pragmatism. If you want a long read with a sparkling plot, real characters, and a strong sense of time and place, this is it.

SUCH A THING

CHRIS BRIDGE

ISBN 978-1-800680-44-9

for Theo, Oscar, Mia and Max

1985

Prelude

It's dark and he is afraid.

All day he has walked the city, mesmerised by its life and its colour: the throngs of people, the bright shops, the tall buildings and stop-start traffic. In his heightened state he has moved to the pulse of the place and felt alive in the way that only a sixteen-year-old can. He has felt the blood in his arteries and the breeze on his skin. His ears have vibrated to the noises: sirens, cars, music from shop doorways, buskers, slogans. Support the Miners. Thatcher Out. *His tongue has salivated to chips and burgers, spices, perfumes, even to the dust and the petrol fumes. His fingers have wanted to reach out and touch every item of this brave new world and he has given way, picked up the slippery bars of coloured soap, run his hands along the racks of leather jackets, tapped on the plastic packets in Woolworths. He has endlessly taken up, read and put back the vinyl record covers that so attracted him.*

As the girls have.

He has seen girls before, but these are different. They wear clothes that show their shapes. They toss their heads and lipstick flashes in the sunshine. They totter on heels and there is nothing submissive or tentative about them. He has been fascinated by the girls.

Then the day dwindles and people go home. Without knowing where he's heading he moves away from the city centre and sees lit windows in houses with small gardens, catches glimpses of families behind the glass.

As he walks he tries to think it out. He's hungry and has no money. He's seen buskers in the city. They play or sing and people give them money. He's observed that people give surreptitiously. He's noticed the way they slide close to the collection box and slip a coin in quickly, then dart away. Only small children make a thing of giving, treat it as a challenge. They walk forward hesitantly, drop the coin, turn triumphantly and then run back.

He can sing. All he needs is a space with people nearby and a hat or something to collect the money in. So he makes his way back to the city centre.

He walks past the eating places, dithers about where to stand, gets moved on by people collecting for the miners and finally chooses his spot.

He stands outside a pub. It's dark and he is afraid. He can hear its liveliness. The people inside sound happy. When they come out he'll sing to them and they'll drop coins into the box and he'll be okay. He has a good voice. Everyone has always told him that.

He stands and he waits. He positions himself in front of the door, under the streetlight. He runs his fingers through his hair to tidy himself up. When they come out he'll start singing.

Not the kind of wonderful songs he's never heard before today. He'll sing hymns. He only knows hymns.

People begin to emerge. He stands up straight like he's been taught and begins.

They stop and stare.

'He's a bloody missionary.'

'I don't need converting.'

More people come out of the swing doors. He knows he needs a different song but he doesn't have any. He tries not to let his voice warble. Unless someone gives him some money he'll be hungry all night. He's fasted before, but always with an end point when a feast will be ready, never like this.

He reaches the end of the first hymn and starts What a friend we have in Jesus. *But Jesus isn't his friend anymore, and he clearly isn't their friend either.*

A girl sways forward, stares into his face. 'Who's a pretty boy?' she croons.

'Come back, Beth. You never know what you'll catch.'

Beth is broad with red lipstick, large breasts and cleavage. She turns to face the pub crowd. 'I could take him home, I could. Put him on the mantlepiece,' she tells them all.

Someone shouts, 'In your bed more like.'

'He's not that lucky,' she yells back, then she gives him another look, laughs and goes away. She's put nothing in the box.

Others come right up to him now and he feels hopeful. Then they put their faces close to his, surrounding him and daring him to sing on. He does just that.

'No,' one of them says, addressing the watchers and the cars in the car park. 'It sounds no better close up.'

Then someone pushes him in the back. He tries not to cannon into the person in front of him but he can't stop himself.

'Who you pushing?' The voice is all fake anger, looking for trouble.

'Sorry,' he says. 'I was pushed.'

Someone yells out, 'He fancies you. He's a pretty boy and he fancies you.'

He gives up on singing. He puts his hands up, tries to back away, but someone is close behind him and he's stuck. He looks round at the faces. There's nothing happy about them. The drink has made them sour.

They're hemming him in. It's as if they are waiting for something to happen.

Most people have already gone. The lights in the pub are out. The car park is empty. There's just this group round him and he can't get away. He feels hands on his back, then he's pushed so hard that he falls and finds himself on the floor with gravel in his mouth. Someone's kicking him in the ribs. Now they all join in. 'We don't like your sort,' one of them grunts, and aims at his face.

'Hey.'

The single word is shouted and the kicks stop. He opens his eyes and a huge man with black hair is pushing his attackers away. Although there is only one of him and several of them, his persecutors are leaving, sullenly moving off as if they are wary of this newcomer.

The big man stretches out a hand and helps him up.

He wants to cry but he won't. 'Thanks,' he says.

'Are you hungry?' the man asks.

He nods.

'Then come with me.'

He looks into the man's face. He expects to see kindness, but the eyes are telling him something different. From a safe distance one of the lads yells, 'Watch yourself, pal. We were only going to beat you up. He'll mess with your head.'

'And other parts of you.'

The laughter cackles in the darkness.

He wants to run away, but the man has a firm grip of his arm and he <u>is</u> hungry.

2019

I

Julia is standing on the narrow bridge in Ronda. She is not about to jump. There are, in Julia's mind, two sorts of people: those who jump and those who make others jump. She sees herself as belonging firmly and exclusively in the second category.

She's always been confident and bossy. She grew up barking orders at her younger siblings. She was the youngest child to be made a prefect in her school, and she graduated from a red brick university with enough qualifications to guarantee that she could, after an initial period of forced new employer humility, spend her working life instructing others. You might think her profession of Human Resources Officer puts her on the soft side of management, but in Julia's case that would be a mistake. Julia is in Human Resources in the same way that other people are in a bad temper or a minor war.

Julia is on her own, on holiday, doing the sights. She booked at the last minute. It's late May. She chose Spain because it would already be hot and she could do with some heat. Spain is beaches or sights. She's never seen the point of beaches so she's doing the sights. So far she has driven from the airport to Ronda, found the hotel, explained to the manager that the instructions for finding the hotel are less than helpful, ignored the red light as she drove into the underground car park, demanded a room away from the main street, got moved, unpacked, and come out for a walk. Her guidebook suggested the bridge, so here she is.

And the view is spectacular. A deep, narrow chasm divides Ronda. Way below her a thin river slips through the gap and heads for a heat-hazed plain. On either side, orange and white rock falls sheer. She can see and hear birds calling from the mid depths. The noise the birds make is a kind of metallic chuff. The rocks echo their calls, amplifying the sound. She watches them sweep from side to side of the gorge and notices they have red beaks. But what is most remarkable to Julia is the sheer drop beneath her feet. The space pulls at her. The stone bridge resists. She is standing where she has lived her life at the point of equilibrium, at the fulcrum of her own and, by implication, everyone else's world.

The bridge and the chasm it spans fascinate her. She wants to know more. If she has to go on a forced holiday she'll use the time to get better informed. The guidebook tells her that this bridge was built in the late eighteenth century, that it stands 130 metres above the river and that, during the Spanish Civil War prisoners were thrown off the bridge to their deaths. Julia looks down. It would be a certain death, she decides: everywhere she looks there are only rocks to break your fall. Then she sees that you can actually walk down there. She makes out tiny people at the bottom, standing on a small, flat patch of ground to the right of the river. How did they get there? Then she spots the paths. These used to be donkey tracks, her guidebook tells her. Residents went down to the fields to tend crops and walked all the way back up in the evening. Was that because the city was defended and the plains were not?

Julia looks down for so long she gets used to the height. She can see the way the spilled rope of a path makes its way to the place where the people are. It's clearly a good spot from which to photograph the bridge she's standing on. She might make her way down there tomorrow. She's here for two nights.

She straightens up and looks at Ronda's whitewashed houses. Some cling to the chasm edges while others scramble the low hills on either side as if heading for safety.

She crosses the chasm, leaves the bridge and steps back onto firm ground. Now 130 metres of solid rock supports her, which is ironic because only recently what has always been a solid foundation to her life has been pulled out from underneath her.

Suspended on full pay! She, Julia Goulden, the Human Resources Director herself, suspended on full pay pending investigation! The very thought of it makes her snort. She knows what suspended on full pay means. She's done it often enough to others. You only do that when you are certain the person is guilty but you can't yet prove it. You only take that step to give the accused person time to think and space to write a resignation letter. You only suspend someone when you have already calculated the severance cost.

She shakes her head as she might on waking from an unpleasant dream. But the charge has been made and she is suspended. Hence the unexpected holiday, hence the sudden interest in Moorish history. The things she's done for the Company! Meanwhile, they owe her a holiday and she's taking it.

After all, they won't be able to prove the accusation because the event complained about never happened, so she might as well have a holiday to fill the time until they exonerate her and beg her to come back to work.

It's seven in the evening and the sun is still warm. The light is immaculate. It sharpens the line between white walls and orange tiles. It glows on the polished cobbles. She should do some more exploring.

She leaves the bridge behind her. She hopes she doesn't look like a tourist. Her height marks her out, and the raised quiff at the front of her hair has always given her a Spanish look. When she walks she doesn't saunter. If the natural gait of a coyote is a lolloping trot, then Julia's natural gait is a long stride. The Victorians would have called it unladylike. In the 1980s it might have been labelled feminist. Now it seems purposeful, determined, and is deemed okay.

But in a tourist hotspot it is also uncompromising. Julia weaves her way through the sauntering throng, making no allowances. Unable to hide what she is really thinking at the best of times, her face shows profound irritation when a couple insist on holding hands and blocking the thoroughfare so that she has to swerve round them, only to nearly collide with a woman who suddenly stops in the middle of the street to point something out to her companion. Julia has no time for tourist shops and no time for unimportant details in the architecture. Her guidebook hasn't said anything about this street ergo there is nothing worth seeing until you reach the square at the far end. A young Asian girl is taking a selfie, just herself and the street. People who have noticed her are standing back and giving her room and time. Not Julia. She is conscious only of the gap in the crowd. She makes for it just as the girl manoeuvres the selfie stick into place and takes the picture. That photo is not destined for Instagram. It shows the girl and the street, but also Julia's out-of-focus face glaring back over her shoulder to see what all the tutting is about.

The square when she reaches it is empty. It's too early for the restaurants to open and the church is already closed. Julia snorts again, looks at her watch and walks on, only to find that she has run out of Ronda. The houses suddenly disappear and all the roads head downhill to the plain. There's nothing else to see. Between her hotel and where she now stands, ancient Ronda had been extoled in the guidebook as different, exotic and pristine. She allotted a whole day to it when she planned the trip, but now she seems to have run through it in little under an hour.

A mixture of post-flight weariness and loss of adrenalin hits her. She slows down but that isn't enough. Her body comes to a sudden full stop. It's as if her feet are stitched into the pavement and her legs are locked. Her right hand continues to hold onto the guidebook, but she doesn't think she could let go if she wanted to. Then her mind follows her body. Its usual mixture of disparagement, irritation and complaint about the state of the world, leaches away. She is suddenly bereft. Every part of her personality is abandoning her. Her memory goes AWOL, like a file misplaced on a computer. It's as if someone up there has pressed ctrl-alt-del on who she is and done it when nothing has been backed up.

She hears nothing, smells nothing. Her eyes are open but she sees nothing. She doesn't move. She's caught on Pause, waiting, and there's nothing she can do about it.

That terrifies her.

She doesn't know how long this state of suspended animation lasts but she becomes aware of movement. A man is walking into the square. He's wearing a Panama hat and walks with an easy swagger. His linen jacket is hooked across his shoulder. He is coming straight towards her. At the same time, she's aware that the restaurant doors are opening, that waiters are emerging carrying tables and chairs, cloths and cutlery.

The man is very close. He stops.

'Are you alright?' he asks.

She has to react now. She absolutely has to snap out of this and say something.

'Yes, perfectly alright.' As the words leave her mouth she drops the guide book.

He bends down and picks it up, wipes the dust off it but doesn't immediately hand it back to her or walk away as she'd like him to. He stays where he is.

'Only I saw you come to a full stop and wondered …' He leaves the sentence unfinished.

She relaxes. Bits of her scattered self are returning. Her legs feel as if they might obey her if she wanted to walk away.

'I'm okay,' she says.

And he looks at her as if to make sure. At first his look is a professional, almost medical check as if he wants reassurance that it is safe to leave her alone, but then the look changes. As she relaxes it becomes another kind of appraisal altogether before he smiles, hands her the guidebook back, shrugs his shoulders and walks away.

She watches him go and thinks, what's happening to me? I can move my legs again. I seem to be alright. She takes an inventory, declares the incident over. Then, as she slowly crosses the square, she remembers the look the stranger gave her and thinks, no one has looked at me like that for a very long time.

She goes to the restaurant and sits down without waiting to be invited. There are no menus. Not all the tables have yet been set out with cutlery and wine glasses. The staff are still scurrying to get everything ready.

She has no idea what happened to her back there but she is alright again. 'Waiter,' she calls, in her most commanding voice.

Two hours later, when Julia is ready to leave the restaurant, it's dark. Because Ronda is high up, and because it is only May, the air is now definitely chill. She felt that when finishing her wine and pulled her cardigan a little more tightly around her shoulders. Even though she's cold she studies the bill thoroughly, then pays and adds a generous tip. The food has been good, so she might come back tomorrow. If she does, she wants to be remembered.

The night is moonless. The sky is black, like paint in a tin. Streetlamps ruthlessly eliminate the stars, zapping light that has been travelling through the universe for millennia. She finds she is walking more slowly on the way back to the hotel. It's as if whatever happened to her earlier in the square is not entirely finished. She is conscious of placing her feet and of the way the cobbles have a tendency to unbalance her. When she reaches the Puente Nouevo she stops, stands in the same place on the bridge and looks down again. It may be a trick of being spotlit, but there is only space under her feet, no rocks, no river. On her level Ronda is brilliant. Above her head and beneath her feet there is only the emptiness of space. Between the two is this bridge, and her standing alone on it.

The bridge is warm to her touch, but she's shivering. If she leans against the stone she can feel warmer, so she does. There is something about being suspended between the two blacknesses that intrigues her, so she stays where she is, amused at her preoccupation with such trivia, feeling the warmth of the stone against her legs. As her eyes get accustomed to the darkness she can see movement in the air, but not from birds as it was earlier in the evening. This flight is different, jerky. Bats, she thinks. Looking up, she notices them around her. The lights pull in insects and the insects pull in the bats. She shakes her head. It must be the wine, she thinks, causing this mellowness.

She sets off again, back to the hotel.

× × ×

Martin listens to Beethoven String Quartet, Op 127. Its deep melancholy suits his mood. After the drama of the last few weeks he has fallen into something close to torpor. He's in his flat above the bookshop. He's on his own, not because Leah has rejected him, but out of respect for whatever she might be thinking about him. They nearly split up over the letters and the journal. Yes, he's been back to the Arts and Crafts house since. Yes, the row has been patched up, but they haven't really talked about what happened. He's never told her in detail about his trip to London and his meeting with the woman who is now the Prime Minister. Howard's reappearance has allowed them to resume all the uncertainties of their relationship, but nothing has been resolved between them.

He loves her, but which Leah does he love? He fears it might be the old Leah who has disappeared, that needy, silent girl who begged for his help when she had no one else to turn to. The new Leah speaks and argues and has strong views about love. The new Leah winces when he quotes from his beloved books. Worse still, the new Leah will soon be enormously rich. She lives in a house to die for, the kind of house he'd pay to visit. She is way out of his league.

But he has already spent too long in her Arts and Crafts house to give it up without regret. His flat and his bookshop, which were once all he wanted, now seem constrained and tatty by comparison. He loves the feel of Leah's house, its zest for life, its sheer beauty, the way the stained glass splashes colour on the tiled floor and the panelled walls, its sense of space. If he were there now he could fill it with this music. If he lived there permanently he could fill it with books.

A passage in the music enthrals Martin. It's as if the deaf Beethoven is searching for something light and hopeful which he gets close to but can never quite reach. He searches for it in the forest of the music, but it's like a bird flying through trees. He sees and loses it, then glimpses it again before the melancholy returns.

What do I want from life, Martin asks himself. Not much until I met Leah. I was content with my books and my music. I had built a life out of those two pleasures.

Martin notes the past tense in those sentences, conjured perhaps by the music. But then Leah appeared in his shop and silently seduced him. Later she came to him for safety, began to speak again and made demands. He was torn out of his world. There were suddenly real enemies and battles to be fought on her behalf. All that is behind them now. It's as if he's back in his comfort zone but no longer comfortable there. In the words of John Donne, he is *ruined and rebegot*.

The music gets stuck as Beethoven abandons melody in favour of a series of notes played on a double bass. That's what he loves about this music: its unpredictability, its no longer being bound by conventions. But he's had enough of its sadness and quite enough of his own company. If he could sleep in a separate room from himself, he would.

Aware of the need to be polite, he waits until the music reaches a pause before switching it off. He hates to offend anyone, even the spirit of a long-dead genius like Beethoven.

The room fills with silence. He could phone Leah, have a chat, find out how the land lies, but there are so many reasons why he shouldn't do that. Instead he switches the light off in the lounge and takes himself to bed.

× × ×

In the middle of the night Julia wakes. Her sense of anger and of outrage is back. How dare they? How dare he? That little boy she'd had to discipline for shoddy work, how dare he accuse her of sexual harassment? Harass him! Fondle him! Reach down for … Her single status turned against her. To be painted as a needy, sex-starved older woman; each of those adjectives a separate stab.

And the way he had reported it: bypassing the CEO and going straight to the Chair of the Board. Unheard of, unprecedented. But calculated. The new Chair of the Board, not the old one. All new Chairs need to establish their reputation for thoroughness. So instead of laughing the little twerp out of court he had actually called an emergency meeting of the Board and due process had set in. Two weeks' suspension in the first instance. To be renewed in two week instalments if required. Of course, in these cases the Chair would normally have consulted the Human Resources Director, but that was her, so they hadn't. She'd roast them for that when her chance came. She'd throw the procedures back in their faces, because she knew those procedures inside out. After all, she'd written them.

In the meantime she was not to have any contact with her accuser, not to have any contact with the Company. She was to wait by her phone for them to contact her. Fuck that, she'd thought, and booked this holiday. She has a mobile. They have her number. They have just about enough nous between them to be able to insert the Spanish dialling code. The regulations say she has to be available. Well, she is.

Her laptop has been taken from her. Her password into the firm's data base has been withdrawn. How the IT man, another of the little boys the Company is so fond of employing, must have loved that moment!

All of which means they have access to the details of her dealings with her accuser and she doesn't. Is the IT man in cahoots? Can they alter her records?

Julia leaps out of bed. Her memory is excellent. She'll write an account now, write it on sheets of hotel notepaper. She'll get all the details down clearly and precisely. It will be the next best thing to a contemporaneous account. That should sink him. It's a fight to the work-death between them. When she wins, her accuser will have to resign.

She writes for over an hour until she has it all recorded. The pad of paper is almost used up and dawn has arrived. She reads through what she has written, makes small adjustments, numbers and stacks the pages, then places them carefully in her suitcase. Making sure she's decent she opens the curtains. Last night her hotel window had looked out across the bullring to the plain and south to the sea at Málaga. She remembers a view of buildings and forests, of a twisting road and then the heat haze that made it impossible to see the Mediterranean.

When she pulls back the curtains this morning the bullring is still there, Ronda is still there, but the rest of the world has vanished. A sea of mist fills the valley, nestling precisely to the rim of the cliffs, curling just under the bridge. The light of a rising sun flecks it with gold and yellow. A young couple stand holding hands at the very edge of the abyss. The fog is a carpet they might step onto and walk across if this were a Disney film.

Julia watches the couple: two dark figures against the resplendent fog. Is this a beginning for them? Is this a moment they will always remember? Are there, perhaps – perish the thought – other things than work to live for?

Julia dresses and joins the small crowd of people who have emptied from the town's hotels and guest houses to gather at the cliff edge and capture the sight. It is, she thinks, a kind of choreographed routine: head towards fog, walking quickly in case it disappears; fish phone out of back pocket as you go; take a photo – check; take another photo – check; look around for a better angle, take a third photo – check; turn your back on the fog, take a selfie – check; compare photos with partner; walk back to breakfast.

Is she the only one who has come just to look?

× × ×

Martin has slept badly and woken early. The curtains in his bedroom are too thin. They exclude neither the streetlamp light of night nor the early sunrise of a summer morning. In front of him he has an entirely predictable day: breakfast, open the shop, lunch, close the shop at 5pm, a meal and some more music. If trade is bad he may speak to no one all day. For a moment he wonders what difference it would make if the bookshop stayed closed, but he quickly shakes himself, showers, and settles down to sorting his recent acquisitions.

The post comes early. He can see the door from where he is sitting. He glances across, expecting circulars or invoices. A single card in a crisp white envelope is lying on the mat. Intrigued, he wanders over and picks it up.

The typed address gives no clue. It'll be a posh advert, he tells himself; an invitation to visit the new retirement village perhaps, or a voucher for the Spa in the swanky hotel a few miles north of here. But if there is one thing Martin does know about, it is paper. He has always been alive to its thickness and texture. Show him any single page torn from a book and he can date it and even trace it to a single printing house. This envelope is too good for an advert. Its matt surface is lightly ridged. It feels exclusive. He slits it open and takes out the card.

At the top is a red embossed crest. The lion is turned towards him. The unicorn is in profile. Their bodies are a rich crimson red in contrast to the almost pink colour of the thin lines on the shield and on the crown. Below them is the motto he knows so well.

DIEU ET MON DROIT

Below the crest he reads:

The Prime Minister
requests the honour of the company of
Martin Stockdale
at a reception at 10 Downing Street, Whitehall
on Wednesday 23rd July from 6.30 to 8.00pm.
Dress: Lounge Suit

Then there are details about how to reply and a final note that this invitation is not transferable.

Thoughts rush through his head. Stella hasn't forgotten him. Stella Stelling has invited him to Downing Street. How did she trace him? Of course, he had to give details before she would meet him. He hasn't a lounge suit that will do for this occasion. Can he tell Leah, and what exactly will he tell her? Perhaps he should decline. To step through that door. Not knowing where he stands with Leah means he doesn't have to tell her anything.

Suddenly he feels hungry. It's time for breakfast.

2

After breakfast Julia picks up her guidebook and sets out to explore. Do the ruined Turkish baths first, she tells herself. She heads out across the bridge and takes the slanting cobbled street which, as the descent steepens, segues into steps. She trots quickly down these, passing other people. The old baths are dull. She is in and out in five minutes. The gardens hold her for a little longer. She hadn't realised how low down she is, almost at river level. She can see the point of the building: wallow in the baths, then walk in the gardens. Okay, what's next?

She turns right and follows a path that slants back up to the square she was in last night. The church, Iglesia del Espiritu Santo, is open, so Julia pays her money and walks in. At first she thinks the church is empty, but then she notices an old woman praying at the back of the nave. The woman is wearing a headscarf and her head is bent in supplication. Her lips are moving but no sound emerges. It seems indecent to watch her closely, so Julia turns towards the altar. She spots another woman praying on her own, and then another, deep in the shadows of a side chapel. Three women, all of a similar age. Her age.

No men. Until the priest comes quickly into the church, crosses himself and moves towards the altar. But then he sees Julia and walks towards her instead. He starts talking in Spanish. Julia doesn't do Spanish, so she listens politely, but when the priest pauses he spreads his arms as if welcoming her to the church. When he touches her shoulder by way of a blessing she is appalled and steps back. Who does he think I am, she wonders to herself. One of the lost women who come singly to pray? One of his old women?

The priest is young and ashamed of his gesture. 'Turista?' he enquires.

Julia understands the mistake he's made. She has no hat, no camera, she's plainly and smartly dressed, and she's holding the guidebook to her chest with both hands so it is covered. She holds the book out now, lets the man see the photograph of Cordoba on the cover. 'I'm a tourist,' she adds, quite unnecessarily.

He nods, smiles, gestures to the whole church and walks away.

Julia abandons her visit and steps outside, out of the gloom of the interior and back into the sunshine. I am not a sad old woman, she says to herself. How dare he?

'But I am lonely.' The words come from nowhere. Julia is quite certain that wasn't what she was thinking about. She hates anything maudlin and abjures self-pity. In spite of all this, the words came and spoke themselves and she has to admit there is a truth in them. She is not just alone. She is lonely. And the lack of work, the eating dinner alone in the restaurant last night, that strange episode in the square, the not being permanently exhausted: all these things she finds unsettling. Perhaps most unsettling of all was the admiring look that man gave her yesterday evening, that quick appraisal of her and the smile that followed.

I'm over forty, she reminds herself. Those days are past.

She turns, exits the square on the left hand side and works her way around the wall. She's looking for one of the paths down that she noticed last night. In the corner of the square she finds steps that seem to be heading where she wants to go. She follows the steps, quickening her pace, almost bounding down the mountainside. No, she doesn't want to buy iced water. No, she has postcards.

The path winds and is dusty underfoot. It goes close to the edge where some of the rocks are polished. It wouldn't do to fall.

Then she reaches a kind of platform. Up above her is the Puente Nuevo, the new bridge she crossed last night, with its three arches at the top and one midway. From her new vantage point she can see that the cut stone and the natural rock are both the same colour, so it's difficult to spot where the construction begins and the natural rock ends.

'Please.' A young man is offering her his mobile phone. He gestures to the girl he's with. 'Would you?'

'If I must. What do I press?'

He shows her, then goes to pose with the girl. They don't look at the camera but at each other. It's rather touching: two dark haired young Spaniards looking into each other's faces with the same dark eyes, and behind them the soaring bridge and the rock wall.

Julia takes the photo. The couple relax their pose, take the camera back, check the picture and are effusive in their thanks.

As she walks more slowly back up the hill she thinks about her family. She remembers Dad's funeral. She gave the address. She was in charge, and when James challenged her authority she simply slapped him down. Leah was silent and could be discounted as a rival. Danny was obsessed with fitness and spoke little. Then Patrick swept into their lives and everything changed. Suddenly Leah was more in charge than she was and Martin, Leah's young man, knew more about the conflict with the Church of the Living Saints than she did. In the week before Patrick's death, she found her status had diminished to the point where she was being given orders by Leah and sent off to carry them out. Then Patrick died and Danny disappeared. James came within a whisker of being the Prime Minister's Chief of Staff. She remembers the shock of seeing him on the news, in the background, looking important and triumphant. Can things go back to how they were before Patrick? She rather doubts it. As soon as the Goulden Trading Company is sold and the money distributed she will have nothing to contribute to her family and, should she lose the harassment case, no work to go back to.

The hill is steep but she won't allow herself to pause. She's determined to reach the top without stopping.

When Julia gets back to the square she stands and reads her guidebook while she gets her breath back. The bullring doesn't interest her. There is the Mondragon Palace still to visit and really that's it for Ronda. She looks at her watch. It's only 11 o'clock.

× × ×

Leah is standing in the hallway of their Arts and Crafts home. She's facing the front door which is open. Through it she can see the gravel drive bathed in May sunlight. The lilacs her dad planted are about to flower. Her mother, Izzy, is framed in the doorway. She's turned towards her daughter and is looking older, even with the light behind her. Izzy's face is now lined with grief but driven by an eagerness to be gone. Leah looks at her mother and worries for her. There is something wild and manic about her these days.

'I'm going into York myself later today,' Leah says. Her voice sounds patient. It carries in it no hope that her mother will listen. 'We can go together. I can help you search.'

Izzy has her car keys in her hand. 'He's out there somewhere,' she says. 'He can't find me so I have to find him.'

Leah tries again. 'If you wait until after lunch you can give me a lift. I have to be at the Job Centre for my two thirty appointment.'

'I have to go now and find him,' Izzy says. 'He's out there somewhere and he's alive. I've always been wrong about him. First I thought Patrick from the cult was the son I gave up for adoption and I was so happy to find him. Then he turned into a monster and I blamed myself. Last March that Patrick died. My son, the real Patrick, is out there somewhere. I feel as if I've been given another chance and I just have to find him.' She aims the key fob in the direction of her car, presses and the lights respond. 'I've got to go now. I may see you later.'

The older woman turns and scurries to her car. The younger woman watches and shouts, 'Good luck,' then turns and goes back into the house.

Leah sighs as she goes towards the warmth of the kitchen and notices that the bowl for spare change is empty. She knows Izzy will have scooped the money up and filled one of her pockets. If she is going to spend the whole day interviewing the homeless she will need lots of change. Leah picks up her coffee, takes a sip, winces and decides to make a fresh cup.

The search is hopeless. Leah knows that. Izzy's real son walked out of the Church of the Living Saints after a particularly severe punishment beating when he was sixteen. If he's still alive he'll be fifty. Izzy called her baby Patrick. That was the name on his birth certificate, but he was probably adopted within the Church and his name might have been changed by his new parents. It might have changed again when he left the Church. Thirty years is a long time. People travel. People emigrate. He could be anyone and he could be anywhere.

Or dead. That is a real possibility. When he ran away he had no knowledge of the world outside the cult he was brought up in. Did he succumb to drugs and alcohol? Did he die of Aids? If he's lived on the streets for more than thirty years he'll look much older than fifty.

They've been to the police, but records from thirty-four years ago have never been transferred to computer. Paper files from that period are archived in enormous warehouses. Her half-brother walked out of the cult into the city of Leeds and vanished in 1985. Finding any record of him when they haven't even got a certain name is impossible. The police were sympathetic but shook their heads. When Izzy persisted they told her about manpower and resources, told her to give up and concentrate on finding Danny.

Leah takes her coffee to the table and sits there to drink it. The sun is shining outside. It's 9.30am and she's still in her pyjamas.

Today is an important day. She's going back to the Job Centre. She must find paid employment and have the structure of work. This time she'll take any job they offer. Izzy no longer needs her, and Leah needs activity and routine. She can't live her mother's life for her. She has to live her own.

× × ×

Izzy parks in the Tower car park and makes straight for Coney Street, but right outside the Regimental Museum she finds her first rough sleeper. He's wearing a heavy wool coat and a beanie. His face is bearded and either too sunburnt or dirty or a mixture of the two. He looks spaced, as if he has emptied his head and sent his mind off somewhere else to be happy. His legs are stuck inside a green sleeping bag.

Izzy stands in front of him and waits for him to notice her, but he doesn't. She digs in her coat pocket for loose change.

'Excuse me.'

His head turns slowly towards her. Now she can see his whole face she knows he will be no help, but she has to start somewhere. 'I'm looking for my son,' she explains. 'He disappeared years ago. I suspect he's homeless and I want to find him.'

'Name?' he asks.

'Patrick.'

He sits and thinks. 'I don't know a Patrick,' he says, and turns away.

'Perhaps you can still help me,' she persists, and holds out the money. 'I want to talk to someone who was sleeping rough in the Leeds or York area thirty years ago.'

'Won't do you any good. He's either dead by now or he won't be able to remember.'

Izzy stands her ground. 'Well, who's the oldest round here then?'

The man looks at her and at the money in her hand.

'That'll be Dougie.'

The door of the museum opens and a young, uniformed soldier steps outside. Izzy thinks he can't be more than seventeen.

'On your way,' he says to the bearded man. 'We don't want your sort cluttering up the steps.'

'My sort! I was in the regiment. I've served.'

The young man clearly doesn't believe him. 'Where?'

'Bosnia, Kuwait, Afghanistan.'

'Never.'

The sleeper glares, then suddenly climbs out of his sleeping bag, stands and salutes.

The young soldier stares.

'Stare away, Sonny,' the sleeper says. 'I'm your future. I'm what you'll look like when they've finished with you.'

'Is it that bad?'

'I lost friends,' the man says. 'I saw stuff, the kind of stuff it's difficult to forget.'

'Stay there,' the young man says.

'I was intending to.'

The young soldier scoots back into the museum.

The bearded man in the overcoat picks up his sleeping bag and, moving surprisingly quickly, vanishes round the corner. Izzy follows.

'So you're not an ex member of the regiment,' she says.

'No, but the patter helps with the money and enough sleepers are ex soldiers.'

'Is Dougie real?'

She's still clutching the money.

He nods.

'And where can I find him?'

'He lives in a green tent. It's hidden under the wall behind one of the bushes at this end of Skeldergate Bridge.'

'Thanks.' She hands him the change.

× × ×

Leah approaches the Job Centre and walks in. Nothing has changed since her last visit. The same woman approaches her and asks her name. She's put into Mr Huyton's queue. The same GS4 men are standing round.

When it's her turn to walk forward she sees that Mr Huyton has remembered her. He grimaces, asks her name, then looks at the screen.

'They need asparagus pickers,' he tells her. 'It's seasonal work. Minimum wage. You have to provide your own clothing, wellingtons and gloves.'

She's ready to say yes to anything but waits in case there is something else.

'If you can stick the asparagus there's fruit picking later. I'd say you have a chance of stringing several jobs together until the summer ends. The growers are a tight knit group. If you work hard your name will be passed around.'

He looks at her. 'Last time you turned such work down. I have to warn you that if you turn this opportunity down you'll run out of options.'

'I'll take that if there's nothing else,' she assures him. 'I need to work.'

Mr Huyton studies his screen again. 'I remember you from last time. No qualifications, you said. No skills, you said, but good with people. If you want something indoors, something that might last longer than seasonal work, you could try care homes. They are always short of care workers and they don't always ask for qualifications. They'd train you.'

He studies her again. 'There's something about you they might take to.'

'Nursing?' she says.

'It's not nursing.' He decides to be brutal. He hasn't forgiven her for what she said to him last time. 'It's wiping bottoms and changing beds. It's lifting and carrying, feeding and clearing up afterwards. And all that on minimum wage.' He looks at her again. 'In case that isn't bad enough, it's anti-social hours, night shifts and weekends. Think you could cope?'

She hesitates.

'Oh, and there's no promotion. And no one values care workers, so you may end up just like I have.'

'I'm sorry I ever said that,' she tells him.

'Well, at least you're honest. Honesty is one of the key qualities care homes look for. Compassion and empathy are the other two. Does that sound like you?'

She nods. 'Have you a contact, an address?'

He prints the details out and hands them to her.

'Good luck.'

Leah nods and leaves, clutching her piece of paper. She walks to the bus stop and the bus is waiting.

The ride is all blossom. She looks out of the window at blocks of yellow rape, at pink blossom on the cherry trees, at white hawthorn hedges and yellow dandelions. The grass is a luxurious green. Even the oaks are breaking into pale green leaf. I'll be a care worker, she says to herself. I'll look after those who don't have many springs to come.

She gets off the bus and walks to Martin's bookshop.

She opens the door. The bell is broken and he hasn't repaired it, so she can walk in and look at him without him looking up. He's sitting in what she calls his throne, cataloguing, picking up books from a pile, pricing them and adding them to the list. He works slowly and diligently. What she sees is what she has always seen. He has an open face, pale because he doesn't spend much time outside. His tufts of brown hair are never quite under control. He's wearing an open-necked shirt, a winter-weight pullover and tatty jeans. His body is too soft to be really attractive, too soft because he does no exercise. She looks at his forehead. The tufted unmanageable hair has no grey in it, but it is already receding. She knows he will be bald one day.

She looks at him as she first looked at him, but he seems different now. They have been through too much together, so his hands will always be the hands that picked up the rock to kill the injured deer. His mouth will always have shouted at Danny that they mustn't take the law into their own hands. His eyes will always have been compassionate after the rape when she came to him and he didn't have to take her in, buy tulips, feed her and play her music.

She walks quietly towards him. When she is very close she examines the nape of his neck, sees he needs a haircut because hairs are growing down to his collar and covering the horizontal lines that are already there.

He is so absorbed in his work that he isn't aware of her presence, so she stretches out her hand and touches him on the shoulder.

Startled, he looks up. His eyes widen, then contract as if he is asking her a question. Their bed at home would be more comfortable but this might be fun, so she nods. He smiles and flicks her shoulder with his hand, which was always their signal. Quickly he locks the door and puts up the Back In Ten Minutes sign. He has temporarily forgotten about the invitation, and she has failed to notice the posh envelope.

She leads the way upstairs and he follows.

× × ×

Izzy is standing outside the green tent. She only spotted it from above. It's well hidden from the side now that the foliage is greening York, replacing spring openness with summer secrecy. She doesn't know what to do. How do you knock on a tent door? She thinks Dougie must be inside, but the traffic noise stops her hearing small sounds. She clears her throat and listens. Nothing.

She's come this far. There was no point if she doesn't keep trying.

'Dougie, Dougie are you in there?' Her voice sounds loud. It has to be loud enough to wake him, but what will strangers think of an old woman shouting at a tent door?

'Douglas, are you there? I need to talk to you.' That was as loud as she could manage. If he doesn't emerge now he never will.

She listens, spots the tent wall bulging and hears a cough, a long unpleasant clearing of the throat. Then a zip starts its slow unlocking. She digs her hand in her pocket and waits.

A smell emerges before the person. The smell is obnoxious, part toilet and part animal. Then a head pokes out. For a moment Izzy thinks she's been had. He doesn't look old enough, but men who sleep rough tend to look the same: bearded, unkempt, dark clothes, the beanie that clearly never leaves the head.

'What do you want?' His voice rasps as if there is an extra h in each word.

'Information. I'm looking for my son.' She holds out her hand.

She knows this works, even when they are stinking drunk. She's calculated that they all feel lost and dream of someone searching for them.

Dougie pulls himself out of the tent and she backs

away. She's learnt that too: always keep the money just out of reach.

'Tell me,' he says. He's far enough away not to grab the money but too close for her not to smell his breath.

'My son went missing in Leeds. He was tall with naturally blond hair. Do you know the Leeds scene?'

Dougie nods and the hope rises in her.

'I've been in Leeds. What were his name?'

'I called him Patrick. I don't know what other name he might have been using.'

'How long ago?'

'Thirty years.'

'Not a chance, lady. I were only nine, living in a house in a street on a hill that still had its cobbled road. Me mam were alive then. I didn't fall into this caper until I were gone twenty.'

Izzy clutches at the usual straws. 'And when you did go homeless, did you ever run into a man with blond hair who was a bit older than you? Someone who liked to sing?'

Dougie has lost interest in her now. She can see he's just waiting for the money.

'If you ask me, there's too many as can sing a bit. I likes to be quiet, that's why I'm here.' He points at the tent and the space.

'Think Dougie, please think. Did you ever run into a tall man with blond hair, just a little bit older than you are?'

He seems to respond to her desperation. 'Look lady, I don't really know. Them were my lost years.'

He stretches out his hand and she gives him the money. He takes it with a decent show of reluctance. 'I could lie to you lady, string you along so you'll come back, but I'm not like that, not like some.' The money has vanished into an inner pocket. He's turned and is climbing back into the tent.

Izzy pushes her way out through the shrubbery. She came close then. A gap of only seven years. She knows she'll carry on searching.

3

Danny finds himself in limbo.

Stella Stelling is now Prime Minister. He, Danny, made that happen. His information and photographs did for Jud Mindsett and ditched his clever brother, James. Michael had fed Danny his lost photos of the Borstov-Mindsett meeting and he, in turn, went to The Guardian. They wanted to use his name, but he insisted on being a *high placed source in the security services*. Only Michael and Stella know his identity. He'd love to tell James, but to his family he is the brother who disappeared.

By the time of The Guardian revelations, Jud had already won the leadership contest, but the margin was tight, just a few hundred votes. Crucially, Jud hadn't been to the Palace and kissed hands. This left him as the Party's chosen candidate but not yet the Prime Minister. Danny doesn't know the detail of what happened next, but suddenly Stella Stelling was standing at a lectern outside Number 10 Downing Street. The previous

Downing Street moggy must have been evicted because there, in the background of the shot, was the pampered cat he'd stroked when he went to see her.

It's ten days since all that happened and Danny's heard nothing from the new government. Should that surprise him? When he visited Stella Stelling she seemed genuine. 'I am grateful for your coming to see me. If I can ever do anything for you in the future…' she'd said. So she'd offered him a job, hadn't she? Michael had suggested he join her close protection team, but he'd turned that down because he wasn't ready to reappear. Perhaps that was his chance and he'd blown it.

So he's stuck. He's homeless, jobless, penniless and in danger. Jud Mindsett isn't the only one who will be pissed off at what he's done. Borstov must want him dead. Even Putin might have heard the details of how his plan to put another idiot in power in a western democracy crumbled because of a single, rogue operator. The Russian Federation know he was working for British Intelligence. They took his photograph, didn't they?

Then there's the matter of Harry. Harry employed him as a deep watcher, gave him instructions which he disobeyed. Was Harry working for a Mindsett government? Was Harry working on both sides? Harry gave him a flat and a salary. Harry knows exactly where and when the photographs published in The Guardian were taken. Harry will not think kindly of him. Danny presumes the flat is out of bounds and the salary terminated. That means he is back sleeping rough with nothing to show for his brush with great events.

Just when he needs him most, Ivor has disappeared. Danny has been to Ivor's drinking haunts, expecting the tall thin Russian to walk through the door at any moment and order a vodka. But Danny has ended up drinking alone and thinking disturbing thoughts. In all the contact they had before the election, in all that comradeship, Ivor made every move. It was always Ivor who found Danny, never the other way round. Most tellingly of all, Ivor gave him no way of contacting back, not a phone number, nor an address, nor the name of the place where he worked.

Danny lists his options. None of them is tempting. He could contact Harry, ask if he is still employed now that the election's over. Might he be able to convince Harry he had nothing to do with the leak to The Guardian? But Harry knows about the photographs. Harry almost certainly wiped them from his phone so he couldn't use them. It's not an option.

He can go back to his own house. On the table is a lottery ticket worth £2.5 million. There's still time to cash it in, open a new bank account in a new name, somehow get round the money laundering restrictions. At least then, if he gets a sniff that someone is looking for him, he has cash if he needs to disappear. At least then he can fund trips abroad, bribe his way across borders, give whichever branch of the Russian secret services might be after him, the FSB or the GRU, a good run for their money.

But that would risk reappearing, and he isn't ready for that. He left his old identity so that he could escape Dad's wealth, achieve something by himself, make a life that will surprise, preferably astonish, his family. To do that he has to have something to show them. As things stand, he has a story and nothing else. He hasn't achieved the permanent breakthrough that he craved and, until he has, he's not going home.

He could go back on the streets, find Shaun, pair up again. But he knows he doesn't belong on the streets.

Shaun knows it too. The others who sleep under the railway bridge were never convinced that he belonged with them either.

He walks the London streets while he weighs his options. He likes to walk beside water. Is that because it is as fluid as he feels? Often he finds himself standing on a bridge staring into the Thames and feeling its enormous weight moving under him. It's remorseless. It pulls at mooring posts, pushes back at the prows of boats moving upstream. In its grip it carries logs and sometimes whole trees. In wind its surface turns scaly. At high tide it licks along the walls that only just control it. At night it is at its most powerful. That is when he feels the way it tugs at the very city it intersects. The river's power attracts him.

Power attracts him. Danny knows that about himself now. When Ivor drank vodka to escape, Danny kept pace out of politeness. He doesn't like being drunk. Drugs don't attract him. Love and sex have never pulled him out of shape. He feels immune to these lesser temptations. He has even watched his body lose its tautness without regret. He's not a natural glutton.

But he does have an addiction. Now that he recognises it, he realises that he has been aware of it for a long time. The knife he held in his hand as he challenged Patrick, the baseball bat he weighed before his second charge, the thought of the photos on his phone as he travelled back from the West Highland Way, these were all clues. He enjoys danger. He wants to stay in the thick of things. The kind of influence he had in the Party election may never come again, but there might be lesser moments, equally satisfying.

His walking today has brought him to his old home. It already looks neglected. He can see the paint damage where they forced the door open. He notes the dust on the windows which he always kept clean. If they know about him they may well know about his house. But he sees no sign of watchers. He notes no cameras. He'll take the risk.

He goes round the back of the house and climbs the sycamore tree. He'll force a way in through the bathroom window. He spots footmarks on the tree. He suspects someone else has been up here. The window has been pushed closed, but the catch is broken. He sees the marks where an instrument was inserted to force entry.

Wary now, he slips in through the window and lands on the rim of the bath. He notices at once that the lavatory handle is missing. How odd. He listens. He doesn't think anyone is in the house. There are two sets of footprints in the dust on the bath. One for entry, one for exit. Nevertheless, he is cautious as he opens the bathroom door and goes downstairs.

Whoever has been in the house hasn't touched his documents or the lottery ticket. Danny checks the water has been left turned on, then runs a bath. He shaves slowly and painfully, getting rid of his street persona. He scrubs himself, then finds some of the clothes he left here. He dresses smartly. He does this automatically. The hand that reached for his suit and chose it out of all the clothes that were hanging there tells him he is not going back to the streets. He desperately needs a haircut. He'll fix that.

When he's ready he tidies the bathroom and looks at himself in the wardrobe mirror.

He expects to see the old Danny, but he doesn't. The man who stares back at him is slimmer. That doesn't surprise him. He knew he had lost muscle tone. What does surprise him is his face. It looks different and the difference isn't only that he's thinner in the cheeks. It's in the eyes. It's in the way he looks at himself. There's something about this new look that he recognises. It isn't frightened. It isn't wary. At first he calls it grown up, but he still isn't satisfied. He tries relaxing his face and smiling, but the look quickly returns. It's very focussed, almost cruel, and he remembers a photo of a hunting wolf, one that screamed of single mindedness and determination. Is that who I am now, he asks himself.

He lets himself out of the front door and slams it shut behind him. He ignores the pile of post. It will all be for the old Danny, not this Danny, so he never notices the posh envelope among the rest. The lottery ticket is still on the table.

As his hair is cut away, falling on the floor in great brown chunks, the wolf look becomes more prominent. The barber tries to engage him in conversation, but Danny is in no mood for that. In his former life he would have been happy to talk squats and lifts, all the chatter of those who work out. In his past life he might have kept a conversation going. Not today. He's monosyllabic and, when the barber gives up, Danny's content to watch a new version of himself being confirmed. His hair hasn't been this short for a long time. He looks like an executive, like a floor trader. He is intrigued and pleased.

None of which solves the problem of what he does next. He has lived two lives and abandoned both of them.

When he walks out of the barber's shop, the cold around his newly cut head is invigorating. He knows what he wants. He'll wait for a call from Michael. If the call doesn't come, he'll seek a meeting. Meanwhile, he heads for the river. He has money in his pocket. He suspects he'll fill in time by completing the West Highland Way. He stored his walking gear in left luggage and can easily redeem it.

× × ×

Two weeks ago James Goulden was a rising political star, credited with the brilliance of the campaign he had run on behalf of Jud Mindsett. The cartoonists had sharpened their pencils to do justice to James's trademark mass of dark hair in ringlets. Those who didn't know Jud Mindsett were attracted to James's self-confidence and flair. Those who did know Jud Mindsett for the self-serving incompetent he had always been, were in awe of James's ability to transform such an unlikely candidate into a potential Prime Minister. The country had noticed James. The world had begun to hear of him. Impossible-to-elect candidates everywhere in the democratic world had jotted his name down and discovered his phone number.

Jud had won by a whisker. Those who despised him had come crawling to James, hoping for Cabinet posts. James had felt the spine-stiffening, body-tingling effect of power. For a few hours he had stood at the centre of the political world. For those few hours he had become the man he always dreamed of being.

Then it all collapsed. Like going from gold medal winner to drugs cheat, from bishop to convicted child abuser, from dictator to being discovered hiding in a drain pipe, James's fall was spectacular. The television screens abandoned him. Journalists who scorned and then fawned now hound him. They camp outside his house, but the only questions they want to put are about the dirty tricks campaign he waged.

On the surface, Jud Mindsett seems to have fared better. Yes, Stella Stelling is Prime Minister, but at least Jud Mindsett has his old job back. This may seem like an act of forgiveness on Stella's part, but it's the opposite. Back as Junior Minister for Transport, Jud is faced with sorting out all the problems he caused. He has a contract to renegotiate with the rail company. He must persuade them to give up a clause they inserted stating that the tax payer would refund the company for days lost through strike action. Before he challenged Stella, his civil servants treated him with some respect and did his bidding. Since the débâcle they treat him with disdain. In the Commons he's shunned by those who only a few weeks ago were begging him for a job. He is a political pariah living in the isolation reserved for those who lie and are stupid enough to get caught out. His wife has left him for much the same reason. His mistress has developed other interests.

Jud has no further contact with his old college friend, James Goulden. James recalls Jud's last words to him: 'You always were a cocky sod, James. I had to make sure you were implicated.' James shook his head in disgust and walked out. They haven't spoken since, and Jud never paid James for the work he'd done. There will be no mending this breach.

After the débâcle James went home and hid, hid from the journalists waiting outside his front door, hid from his landline and from his mobile phone.

But he is unable to keep that up. Three days later, in a fit of self-pity, he phones Roz. Before she can say anything he tells her she was dead right about Jud, and he should have listened to her. She says three words only: 'But you didn't,' and ends the call. In exasperation James switches his own phone off again.

He knows he deserves that reaction. He knows he's finished as a serious player. He knows it wasn't entirely Jud's fault they lost. He even wonders if he would have been up to the job of Mindsett's Chief of Staff. He watches Stella Stelling on television and is intelligent enough to recognise that she is and always was a far better candidate. He tries to imagine a Mindsett premiership: his self-adulation, his laziness, his inability to make his mind up, his utter lack of any attention to detail, his need to constantly look over his shoulder to check if the Russians will allow his next move. It would have been a nightmare. And who would have been promoted to Cabinet posts if Ministers had to be neither as intelligent nor as competent as Jud himself? Even in his Party there would never have been enough suitable candidates to fill the spaces around the Cabinet table.

Then he considers the kind of events that can derail even the most adept of leaders: a cyber attack, an unexpected recession, even (heaven help the country with Mindsett in charge) a global pandemic. Could he have guided Jud though such an occurrence when he, James, had been outwitted by Jud in what will now go down in history as the Mindsett Treason?

It is better thus. It was right to lose. If they had lost narrowly but fairly he would have a future. To take a stupid man like Jud and nearly shoehorn him into Downing Street would have made him for life as a campaign manager. If that had been the story he would be in demand, but the way they lost, the ignominy of that revelation about Jud's meeting with Borstov, means that any candidate hiring James to manage their campaign would automatically drop ten percentage points, except perhaps in the United States or Brazil.

No, he is finished and will have to fish around for any kind of work. Who will hire him now? That *high placed source in the security services* has finished him off.

He waits until the journalists are no longer camped outside his door. Only then does he feel that it's safe to reconnect his phones. He still takes precautions. When he goes shopping for food and whisky he chooses the rainy days so he can hide his hair under a hood. That way he can pass unrecognised through the throng he once hoped would always know who he was.

After several days of complete silence his mobile rings. Now that he is as certain as he can be that the story has moved on he feels it's safe to answer, even though he doesn't recognise the number.

'James,' he says. If he had won, that would have been sufficient identification, but he needs to be a little more humble today. He'll identify himself in the normal way. 'James Goulden.'

The voice should have told him at once that this isn't going to be an opening he can possibly consider.

The accent is northern, the diction uneducated, the first question unnerving.

'Before we go any further, can I just check that you are white, and that your family has for at least four generations been entirely white?'

'Yes,' James says, wondering where this is going, but at least pleased to be talking to another human voice.

'Only on some of your television appearances you have looked, shall we say, a little tanned, and with that afro-inspired haircut of yours we did wonder.'

This is rock bottom. James knows he should slam the phone down, but what else does he have to do if he does, and who else will ever talk to him? So he answers the question. 'As far as I know, my family came over with the Anglo Saxons and have stuck to Anglo Saxon partners throughout the ages.'

The voice sounds worried. 'You say you came over. Does that mean your family were at one time immigrants?'

James takes a deep breath. 'The Anglo Saxons invaded this country after the Romans left and before the Normans arrived.' He adds, 'That's an awfully long time ago.'

'Invaders,' the voice says. 'That sounds much better that immigrants. I'm sure we can go with invaders. It sounds powerful and it sounds like a white thing to do.'

'So now we've got that sorted out, why have you phoned me?'

The next bit comes out in a rush and in a sing-song voice as if it's been rote-learned. 'We believe that the white race is under attack, that the once dominant white race will be extinguished within a few generations unless we act and act now. We are not racists. We hate racists. We have nothing against individual black persons of a certain skin colour, but we cannot accept the sheer volume of black people in this country unless, it goes without saying, they work for the NHS.'

James hears someone prompting in the background.

'Or care homes.'

'Right, I think I understand your position. How can I help?'

The voice changes. 'The trouble is that we are none of us the brightest cookie in the box and, in spite of the fact that we have a just cause, we keep saying the wrong things and come over as stupid. We need someone to put an acceptable face with good grammar on our organisation, then we can begin to make real progress.'

'What progress do you want to make?'

There's a silence. Then, 'Can you say that again?'

He'll put it more simply. 'What do you want to make

happen?' James asks.

'We want to create more all-white babies, so we want to encourage whites to marry whites.'

'How do you intend to do that?'

'Abolish love between the races.'

James speaks slowly to help the conversation along, but only succeeds in seeming patronising. 'Love,' he tells his interlocutor, 'isn't something you can legislate, that means pass laws about.'

'Why not?'

'It's a feeling. It's colour blind.'

There's a silence.

'Look,' says James, 'are you offering me a job?'

'Of course not. We have no money, but we felt that you were a kindred spirit, that if you were our spokesman we could become a force. We could then get funding for a real campaign, at which point we might be able to reimburse you.'

'I'm sorry,' James tells him, 'I need to earn and I need to earn now.'

'Then you're not the principled person we took you to be. We thought you were one of us, but in fact you're just a…'

James cuts off the caller and blocks the number. He's broke. Until the family firm is disposed of he has no money to live on. He subsides back into self-pity.

4

As James pours himself a whisky and Danny heads back to the river, Leah is approaching the care home. She too is dressed for the occasion. This is her first job interview and she doesn't want to mess it up.

On the bus journey she's thought about what to expect: decaying elderly people with all their bodily functions requiring assistance. She imagines them sinking deeper into forgetfulness, waiting for God to call them. Leah has had little dealing with the old. She never knew her grandparents. Is this the right thing for her?

It has to be. She's bored at home all day. Martin is back in the bookshop. Danny is still missing. Izzy is fully occupied searching for her son. It has become perfectly clear to Leah that she has to make a life for herself.

This could be a start. It's a small care home, only thirty beds. The home is by the river and next to the Priory. It's hidden from the road. Leah gets off the bus and rereads the instructions. She walks past the Priory and takes the first turn down a single track drive. The drive has her confused. It seems to be heading for the river and the flood plain. She can see no trace of a care home. She's hesitating, then she sees the sign *Care Needed, Elderly*. It must be down here after all.

On her right is a stone wall with several brick buttresses. In front of her is a beautiful sycamore tree, just in leaf so she can make out the huge skeleton of branches. Now she can see the home. Its frontage looks across the fields. It has an open view.

The house itself is old, built out of pale sandstone. She'd guess that it is Victorian. To the left of the front door is a carved urn that must be much older. Perhaps it belonged to the Priory. It looks more like a font than a planter. Now it spills pansies. A laburnum arches over the lawn in front of the home. It's in full flower, and the yellow petals echo the curve of its single stem. Her heart leaps. This might be an okay place to work. She rings the doorbell.

There's no reply, so she turns the handle and walks in. It doesn't smell of old people. She can see a lounge on her left with a circle of chairs. There must be a television on somewhere because she can hear commentary. In front of her is a room labelled Office. She knocks on this door and waits. In the silence she hears nothing to disturb her.

It's a big moment for her. This is a step she thought she might never take. Mr Huyton tried to put her off, but she wrote her application and has been called for interview.

The door opens, revealing a somewhat cramped space with three computer stations visible. There are shelves with files and boxes of supplies. Several coloured folders have room numbers on their spines.

A tall lady with jet black hair, neatly parted along a central line, is standing there. She's plump and her face is friendly, if somewhat harassed. She's wearing black leggings and a pale blue top. 'Leah Goulden?' she enquires.

'That's me.'

'I'm Helen. Come in. You found us alright?'

Leah is nervous. She doesn't want to say the wrong thing, and getting this job is important to her. She'll have to face fields of asparagus and rows of strawberries if she fails. She licks her lips. Today of all days her speech has to work.

'Yes. Thanks for the instructions.' A pair of grey eyes is assessing her. Helen has the letter of application in front of her. Leah senses a vibe in the room and she needs to understand it. Eagerness, she thinks, as if they might need her. She'll take the initiative.

'Thank you for inviting me for interview. I can't seem a very promising candidate on paper.'

The grey eyes flick up from the letter and then look down again. 'Somewhat unusual, even for us,' Helen says. 'Tell me about not speaking, then speaking again.'

'I was nine. My family bullied me. One day it got really bad, so I stopped speaking. The odd thing is that from that moment the bullying stopped. Instead they ignored me, which was preferable. Looking back, I think it might have been a control mechanism.'

'And the starting again?'

'Before I answer that I'd like to tell you why I have no qualifications. Because I never spoke they thought there was something wrong with me. I was sent to a special school. The school did lots of things, but it didn't enter people for examinations.'

The grey eyes are watching her. 'Lots of our girls have few or no qualifications.'

'I started talking again because I had to. Until that moment I had got by without saying anything. When I was … attacked…' Will Helen pick up the hesitation? '… I needed to respond. My boyfriend helped me, was very sympathetic. It just got too complicated to write everything down.'

'When was this, if you don't mind me asking?'

'Just over a year ago. I suspect you want to know if I'm alright again?'

Helen nods.

'Yes, I am. I was protecting my mother at the time, and the man who attacked me is dead.'

Should she have said that last bit?

'I hasten to add that I had no part in his death.'

Helen smiles. 'You don't look like a killer.'

And at that moment Leah knows the job is hers.

They talk for another half hour. Leah has relaxed. She talks about Patrick, about how she had to rescue her mother, how she didn't want to tell her mother what Patrick had done to her. The word attack changes to rape. Helen listens and nods.

'Okay. We'll give you a chance. We'll train you. For the first week you'll follow an experienced carer. Then you'll be on your own. I trust you're happy to work nights?'

Leah nods. She doesn't know when she'll see Martin, but they can work that out.

'One month's probation in the first instance?'

Leah nods again. 'Thank you,' she adds.

'Right, I'll show you round.'

Leah follows Helen into the lounge.

Women sit on one side, men sit by the television. The room has wheelchairs and frames everywhere. Faces look up as they come in, and Leah immediately senses that the residents are not the elderly and vulnerable as she had imagined them to be, but individuals. A scrawny man with a mass of white hair grabs her hand as she walks past him. It feels odd, but she lets it happen.

'Tell me,' the old man says, 'how far is a long way off?'

Perhaps the interview isn't over.

'Good question,' Leah tells him. 'I'd say the other side of Malton.'

Helen is smiling at her. 'Eric, this is Leah. She's going to be working here.'

Eric lets go of her hand.

'My daughter's coming soon. What day is it?'

'Wednesday.'

'No, she doesn't come on a Wednesday.'

The rest of the tour is a blur of rooms and names. It actually feels homely. Every room has a view outside.

Finally, Helen knocks on the door of Room 10. Before she goes in she whispers to Leah, 'Wendell's been with us for several months. Like you when you were younger, he doesn't talk. There's nothing physiologically wrong. I wonder if you might help?'

They walk into the room. Wendell is smartly dressed. His trousers have creases. His shirt is newly ironed. As Helen does the introductions Leah looks into his eyes. She has never really examined older people, but she thinks she sees intelligence, pride and something else: that he doesn't like being old.

Back at the door of her office Helen reaches out and shakes Leah's hand. 'Welcome to the team,' she says.

Leah is to start in two days' time. She'll work days to begin with, twelve hour shifts, eight until eight. When she's trained she'll transfer to nights.

On the bus heading home the image of Wendell flits in and out of her mind. There are lots of reasons people stop talking.

× × ×

'Patrick, you say? His name might have been Patrick?'

Izzy is conducting an evening search. This man is the right age. She's established that he is local. He occasionally sees family in the area, so he's stayed around. His way of life can be read in his face. If I were to wash his face, Izzy thinks, nothing would change. The dirt and the weather have become a patina, a part of him. There's no way he could ever get clean. Could her son be like this? If he is, is it even remotely possible that over time she might clean him up, make him respectable?

The rough sleeper is sitting on the pavement at one end of Lendal Bridge. Izzy has to crouch down to hear what he says. Inside his collar she notices that his skin is surprisingly white.

'He disappeared in Leeds in the 1980s. He might be religious. He was brought up in a cult. He might talk about God.'

It's a particularly cold night for May. The wind has turned and is driving down from the north. People who pass her are back in winter coats. Izzy has come at night because she's learnt nothing useful from those who beg during the day. She wonders if the night crowd are the same. She's never seen this man before.

'Might you know him?' Izzy asks.

'People move around. The police and the community force keep moving us on.' The man spits on the ground. It's a horrible noise as he draws up whatever is irritating his lungs and exhales it.

Izzy winces and waits. Her son might be like this.

'But if you want to find him you need to know where

people sleep and just who's around. I doss down in Rowntree Park.'

He stops. Izzy wishes he'd get a move on. It takes him so long to say anything.

'Now last night a new fella joined us. About my age. He'd been drinking and he had it on him still. He sang somethink, kept the rest of us awake. I think it was an hymn.'

Hope rises as it often does. Deep down Izzy believes that effort has rewards, that hard work will bring her what she craves.

'Might he be there tonight?'

The man looks up and down the street. There are few people about now. It's both late and cold.

'Shall we go see?' he suggests.

Izzy stands and is glad to be upright again. The man gets up, sweeps his sleeping bag over his shoulder, and pockets the lure money from the coffee cup. Then he kicks the cup into the river. Izzy wants to tell him off for littering, but she doesn't.

'Come on,' he says.

Izzy follows him. It's dark and she knows she's being stupid. They cross the bridge and turn left, walking along the river with houses on either side. Before they reach the next bridge he swerves left and goes underneath, moving closer to the river. Now there are houses only on the right. The river on her left is moving with them. They pass a couple of houseboats and approach the entrance to a caravan park. Tall trees already in leaf darken her mood and increase her sense of isolation. The park gates are locked. He ducks under the fence. So far he hasn't spoken at all, but now he says, 'We sleep under the café. It's warmer there.'

She's aware of a children's playground on her right and still water on her left. But they are beyond the street lights now and there is only a thin moon, so what she sees is a kaleidoscope of dark patches. She thinks there must be geese roosting on the lawns. Small shapes scuttle out of their way as they walk. The path has slippery patches and she hates to think what she must be treading in. She knows she shouldn't be doing this, but she is determined to follow every lead. If he is here and she didn't follow because she was scared, could she ever forgive herself?

They reach a crossroads, or rather a point where two paths meet. The sky is slightly lighter to her left and there's more water that way too. He stops suddenly. How will she recognise her son in this blackness? She tries to pierce the darkness under the edge of the buildings, but she can make out no huddled sleeping bags.

He's saying something to her. He's talking in a low voice. She has to concentrate to hear him.

'Your money,' he says. 'I want it all, every last bit of it.'

'Why?'

She's clinging on to the possibility that there are sleepers here, that Patrick might be as close to her as he was when she gave him away, that the money might be for the group.

'Are you thick or what?' he says, still keeping his voice low. 'Hand it over.'

How will she get out of the park and back to the city? Can she remember the way? She digs her hand into her pocket and gives him the change.

'All of it.'

She roots around, hands over a bit more. 'That's all.'

She turns to leave him but he has hold of her. 'Your purse.'

'I didn't bring one.'

'Your card then. You must have one.'

She shakes her head at him, realises he can't see her. 'I don't have one.'

The hand doesn't let go. It turns her. Another hand invades her coat and finds the inside pocket. This pocket is zipped. He'll need both hands to undo it, so he'll have to let go and then she can shout and run. Her eyes are still adjusting. She can see houses and streets behind the dark buildings. Someone might still be up. Someone might hear her. Where are late dog walkers when you need one?

But he does it one handed, opens the zip and extracts the thin purse whilst keeping hold of her. There's nearly a hundred pounds and her bank card in there.

He lets her go. She still has her car keys. She watches him feel through the purse contents. 'That's more like it,' he says. 'Now, be a good girl and run along.'

'Where's Patrick?' she asks, standing her ground.

'How the fuck would I know?'

He vanishes quickly into the darkness, the way they came.

Izzy turns and stumbles away. She won't be able to tell Leah about this, or Martin. They'd be sure to lecture her and not let her out again. She'll have to keep it to herself.

Frightened now, she heads to the street behind the dark buildings. The exit gate is locked but workmen have left a gap. She squeezes through and she's among houses again. She turns right and walks briskly. The river is somewhere further on. The city must be in front of her. At the crossroads she turns right again. A police car is coming along the road, no siren, just cruising. She steps into the road and waves it down.

It's a policewoman. She's pleased about that and leans into the car. 'I've been robbed.'

'Get in.'

Izzy climbs in and the officer drives a little further until she can pull off the road safely.

'What happened?'

Izzy tells her story, explains about her lost son, tells the officer she knows she was stupid. The officer listens.

'A hundred pounds and a card you can cancel as soon as you get home. You got off lightly. Would you recognise him if you saw him again?'

Izzy isn't sure.

'Do you want to make a statement, press charges?'

Izzy shakes her head.

The officer starts the engine. 'Where are you parked? I'll take you to your car.'

Izzy tells her. They drive in silence. When they reach her car the officer turns to her.

'I want to tell you not to go on searching. After all this time, without a name, you have no chance. He could be anywhere in the world, or dead.'

Izzy is tired. She wants to get into her car and drive away. 'Are you a mother?' she asks.

The officer nods.

'I feel so guilty,' Izzy explains. 'I held him in my arms. I could have protected him. I could have raised him myself. Instead I gave him away to a cult I knew was no good for him. I have to live with that.'

The officer smiles, pats her on her arm. 'It's what we mums are best at: guilt. Learn to live with it. I do.'

Izzy shakes her head.

'Has your son ever come looking for you?' the woman asks.

'No.'

'Then there's your answer. Have you other children?'

Izzy nods.

'Then spend more time with them. Goodnight.'

Izzy climbs out of the car.

'Thank you for the advice,' she says. 'I won't be taking it.'

× × ×

Danny has gone back to Scotland. He spent last night camped down by the Bridge of Orchy. Now he's on the old Military Road heading for Glencoe. The cloud is down. On his left, enormous mountains have shrunk to just their feet. To his right, the many lochans of Rannoch Moor are steel and pewter grey. It isn't actually raining so he walks bareheaded. His scalp is still sensitive following the haircut, and that's how he knows the weather is changing. A wind is pushing down from the north.

He is utterly content. Walking has revealed to him his real strength. To place one foot on the rough track, then lean forward and place the other, confident that he could do this for hours, knowing he's the fixed point and the landscape is slipping away behind him, is wonderful. He feels the life inside him. He's conscious of the way his muscles work. His feet are alive inside his boots, tapping out their rhythm across this country. He's even conscious of the way he is breathing and of the clean, cold air in the tissue of his lungs.

As he walks he listens to all that is not quite silence. Last night's rain trickles, gurgles and cascades down the fell. Occasionally the track crosses the roar of white water. As these sounds subside he is aware of piping calls from birds whose names he doesn't know. The cloud turns fluorescent as the track loses height. Occasionally Danny can see a yellow disc of sun travelling with the cloud.

As he rounds the corner underneath the ski centre it happens. He's passing the low white form of Blackrock

Cottage when the cloud breaks and lifts as if it is being sucked away. There in front of him is Buachaille Etive Mor. Now the water glints, sparkles and shines. Rock faces flash like mirrors high on the mountain's northern edge. To his right he can hear road noises, but Glencoe is grand enough to drown out the incursions of modern traffic.

He stops walking, just stands and watches as mountain after mountain on either side of the steep defile slip out of the clouds and shimmer.

His phone pings. There's a message from Michael. It says simply *We have a job for you. Are you available?*

It's what he's been waiting for. They haven't forgotten him.

He texts back. *Yes, but I'm in Glencoe. I can be back in London tomorrow.*

He pushes the phone back in his pocket and stares at the valley in front of him. The sky is now a clear blue and the water responds, takes up the same colour.

When the phone pings again he doesn't immediately pick it up. Above his head a large bird is climbing into the air with great speed. He watches its pinions as they splinter the sunlight. Soon it is only a speck in the sky above him.

The cloud has vanished. Snow glistens in patches. It would be perfect to cross the road and climb the Devil's Staircase. After that there would only be a short, easy day of walking from Kinlochleven to Fort William and he'd have completed the West Highland Way. It's tempting to carry on, but he mustn't keep Michael waiting. He extracts the phone from his pocket and sees there's another text giving a time and place for their meeting.

He heads for the road. There's a bus stop by the ski centre. He'll catch the next bus to Glasgow, away from all this. He can be in London tomorrow.

5

Julia is now in Seville. She drove here yesterday. This time she ignored the written instructions and relied on her Sat Nav. She's glad she did that. Seville is a complicated city, but Sat Nav made the journey straightforward. Using the written instructions would have been impossible.

There's been no word about her 'case', only a silence she distrusts. The twerp is still employed. He has the audience denied to her. He can patrol round HQ encouraging sympathy for his predicament, particularly from the men. Particularly, Julia thinks, from the men I've had to have words with. They'll love his story.

It's eight days since she was suspended. That means they have six days left to call her back or extend her suspension for another fortnight. That would be devastating. That is only ever done in rare cases and would need the Board's approval.

Meanwhile she is about to enter the Alcazar. Being organised she has pre-booked her ticket, and she presents herself precisely on time at the entrance. It's hot and the orange trees are in blossom. She's walked from her hotel across the river, and all the way she's been aware of a sweet smell, as if the city has sprayed itself with perfume. The aquamarine river slid sinuously under the bridge when she crossed it, and the contrast between the pure white blossoms, the new green leaves, and the paler green of the river has been exquisite.

Keen to gain something from this enforced holiday, she walks in through the gates with her guidebook. Founded in the 8th century, the Alcazar was built on the site of a Roman barracks, then expanded to become the court of the Abbadid dynasty. When Mu'tamid was ruler it housed a harem of eight hundred women. Julia stops there. Sex has never been very important to her, but the idea of being one of eight hundred women waiting for your turn doesn't appeal. What kind of queue would that be? Say Mu'tamid manages one a night at his age. Eight hundred days is two years and seventy days. That's one hell of a wait. What if he gets ill and you are shunted down the queue? Eight hundred women! Eat your heart out, Mormons. Think of the rivalries, think of the bitchiness you could generate amongst eight hundred women. Did they have a Human Resources Department in those days? They'd certainly need one. Mu'tamid also planted the gardens, apparently growing plants in the skulls of his decapitated enemies.

An image of the twerp floats into Julia's mind. She can imagine his skull just to the left of the bird bath in her garden. What would she grow in it? Belladonna, monkshood, poison ivy?

She walks into the building itself. What does a bloodthirsty, randy old man build for himself by way of a palace? Something grand but also something exquisite, apparently. She's never been in a building like it. Arches lead into courtyards. Water flows through pools, cooling the air, and everywhere there is plasterwork of the highest quality. The rooms have numbers that don't seem to correspond to sections of text in her guidebook. She's examining a map and comparing it to the one in the book when someone speaks.

'How are you?' the person asks.

Julia doesn't think the words can be addressed to her, so she continues her comparison between the map in the book and the reality of the room she finds herself in.

'You did have me worried, you know.'

Julia looks up. It's the man from the square in Ronda, the one who came towards her when she had her turn.

She's startled. 'Fine,' she snaps. Then she remembers his look and adds, 'I think I just needed food.'

He doesn't immediately go away. He's looking very relaxed. His linen jacket is over his shoulder again. He's wearing the same Panama hat, but he's more tanned than she remembers.

'Thanks for your concern.' She turns back to her book. It's a matter of which way round she holds the page. Now she understands and sets off.

She is aware as she walks that he is standing watching her. How irritating! Sneaked looks back tell her that he has nothing with him except his jacket. She heads on, reads and looks. The plaster is odd. It's Muslim craftsmen working for a Christian ruler. Why, she wonders. Didn't they hate each other? Julia likes consistency. She stands and studies the plasterwork. It has been damaged. Not all the colour remains. No portraits, no pictures of nature, just patterns, like the tessellations in her school maths book.

She's standing in the Patio of the Maidens. Apparently, at the time of Moorish rule, the Christians presented an annual tribute of one hundred virgins to the Moorish ruler. It doesn't bear thinking about. Hardly a Christian thing to do, in Julia's judgement. She looks round the room. It's filled with light. Even with this number of visitors she can see the way sunlight on the water is reflected onto the plaster. With fewer people you'd hear the fountain too. Here and now there are people everywhere, people and cameras and tour parties following colourful tassels tied to poles. Some guides shout. Others whisper into a microphone to people with earphones. She can tell the nationalities. Delight seems reserved for the Chinese. The Americans, escaping Trump's USA, wear lanyards and walk with the swagger of rulers. Julia looks round and snorts. Then she catches sight of him again. Even in this throng he stands out, she has to admit that. He has a certain presence and no camera. He's tall and there's a stillness about him. Is he following her?

Stupid thought. He's just in the same building. Everyone's going the same way.

Nevertheless, she'll check. She's just curious enough about him to do that. She stands still and reads the guidebook. Apparently, the goldfish in the pool are not just there to look pretty. They deal with the mosquitos by eating the larvae. The six original orange trees have been replaced.

He's passed her so she can now follow him. She notices that he walks slowly, just looking around. Very self-sufficient, very content. He doesn't look at maps or read interpretations. He takes it all in and then moves on.

She sees him turn and look back at her. She's sure this is deliberate. What kind of a man is he?

Inside and outside are merged in the Alcazar. Refusing to be swayed by the hypnotic beauty of the plasterwork, Julia muses on what it must be like in winter. Did they actually have any enclosed comfortable rooms for private use?

Only when she is out of the palace and in the gardens does she interrogate her phone. There's been no attempt to contact her. What the hell are they doing?

× × ×

Danny is dressed in his suit again. His climbing self is carefully stowed back in the left luggage office. This is the meeting that will determine his future and he needs to be smart and on time.

'I'm here for a meeting,' Danny tells the receptionist.

'Name?' the woman asks. She's po-faced and efficient. She examines him through black-rimmed heavy glasses.

He hesitates.

'You can't have forgotten your name.' She smiles. 'Who are you?' It's meant to be an encouraging smile, but it puts him in his place. This great glass atrium is clearly her territory. It's much too important a building for her to let in someone who doesn't even remember his own name. As she waits she taps her finger.

'I'm here to see Michael.'

This time she giggles. To prevent her asking 'Michael who?' Danny shows her the text with the time and the place.

'Oh, that Michael,' the woman says.

Her attitude changes. 'I'll let him know you're here. If you'd like to take a seat he'll send someone down to collect you.'

Danny sits and watches her as she takes calls and gossips with those who come to the desk and sign in. Then Michael himself steps out of the lift and crosses the floor towards him.

The woman clearly can't believe that he has come himself. She stands up and walks towards them.

'Hello Sir,' Danny says, as he takes Michael's outstretched hand.

The woman arrives, flustered. 'He has no security badge because he couldn't give me a name,' she explains.

'Quite right,' Michael assures her. 'We must make sure we give him a name before he leaves. Then at least you'll be able to sign him out.'

He gestures for Danny to follow him.

They walk into the lift which has stayed because it's attended. Under the scrutiny of the operator they stay silent until they reach what turns out to be the top floor.

'I hardly recognised you,' Michael says. 'Last time we met you looked different.'

'Join the club. I hardly recognise myself.'

The room is opulent. It has immense glass windows that look out across London. Michael gestures Danny into a chair.

A girl has followed them into the room. Danny orders coffee and has time to study his patron while they wait for it to arrive. Michael's height is unnerving. His hair adds a couple of inches. It's swept back, luxuriant, but turning grey. He sits in his chair as if he prefers standing. He looks exceptionally smart.

The moment they are alone, Michael begins.

'First, I want to say thank you. You made all the difference. It was touch and go right until the moment you went to The Guardian. I'd have liked to have been there when you walked in dressed as you were, the dirt of the West Highland Way still clinging to you.'

He quickly becomes serious. 'The Prime Minister wants me to pass on her thanks.' Michael pauses. 'What she actually said was, 'Tell Danny that if it wasn't for him, I wouldn't be stuck here, spending eighteen hours a day dealing with endless stuff I don't really understand."

Michael shrugs. 'So, would you like to work for us?'

'I'd like some work. I need to earn. Who's us?'

'At one time we used to dodge that question, but not anymore. If I remember rightly, The Guardian described you as a *high placed source in the security services*. What I'm offering is a junior post in this Security Service. Will you take it?'

Danny will take anything, except … 'Will it be working for Harry?'

'He's been posted.' Michael says this with finality, as if Harry has been shoved into a letterbox.

'Then, yes please.'

'Good. You will need training. You will have to prove yourself.'

'And be vetted?' Danny asks.

'No, that's been taken care of. Your service up to the present is already on your record. Your pay has been backdated, and you can keep the flat at least until you've passed your probationary period. You don't have to do the preliminary tests either. In your previous role with us you showed aptitude and initiative. Your guesses were good and you proved your ability to blag your way into a guarded property, which is one of our standard tests, when you talked your way into Stella's house. Okay?'

'That all sounds fair enough.'

'Good, but I do have to hand you down the chain of command. You won't be seeing me or reporting to me in future.' Michael goes to press a button on the intercom.

Danny stops him. 'What's happened to Ivor?'

Michael looks him straight in the eyes. 'His visa ran out so he returned home.'

'To the Russian Federation?'

'Yes.'

'But he was an asylum seeker.' As Danny says this, he remembers that he has no idea what Ivor really was.

'He let his application lapse, Danny. Then his visa ran out.' Michael presses the button. 'The law has to take its course. We have to support the law, or have a watertight reason for not doing so.'

Another young woman walks into the room. She's Danny's age, stern rather than beautiful with a good figure. Danny would guess she works out to keep herself like that. Her face is thin and framed with long black hair.

'I'm Chloe,' she tells him.

Danny stands. She doesn't offer to shake hands.

'I haven't got a name,' he tells her.

'I know that.'

She is close enough now for Danny to look into her eyes. He sees nothing there but professionalism. He's never worked for a woman. Her eyes are telling him that's all this is: a purely professional relationship.

'You were Daniel Goulden before you disappeared,' she says. 'On the streets you became Patrick. We'll find you a new name, one you can settle with, and then a whole host of names you can wear and discard as operational needs dictate.'

Her voice is wholly businesslike. She has no ring on her finger. Something about her reminds him of Julia at her most bossy. He has spent plenty of time with women, but only in a dating sense. Much of his life – in the gym, on the streets – has been with men. Well, he supposes this is the modern world. He doesn't have a choice.

Danny looks at Michael. He is already focussed on what comes next. He wants to ask about greater powers for the security services. He wants to thank him and say he won't let him down, but the moment has gone.

'Come with me,' Chloe says.

Michael is already reading papers. He doesn't wish him luck.

They go down to the third floor. These offices are closely crammed and full of people. No uniform, Danny notices and not much activity. Lots of looking at screens. Is this the life he wants for himself? Chloe leads and he follows. They reach a door without a name and Chloe walks straight in.

The moment the door is closed she begins. 'I should warn you that you are not the pin-up of this place, much as the boss may love you. Our life is hard enough without the saintly Stella making it harder. She …' the word is said with contempt, '… is set to announce that there will be no new powers granted to the security services. How the hell are we meant to protect this country against our enemies with our hands tied behind our backs?'

The room has a table and chairs. On one corner of the table is a pile of papers. She hasn't invited him to sit, so he doesn't.

'Mindsett would have given us what we wanted. You, single handedly, emasculated this Service, made the life of everyone in this building impossible. And as for claiming to be a *high placed source in the security services*, you can imagine how that went down.' She stares at him. 'Sit.'

He stays standing.

'It has fallen to me to train you, and to protect you from everyone else in this building. First, we need to fill in these forms.'

Danny sits and pulls the forms towards him.

'What name do I use?' Danny asks.

'Choose one for yourself,' she tells him. 'That's a long tradition of this Service. Fill in the forms and then come and find me.'

Danny thinks. He won't use Patrick and he is Danny only to his family. Names are difficult. When he comes up with a name, everyone in his new work will use it. It will be shouted at him, whispered to him, read out flatly on a list, shortened, perhaps turned into a nickname. And all the time they use this name he must answer to it, learn to live inside it. He tries many names, puts them on and discards them.

Then one springs to mind. Colm. Not Colin. Colin is a nondescript name. Colm has a bit of class. He'll tell everyone his mother is Irish. He writes the name on the form. It's nice and short. No one will hear it correctly first time and he will correct them. If they are determined to hate him, he will at least insist on them saying his operational name properly.

He finishes the forms and walks the corridor until he spots Chloe. She's alone in a room, reading a file.

He introduces himself. 'Hello Chloe. I'm Colm.'

'Spell it.'

'C O L M, pronounced Collum.'

'Sit down,' she tells him. 'We have a case.'

'We?'

'It's on-the-job training. Because you are such a special asset I've been told to work with and train you at the same time. A pity. I'd have loved to take you through the whole training rigmarole that I went through. I'd have particularly relished the unarmed combat session. You fancy yourself in combat, I hear. There'd be no baseball bats and I'd wipe the floor with you, Colm.'

'It's an Irish name,' he explains. 'I didn't want to be

mistaken for anyone else.' He pushes his completed forms across the table to her. She picks them up and neatens the pile. Then she reads him a lecture on secrecy, spells out that he must never go to the newspapers again, and makes him sign the Official Secrets Act, emphasising the penalties for non-compliance. Finally, she indicates the file she has just been reading.

'One of our old spies is missing. There's evidence in his file that he may have gone rogue. It's possible that he has information damaging to this country's interests. We need to find him.'

She pushes the file across the table. It looks enormous. Danny hasn't read anything of any length since he left school. Chloe is watching him closely as he opens the file.

Even the name of the agent is a problem. How on earth do you pronounce Juozas Žemaitis?

Danny settles down to read. On the first page he finds a simple summary:

1931 Juozas Žemaitis born Vilnius, Lithuania.
1947 His father, Antanas Žemaitis, a leading Lithuanian partisan, shot by the KGB.
1947 Juozas Žemaitis's family flee to England.
1953 Aged twenty-two Juozas Žemaitis joins the Service. Code name Baldr.

The rest of the file is in contemporaneous notes, some of them detailed. Danny establishes that once Juozas's training is complete he is sent back to Lithuania. There he quickly establishes a network and sends what his handlers refer to as excellent reports on Soviet troop movements.

Up to this point Danny has found concentrating difficult. Now he becomes absorbed in piecing together the back story of this missing spy. He doesn't notice Chloe leaving the room.

Time passes for Juozas. He stays eight years in Lithuania with very few trips to London. As Danny reads on, the story becomes personal. Danny is fascinated by the contemporary handler notes. Juozas Žemaitis is commended for his zeal, for the risks he takes, and for his determination. In 1963, aged thirty-two, he returns to London. He has an outstanding record for veracity. Russian defector testimony supports his conclusions. He's offered promotion within the Service which he refuses, seemingly because it would mean being desk-bound in London. He continues to manage his agents in the field. At this point he is a legend in the Service. In 1969, aged thirty-eight, his role is expanded to include Estonia and Latvia. He continues to visit what he now clearly regards as his domain. Suddenly there are blemishes in the record. Juozas changes his code name. The files start to refer to him as Vidar. This change is frowned on and has to be sanctioned at the highest level. Because the intelligence flows well, the top floor sanctions the change. Danny gratefully goes with the new code name, Vidar, because it's so much easier to pronounce.

After Vidar returns to Lithuania, the partisan groups change tactics. They seem better informed and able to be more effective, scoring several notable successes. The file Danny's reading should be happy with this, but it isn't. Head Office wonders whether the partisans are receiving and acting on intelligence that might have come from Vidar himself. Danny finds a note attached to a report. It reads *It is not the intention of this Service to get involved directly in supporting local opposition groups, which often prove leaky and unreliable.* No one has countersigned the note and the matter seems to be dropped, to be superseded by whiffs of scandal round Vidar's sexuality.

He's brought back to London for interrogation. How typical of the British, Danny thinks, to haul him back about his sex life when he might be betraying his country on the side. Vidar is interrogated, but denies all the charges against him. Danny reads his interrogators' frustration in the file. Because Vidar is himself the Baltics go-to man, it is difficult to challenge his assertions. The inquisitors find they have nothing to go on and so the matter is dropped. The Service has other concerns.

It's clear to Danny by now that the Baltics were regarded as unimportant by the British. The Service is looking elsewhere: at Russia, Hungary and Poland in particular. Vidar is given free rein in what has become his own fiefdom.

And the pattern of Vidar's activity changes again. There are no further comments on private wars, no partisan collaboration. Instead, a number of extraordinary incidents are recorded in the file. In 1987, Service microphones embedded by Vidor's teams in the walls of the KGB headquarters in Tallin start to emit noises at random. The noises are soft and intermittent at first, then change note and become so penetrating that the building has to be abandoned and the prisoners moved out. The noises are so loud that they are heard throughout the town, and the exodus of the hated KGB men is even reported in the local paper before Soviet sweepers are called in. It takes them more than a week to locate and remove the implanted bugs.

Vidar's handlers wonder if he's going rogue. Vidar is four years off retirement. His handlers fume about the waste of electrical resources, fail to see the joke, which has spread across the Baltics. There is nothing better if you are a subjugated people than swapping stories about someone getting one over on your invaders.

The speaker incident is followed by what became known as the soap incident. A Soviet barracks is made uninhabitable when a large quantity of washing up liquid is introduced into its water system. Tanks of fresh water have to be brought in. Soldiers and cooks have to fill containers because the attempt to flush through the pipes only results in bubbles and airlocks. The barracks water system isn't self-contained and local houses find their toilets full of bubbles. This joke even reaches as far as Russia itself. The suspicion is that Vidar was involved, but there is no evidence against him.

At the same time much is changing in the area. The Soviet Union is on the verge of collapse. In 1989, what became known as the Pan-Baltic Human Chain marks the fiftieth anniversary of the notorious Nazi-Soviet non-aggression pact. In this fantastic act of peaceful defiance, two million citizens of all three Baltic countries join hands to form a continuous human chain, linking them together from sea to sea. The unbroken chain stretches for 675.5 kilometres.

Danny is conscious that he is getting to the end of the file. In January 1991, Soviet troops and paramilitary police storm the radio and television station in Vilnius. Fourteen people are killed, but the attempt by hardliners to push back the tide is doomed. Later that same year, on 6th September, Lithuania gains independence and Vidar leaves the Service. He is a national hero and he retires with honour.

One final note in the file intrigues Danny. There are independence celebrations right across Vidar's patch. Vidar is invited but he never attends any of them. At the end of the file is an anonymous contribution written after 2000. It states that, following independence, there is no evidence that Vidar has ever been back to Estonia, Latvia or Lithuania. Danny pauses there, stunned, and reads back to double-check. In 1991, Vidar finally helped to achieve independence for Lithuania. He's fought for this all his professional life, at great personal risk, but he never celebrates his success. The man who turned down promotion so that he could stay in the Baltics never went back when they were free. Why? The file has no answer.

Chloe has been back for some time. Danny closes the file.

'Well, what do you make of Vidar?' she asks.

Danny is not ready to be quizzed by this frightening woman. 'I need a coffee,' he tells her. 'I need some lunch.'

6

There's a café in the Alcazar garden. Julia queues up, orders and collects a coffee, then finds the one table that's free and sits down.

There are palm trees and myrtle hedges in front of her. Occasionally a fountain shoots itself into the air and disappears. What if there is no phone call or email? What if the fourteen days go by and there is nothing?

She knows the answer. In those circumstances the case lapses. Unless they've written to her, of course, but her cleaner has been instructed to check her post every day. If there is no letter and no phone call, they will be guilty of not following the procedures and she can go back to work.

But will that be enough? No victory party! No formal vindication from the Board!

She has her return flight booked. She'll be back in England before the fortnight ends.

She won't check her phone again. They are not having her strung out on a phone call, waiting and waiting.

She looks up and sees him standing there. His jacket is still over his shoulder. He too has a cup of coffee, and a quick glance round tells her that there are no empty tables.

'May I?'

She doesn't say anything. Instead she flips a hand over and leaves it palm upwards.

He smiles. It's enough of an invitation. 'You can tell them I'm your carer if you like.'

How could he know she was wondering what those sitting around her might think? But, of course, he can't know. It was just a lucky guess.

He puts the coffee down, hooks the jacket over the back of the chair and sits. There's something theatrical about the gestures.

'You do seem to need a carer, or rather you did the other night.'

He's not only sitting down at her table but he's going to talk, remind her of that embarrassing moment in the square in Ronda. Can she close him down by staying silent so that he gives up? To say anything might be fatal.

'Any moment now you'll hide in that guidebook of yours.'

Her hand was going towards it. She frowns. She knows how he did that. He just watched her hand move. There's nothing special about him, she decides.

She's conscious that he's looking at her, studying her features. He can't be English, she thinks, or he'd turn sideways and ignore her. But his English sounds, well, English.

'You look unhappy,' he says. 'You looked lost and unhappy the other night. That's what I noticed and why I was concerned. You look better this morning, but not yet mended.'

This isn't happening, Julia tells herself. He can't be English if he tells a complete stranger what he thinks. He has blond hair. He might be German or Scandinavian.

She doesn't think he's Dutch.

'I'm alright. Thank you for the other night.'

Is that clipped enough? He hasn't touched his coffee.

Now he picks the cup up and sips.

'What did you think of the Alcazar?'

He's asked her a direct question and it needs an answer. She won't let him force her into being rude, but she won't say it's beautiful or anything banal. He's looking at her again. She takes a breath. She can use her knowledge.

'I wondered how a man so carnal and so cruel could create something so beautiful.'

He smiles. He's on the pick-up, she thinks. He's that type. He wants me, simple as that. But being wanted isn't simple, is it? No one has wanted her for a long, long time.

'Yes, I like people to be consistent. I like things to be straightforward. I don't read guidebooks like you do. I try to get under the skin of a building. This building has a beautiful skin.'

He makes the word skin sound vaguely indecent, and she reaches for her coffee cup. He's not going to talk about her skin, is he? Is he that sort of man? Might she need to make a quick getaway?

'It's a fortress first and foremost,' he goes on to explain. 'The outside walls tell you that. But everything inside pretends it's something different. You walk through defended walls into a pleasure palace.'

Okay, she'll join in. Was that *I don't read guidebooks like you do* a *dig*? She'll use what she knows. 'In the same way that the Moorish plaster pretends it isn't a Christian interior, largely built after the Christian conquest of the south.'

'I didn't know that,' he says.

She'll get her own back. 'Didn't you feel it as you walked round? Perhaps you should read a guidebook.'

'May I?'

It's the second time he's said that. She hands the guidebook over and tells him the page number. He takes it and starts to read.

Now she's trapped. She expects him to find something quickly and challenge her, but he doesn't. He sits and reads it intently as if he's already forgotten about her, as if she isn't there and he has the table to himself. Five minutes of complete silence between them stretch out into the gardens under the intense shade of the cypress trees.

'You have a point,' he says when he's finished. 'I'd have got the chronology wrong.'

He doesn't hand the guidebook back, but puts it down on the table slightly nearer himself than her.

They are talking and she never meant it to happen. She needs to finish her coffee and move away. She'll say a few more things and then *Nice meeting you*, meaning it wasn't. And she must do that before he asks her how long she's staying in Seville.

She gulps her coffee and waits for what he'll say next, but he lapses into silence. He even moves his chair sideways as if he knows the conversation is over. There's something about him, she decides. Every time she thinks she has him taped he surprises her.

And changes the way she acts. If she was on her own and about to go she'd pick up the guidebook and look for what's next. But he'll laugh at her if she does that, and she doesn't want to be laughed at.

She looks at him. He has a knowing face. It's not yet lined. He must be at least her own age, perhaps older, but the face looks at if it has done some living and some thinking. It's not full of itself, it's far from haughty or self-satisfied. Its natural expression seems to be a slight frown.

There's no ring on his finger and, as far as she can see, there never has been. He's well dressed. He's clean. The shirt's too colourful, needs toning down a few notches, but it's ironed and it fits him. Not English, she decides again. English people dress for comfort and look terrible. He looks as if he knows and cares what he looks like.

As she finishes her appraisal he suddenly downs the rest of his coffee, pushes her guidebook back across the table and gets up. He collects his jacket from the back of the chair, hooks his finger under the collar, and swings it back onto his shoulder.

'Thanks for the use of the chair,' he says, and walks away.

No *Nice meeting you*. No anything.

And she feels abandoned. She even feels dumped.

× × ×

'So what do you make of the file, Colm?' Chloe stresses the m, squashing her lips together to do so. She's like a cat ready to pounce, and Danny doesn't want her to think he's stupid.

They are back in the room after a lunch break Danny insisted on. All through lunch Danny has known this question was coming. He's tried to think about what he's read in the way that Ivor would. He's attempted the Ivor trick of looking at everything from the worst angle. But Ivor made guesses. Danny mustn't do that. He doesn't have Ivor's background. Now, with time running out, he suddenly recalls a school assembly. He's no idea why it comes to mind. It was about a guy called Socrates who finally worked out that he was the wisest man in the world, not because of what he knew, but because he knew what he didn't know.

'I don't know enough to reach a conclusion,' Danny announces.

She is exasperated with him. 'That's all we have. That's everything.'

He bats this back. 'It still isn't enough to reach a firm conclusion.'

Her frown, which is not unattractive, deepens. 'So do you, Colm the wonder man, have a temporary hypothesis?'

'Just lots of questions really.'

'Such as?'

He suspects, as he watches her, that she is determined to roast him, so he talks fast. 'Did Vidar choose Lithuania, or was he sent there because Lithuania didn't really matter, or because be was the only one who spoke the language? After all, how many people do you know who speak Lithuanian? Then he stayed eight years. He did an eight year stint behind enemy lines! Is that normal for a spy? Why did he refuse promotion? Was that because it was a desk job or because he'd have to leave Lithuania? If the latter, what was keeping him there? A woman? A man? A boy? Why did he change his code name? Was the old one blown? Had he been captured by the KGB and turned? Eight years is a hell of a long time to go undetected. What was his link with the partisans? You see, he was essentially a one man band. His interrogators never knew enough to know what to ask him, so could never really put him under pressure. Lithuania was his stalking ground, his fiefdom. Was he in reality a partisan, paid for by London? Did he hate the Soviets because they shot his dad, or was the relationship with his enemy different? If he was a Lithuanian patriot, why did he never go back after September 1991 when the country was suddenly free? The Soviets left and he left the same day. Odd, isn't it, or instructive? The soap suds and the microphone speakers make no sense. The Soviets shot his dad. He blew them up with bubbles.'

He pauses and looks at her. 'How am I doing?'

She nods but stays silent. Danny decides to continue.

'It seems to me that your Service was careless with Vidar,' he pronounces. 'And,' he adds, 'I do have one final question. Gay or straight, loyalist or double agent, what might he have that matters to us now? He left the Service twenty years ago. He's not been back. What's scaring you?'

She's listening behind those glasses, but she doesn't answer any of his questions. Instead she asks one of her own. 'So how do we proceed?'

'You haven't answered any of my questions, especially the last one.'

'This is a real case, Colm. I don't know what's in the files. I haven't been told.'

'But after twenty years of his retirement, why do you suspect him now?'

She pauses, and he knows she will tell him only so much.

'We keep tabs on ex agents. It's good practice and an insurance policy. No one leaves the Service without a certain amount of unfinished business. We know where he was living and he isn't any longer there. The house isn't up for sale; it's been abandoned. His pension is still being paid into his account, but his assets have been moved and we don't know where to. He's walked out of his life or he's been abducted. Either way, we need to find him, check that he's alright.'

'I don't believe you,' Danny says in his best Ivor impersonation. 'You're not a welfare agency.'

She sighs because she'll have to tell him. 'You're quite

right. Something else happened at the same time. We had a burglary in one of our outlying record stores quite recently. A file has gone missing.'

'What was in it?'

She's embarrassed, he can tell that. 'We don't know. As you say, this Service was careless with Juozas, with Vidar. I can't pronounce his real name either. The only information we have about the file is that it was written by Vidar himself and for his eyes only. He was a one-off. His handlers are dead. He's outlived anyone who worked with him. It's just possible he's out there with a file that matters.'

'Have you searched his house?'

'Not yet.'

'It seems like a good place to start.'

Are they becoming a team? It's far too early to say.

× × ×

James has begun to revive. He's been going over the campaign in his mind and has come to the conclusion that he is the victim. Through his brilliance Jud was in with a chance. What blew it was the one time Jud went solo and set up that meeting with Borstov. If that had never happened, they would have carried the day. He, James, had identified Stella's weakness. He, James, had exploited that weakness. He, James, had discovered the letters and journal. He, James, had deployed her own words against her. He, James, had trained Jud in what and what not to say in front of the cameras. If it hadn't been for the *high placed source in the security services* they would be in Downing Street. He needs to identify the source. He'd like to meet him face to face, explain that Jud would have given MI5 more leeway to spy on British citizens, explain to that fool in the intelligence services that he's scored an own goal.

As he tells and retells the story he discovers a sense of outrage. The press, a secret cabal within the deep state, and even the candidate himself had combined to sink James Goulden. The press did this because they hated the fact that he had discovered dirt on Stella which they had missed. James had hurt their pride, and the Guardian article was exactly timed to achieve maximum journalistic revenge. The secret cabal in the deep state hates outsiders, and James feels he is an outsider. He didn't go to the right school or the right university. He isn't fit, in their eyes, to reach high office. Finally, Jud must have realised that he would never be able to cope as Prime Minister so he committed hara-kiri. The truth was that Jud wanted to become Prime Minister and to have been Prime Minister. It was the bit in the middle he needed to avoid. In fact, the more James reflects, the more James realises he is the only individual who emerges from the whole sorry mess with any credit.

And that returning sense of himself makes him rally from his profound depression. He has only to wait. The offers of work will come.

7

It's evening. Julia walks out of her hotel and turns right. There are posh places to eat by the bridge across the river. There is also a busy street halfway there with lots of pavement cafes. To eat in the street with the locals would be different and daring. It's a warm night. She'll saunter and see what grabs her. She likes this city and is no longer striding to get to places quickly.

After leaving the Alcazar this morning she visited the cathedral (disappointing) and walked the intricate old streets (interesting). She admired La Giralda, the Cathedral's annexed Muslim tower. She even noticed its exceptional beauty for herself before reading about it in the guidebook. She spent time sitting down by the river in the sunshine. Intermittently during the day she also pondered what he said to her. *You look unhappy. You looked lost and unhappy the other night. That's what I noticed and why I was concerned. You look better this morning, but not yet mended.* Occasionally she caught a reflection of herself in shop windows and what she saw worried her.

When she returned to her hotel she took a long look at herself in the mirror. A serious woman looked back at her, a woman who still has long hair when she's over forty, a woman who is tall and imposing. She's always liked the quiff of hair at the top of her forehead. This afternoon she questioned it.

She spent longest looking at her eyes. Little lines were forming around them, something under her eyes was softening, falling. She smiled into the mirror and the eyes didn't join in with her mouth. Had that always been the case? She can't remember.

She had a bath and looked at her body in the water as if it was somebody else's. Past childbearing, she thought. Not bad for her age, built for stamina and power. She thought of the photographs of her younger self: the tall girl in the back of the netball team, the big sister who towered above James, the bride who was trying not to look taller than her husband. There weren't many photos of her. The family had never gone in for photographs, and most of the pictures of her from the last twenty years were mug shots for passports and security tags.

Her breasts were still okay. Her muscles had some tone. She'd never cared much about food, so her stomach accused her of nothing. After she'd dried herself, standing in front of the full-length mirror, she'd thought, I'm not yet old. I stand tall. I hold myself well. I am a force.

Now she's come down to the green river and is walking along the path. The last low sun accentuates the contrast between the water and the stone. This city is ancient, has pre-Roman roots, but it doesn't feel old. She doesn't feel old. A pole, perhaps used to moor a boat, tells her the real strength of the water flowing past her. Its force is revealed in the broken circles that rush downstream as if hurrying to catch up. Julia stops and looks; she doesn't know why. The water is breaking into lines like ringlets. Anxious lines, Julia thinks, turning white at the edges before they regain equilibrium further downstream; lines that begin like a young girl's curls, then transform into an old woman's grey serenity.

The Julia of last week would have snorted at what she is thinking. This Julia watches it happen again and again. Then she turns and heads back towards the centre. She needs a drink.

A café on the right, halfway up the next street, is mentioned in the guidebook. It's filling up quickly. She finds a table outside and sits with her back to the wall so she can watch the crowds. She orders a beer and studies the menu, then pushes it to one side. Other people are just drinking. She'll do that. She'll decide about food when she's finished her drink.

The evening is warm. Families parade in the street. It's like an English carnival, but here it is an everyday event. She's not the only single woman sitting there. The beer arrives. The glass is cold. The first sip is the perfect antidote to the world of the twerp and suspension on full pay.

The waiter talks to her in Spanish. She's been taken for Spanish before. Is she beginning to belong?

Perhaps it's a special day. A procession is making its way down the street. She hears the music first and then sees the Madonna riding her chariot, swaying as she is carried along. Mary rides on a platform at head height so she stands out from the crowd. From the platform a red curtain falls almost to the ground. Between the bottom of the curtain and the road Julia notices a series of feet in trainers as they shuffle the Madonna forwards. The carrying must be demanding because every now and then fresh porters join the front of the cortege and exhausted porters leave from the back. For a moment, as the curtain opens, she glimpses the mass of men straining beneath the weight. Then the curtain closes, the band strikes up again, and the whole procession moves forward.

How absurd, Julia thinks. It's not as if the statue is particularly fine. It's a plaster cast and glossily painted. There is something of the pantomime about the whole performance. She notices a man whose job is simply to keep the candles alight. He carries a pair of step ladders, and when the procession stops he opens them, climbs up, then trims and replaces candles. Everyone's watching. Julia is so absorbed in the spectacle that she doesn't see her fellow traveller approaching. She is only aware of him when he swats his jacket across the back of the other chair at her table and sits down, this time without asking permission.

She stares at him. 'You again?'

'My name's Zakk, with two ks.' He offers his hand to her.

'Are you stalking me?' she asks, 'or is this pity because you think I'm unhappy?'

'Neither. I don't really like drinking alone.'

He's cute, if you can be both cute and lived-in. His face is asymmetrical, but he has a smile and he shaves. She can't abide stubble. Bearded is definite. Shaved is definite. Stubble shows indecision.

'Julia.' She takes his hand. Fingers dry not sweaty, grip precise. 'Can I get you a drink?' She calls out, 'Waiter,' before he has a chance to argue.

'Thanks, I'll have a beer like yours.'

'Spill!' she challenges him, when the waiter departs.

'I should tell you that beer is one of the things in life that is important to me. I won't be spilling a drop.'

'Good, I'd hate you to waste what I'm paying for. Now spill. What is this? Why are you haunting me?'

He frowns. 'The truthful answer to that question is that I don't know. The coincidence of us bumping into each other whenever we emerge from our separate hotels …'

She interrupts him. '… is of no significance. We meet in the hot spots of a tour of Moorish Spain. It's bound to happen.' She's being sharp on purpose, laying down a marker.

'But here?'

'You must have been looking for me.'

'I look around me wherever I go. I love crowds and difference. You stand out.'

'My beauty?'

'I was thinking of your height. If you were a tour guide you wouldn't need a flag or an umbrella.'

That remark, she thinks, is out of order, but his eyes stay on her and he's smiling.

His beer arrives. 'Cheers!' he says. 'Here's to coincidence.'

They click glasses. She says nothing. She doesn't know if she welcomes his being there or not. She looks around her. All the tables are full. She doesn't particularly like sitting alone either, but her tour isn't finished. This can't really keep happening. Or can it? Does she want it to?

'What did you think of the Madonna?' she asks.

'I don't do religion,' he tells her. 'I'm a rationalist,' he explains.

'Pure pantomime,' she tells him. 'It's a social statement. Don't take it so seriously.'

'They do,' he tells her. 'Here it's still a sign of conquest. The pluralism of Moorish religious tolerance swept away by Christian exceptionalism.' He watches the disappearing Madonna as she turns left at the end of the street.

'Carried in triumph,' he says. 'Look!'

She looks. Turning a corner is difficult for the procession. The Madonna sways as those on the left side shorten already tiny steps whilst those on the right lengthen their stride.

'Do you like Spain?' she asks him.

'I adore it.'

He's stopped looking down the street and has turned towards her.

'Why?' she asks.

'It's fierceness, its heat, its sense if fun, its history, all those civil wars distilled into this mixture.' He pauses. 'I also think the people have a sense of their bodies and are more in touch with their animal selves than we are.'

He says it with a sense of sadness, a sense of having missed out.

She wants to mock him but hesitates. Sitting opposite her he does not give off animal vibes.

'Goodness,' she says. 'Is that why you've come, to leer at the girls and learn to dance the flamenco?'

He turns on her. 'Don't pretend you don't feel it too. You have to be honest if you want to feel alive. I even think it's changing you.'

She has no answer to that.

After this interesting exchange, conversation lapses. He drinks his beer as if he's thirsty. She sips hers. The waiter is hovering. Clearly the kitchens want to start cooking. She's about to suggest they order when he stands up.

'Thanks for the drink. I needed that,' he says. 'Being on holiday is thirsty work.' Then he pauses before he goes. 'Will I see you in Cordoba? If you want to be certain of seeing me, you'll find me at the Hotel Mezquita. Enjoy your meal.'

When he's gone, and really gone, walked right down the street and turned the corner without once looking back, she reaches for her mobile phone and checks her booking for Cordoba. At least they won't be staying at the same hotel.

× × ×

That same evening James receives another call. This one sounds more promising. This voice is confident and seems to be offering him work.

'Are you available for immediate employment?'

James confirms that he is.

'Could you start tomorrow?'

James confirms that he could.

'You see, we need a spokesman to make our case.'

'What case is that?'

'This is a free country, isn't it?' the voice asks.

'Indeed it is.'

'And that means we have certain liberties as individuals?'

'We have.'

'Good, you sound like a bright bloke.'

'Thanks,' says James, and his heart sinks.

'We are a group of entrepreneurs. We want to use the ancient laws regarding the liberty of the individual to assert our right to use indentured labour.'

James processes that. There can only be one meaning. 'So you want to own slaves?'

'No. All that stuff belongs in the past. We're not talking shackles and transportation. We want to be legit. We want to offer unpaid internships that go on and on. We want to offer apprenticeships that never end, on-the-job training that necessitates continual practice for a lifetime. Everyone needs to drive down costs. This is how we intend to do it and this is where you come in, Mr Goulden.

'How?'

'It's all about names, isn't it? It's all about what you call a thing. You're good at names. Trafficking sounds terrible, so we form a holiday company, that sort of thing. Not *Experience of a lifetime* but *Experience for a lifetime* and hope they don't notice the difference. Tui get paid for moving people between countries, why can't we? It'll save all those drownings and rescue boats.'

James needs to get his head around this. 'Have I got this right? You want to assert your liberty to take away the liberty of others, and you want me to find the words that make it sound legitimate.'

'That's exactly it. You're in PR. That's what you do, isn't it?'

'How can I possibly do that?'

'Look, there are all these people, migrants, trying to get to this country. It's the drugs problem, isn't it? The problem with drugs is that they are illegal. It's the same with trafficking. We need to make it legal. The problem with Britain is that, in spite of the efforts of the last governments, the wage bill is too high. Indentured labour would make us competitive again.'

'That is slavery. That is exactly what slavery was.'

'But we are different. Of course, we offer freedom in the end. After all, we don't want to care for these people in old age. When they have paid us back we will set them free. I mean, that's what a community sentence is, isn't it, paying a debt to society. Community service is unpaid, in other words it's a form of slave labour and it's legal. What we offer will be earned freedom. There's a phrase for that, isn't there? Now what is it?' There's a pause on the other end of the line. Then, 'Work will set you free. That's it. We could put it on the gates, translate it into a number of languages. It will soften the razor wire.'

James sees the picture: the railway lines and the barrack blocks.

'It's been done before,' James tells his caller. 'It didn't end well. No thank you.' He ends another call and sinks back into depression.

× × ×

Martin is back with Leah. She came to the shop and they made love. Nothing of a definite kind was said, but then nothing has ever been definite between them. Martin likes to think that she missed him and wanted him back, but she didn't say so. Once again he splits his time between the shop and the Arts and Crafts house. The arrangement seems to suit them both.

He has yet to tell Leah about Stella's invitation to Number 10. He's accepted it. He wants to join the long list of people who have walked through that famous door. He wants to see inside. The date is still some weeks off. He'll need to tell her soon if he wants her help in buying a suit.

Tomorrow Leah is due to start work at the care home and Martin realises she's nervous.

'What's there to be nervous about?' he asks. 'You've invaded a cult. You've brought Howard back from the dead. You've even stood up to Julia. You can cope with a room full of old ladies and a scattering of old men.'

Izzy is away. Frightened by her mugging she's gone to Scotland to see her brother, Joshua. Martin and Leah have the house to themselves. They've dined in the kitchen and played La Bohème at high volume so that it filled the ground floor with its longing. They've shared a bottle of wine, lit a fire, and made love in front of the flames, feeling the warmth on their skin.

Now they're lying in bed. 'What if I can't cope with the old people?' she says. 'I'm no Julia, but what if I don't like them enough to want to look after them?'

He props himself up on one elbow to look at her. 'What did you feel when you walked into the lounge?' he asks.

'Pity,' she says, 'at first. Then, that I'm glad I'm not old. Their incapacity made me want to skip like a little girl, just to prove I still could.'

'And what did you feel when you met the silent man?'

'That I wanted to understand him. That I wanted to read him.'

'If anyone can reach them, you can. I mean, you're quite scary sometimes when you look at people.'

'Do I scare you?'

'Sometimes.'

'Well, let's keep it that way.'

He reaches out and touches her chin. It's a light touch and hesitant. Her face is out of bounds, unlike the rest of her. 'So, there is an us?'

'Martin!'

'You see, I never really know. Over the Stella/Howard letters I thought I'd lost you. Now we are back here.' He indicates the bed.

She props herself up beside him. 'I'll ask some questions of my own. What do you feel when you look at me?'

'Like a teenager: excited, a bit lost.'

She frowns.

'I think I like that,' he says. 'The not being quite certain. I feel we're still working stuff out.' He pauses. 'I'm glad we made up after the letters.'

She rolls over on her back. ‘A second-hand bookseller and a care worker. We’re never going to set the world on fire.’

‘But we touched power only a few weeks ago. We shook the councils of the wise.’

She ignores him. ‘In a house that is far too grand for us.’

‘I love this house. I’ve always been certain about that.’

‘Enough,’ she says. ‘I need my sleep. Tomorrow I have my first twelve hour shift.’

He kisses her and rolls away onto his own side.

‘Have you set the alarm?’

8

Izzy steps off the train in Inverness and catches the bus to Ullapool. She's still shaken from the mugging. That way of searching for Patrick is closed off to her now. She can't risk another attack. For a week she's stayed at home despairing, moping until Leah and Martin persuaded her to do what they did after the rape and visit her brother, Joshua.

'Joshua and Hilary know a lot about the Church of the Living Saints,' Leah told her mother. 'I know they left before Patrick was born, but they might tell you something useful.'

'Besides, you need a break. You need to forget your recent setback. What have you got to lose?' Martin added.

For a few days Izzy resisted, then she gave way. What else was she to do? What other avenues were open to her? So she's travelled all this way, more in hope than expectation. She's nervous. She's never been to Scotland and she hasn't seen her brother, Joshua, for more than fifty years. It's late afternoon and Izzy finds she's on what is really a school bus. Teenagers from the local school play music, eat sweets, chat. When she last saw Joshua he was their age. The bus climbs steadily and stops occasionally for children to dismount, even though Izzy can see no houses nearby. To either side, grass stretches up to low summit ridges, interspersed with blocks of dark conifers. Then they lose height and run alongside a sea loch. Izzy gets herself ready for the reunion. They've spoken on the phone and Leah has described Joshua to her, but will she recognise her own brother?

Although frightened by her recent mugging, Izzy is still determined to trace her son. The false Patrick called himself Patrick Barr. She wonders if there is anything in the surname. Her brother, Joshua, and Hilary were members of the cult. Might the name mean something to them? It's a long shot. So much time has gone by. She could have asked the question on the phone and not made this journey. But, after losing Patrick and Danny, family means more to her. At home Leah and Martin need space, and she's not had a holiday since the death of her husband, Gary. It's also high time she saw her brother.

The bus follows the loch edge into the heart of the town. To her left, a long wooden pier sticks out into deep water so the fishing boats can tie up. In front of her is the ferry terminal. That's where they agreed to meet. The school children are on their feet already and jostling to the door. She picks up her case and walks slowly to the front of the bus. She steps down, and fresh sea air pulls her across to where two people are standing, waiting.

He's grizzled. The schoolboy she didn't wave to all those years ago is an old man. His mass of hair and his beard are grey and white. His face is weather worn. As she walks towards him she stares at him. He seems fit. He's only just seventy and he walks well. She's imagined this moment, but what's happening is different. They were never a touchy-feely family, and a drone, if one had been flying above them, would have recorded no great speed, certainly no run towards each other, arms outstretched.

When they are still six feet apart they stop and look at each other. Izzy can see at once that he is still Joshua, but a sadder form of his younger self.

'My little sister grew old.'

'I'm sorry,' she says. Just for a second she wants to go back to being ten years old. This time she wants to open the window and wave and shout to her brother before he walks away. Back then, the Church of the Living Saints and all it believed in had stopped her from waving. 'I'm sorry I never waved,' she tells him.

She stands still and he walks towards her.

'Are you still in there?' he asks.

Then he reaches out, and she remembers the way he used to hold her face when he was a small boy. Rougher, drier hands gently hold her and she tries not to worry about her makeup.

Then the hands let her face go and the arms encircle her. She is being hugged, which hasn't happened to her in a long while, and her makeup may not survive this second assault.

'Hello,' she says. 'Hello Josh.'

He's crying. She can feel his tears on her face. She knows that inside the hug she's smiling.

They stand together, then his face pulls away from hers and they each wipe eyes.

A small wrinkled woman apparates beside them. Her grey hair is a mess, but her smile is warm. 'Hello, I'm Hilary.'

Izzy puts out her hand.

'Don't I deserve a hug too?'

They embrace quickly. Joshua picks up Izzy's case and all three climb the hill in silence. There's simply too much to say and to hear, and it all deserves its own space. It shouldn't be wasted as the adjunct to a journey.

They head out of Ullapool and take the side road to the Summer Isles and Achiltibue. Izzy sits in the back of the car and absorbs the view. The gorse is in full flower. Bright yellow clumps, like so many fires, blaze in the early summer landscape. Still water fills every hollow and reflects the clouds.

'How do you like our view?' Hilary asks.

On the left, a deeply gouged mountain dominates, but in front and to the right a hill like a fantastic castle lifts its crenulated ridge behind the birches.

'Beautiful,' she says, and it is. But it's another kind of beauty altogether. The Yorkshire landscape she's used to is softer and has Man's imprints everywhere. This is older and has its own music, is its own self. She'd like to say as God intended, but she's had it with God. You really know where you stand when you've tried something twice and rejected it each time.

'That's us.'

Hilary points, and Izzy is disappointed. At the end of a track are two low modern houses. One seems to be a holiday home.

Joshua carries her case in. 'You'll find us savage,' he explains. 'We don't really do visitors. The last people we entertained were Leah and her friend. They didn't stay the night. By the way, how is she? And how is that strange young man of hers?'

'Martin? Martin and Leah seem to have an on-off relationship. But you don't know what happened, do you?'

'Save it for Hilary. She'll want to know every word.'

It's after supper. The story has been told.

'That daughter of yours, she smashed the Church that cost us our lives.' There's glee in Joshua's eyes. 'I told her not to try and she took no notice of me. Good girl. I'm proud of my niece. And Patrick, the man who raped her, wasn't your son.' He smiles at that. 'You know, that's the strangest thing of all. Until now, until you told us about the cult foisting Patrick on you to get the house and the money, I think somewhere inside me I still believed they might be right and I must be wrong. Little sister, you've freed me. I could hug you again.'

'But they are still there,' Hilary objects. 'They may have put a woman in charge, but she sounds as shitty as all the others.'

'It didn't feel like that. When Martin, Leah and I went there to get the information about my real son, the place was a shadow of its former self. Yes, Katherine is God's Woman, but many have left and they aren't the force they were. The man I thought was my son is dead. I wonder who he really was.'

'I wish Dad could know this,' Joshua says. He speaks harshly. 'I'd like to ram it down his god-terrified throat.'

Hilary takes a long swig of red wine. 'Just because he was wrong? Passionately wrong, I grant you.'

'Because he was so certain he was right.'

'That's the same thing. Right, wrong,' Hilary muses. 'I lost a husband I never loved. I lost children who didn't love me. Because of that Church I seduced a boy who came to live with me and I have lived with him, very happily indeed, ever since. How frustrated would I be now if the Church of the Living Saints hadn't had the good sense to cast me out?' Her wine glass is empty. 'Yes, I occasionally wonder what happened to my children.

Should I go searching too?' She pauses. 'I think not.'

Izzy sits up. 'But I must, and I may need your help. I must, because he walked out of the same Church that has dominated all our lives when he was only sixteen. Imagine that! He walked out and knew nothing of the world. He wasn't like Joshua with a kind woman to look after him. They let him walk out and washed their hands of him because in walking out he became like a spiritual virus that could infect them all. The police tell me I have no chance of finding him and should give up at once. I've talked to rough sleepers. There are those who've been on the streets for thirty years. He might still be sleeping rough. I suppose what I'm saying is that I must at least exhaust every single avenue before I give in. The Patrick who is dead called himself Patrick Barr. Does that surname mean anything to either of you? The name rings no bells with me, but then Joshua and I called everyone by their first names.'

'There were Barrs,' Hilary says. 'But they were older than I was, quite a lot older. If I remember rightly they were childless. I suppose they might have adopted your son, Isabel, but they must have been over fifty if that's what happened.'

'Over fifty when they first adopted him, so around seventy when he walked out. They've been dead a long time.'

'Perhaps the cult is still lying to you.'

The two women turn and look at Joshua.

'If you were lied to before, and the cult attempted to insert a cuckoo into your nest, there's no proof they aren't lying now. They may be giving you an impossible search so you don't find out the truth. The surname might be invented.'

'I don't need this,' Izzy moans. 'I want a positive trail that I can follow.'

'They are capable of anything. Leah knows that.' Hilary is speaking slowly, as if she is wondering whether she should complete the statement. 'In one corner of the grounds there was a spot no one was allowed near.' She hurries on. 'I'm not saying that your son is dead. You do have a photograph of when he was sixteen. But perhaps not all babies and children survived. If you ever go back to the cult to ask questions, ask about that plot, suggest the police dig it up and carry out DNA tests. Use it as a threat. It might work.'

Joshua nods, 'Some Magdalene homes in Ireland had infant graveyards. It's happened elsewhere.'

Izzy doesn't want to hear this. She gets up and moves to the window. She came here for hope and she's finding the opposite. It's 9pm on a late May evening. The clouds are changing colour and the small lochans are stained with pink and yellow. Joshua has got up and come to stand beside his little sister. He names the mountains as he once did for Leah: 'Quinag, Suilven, Canisp, Stac Pollaidh, Col Mor, Cul Beg, Ben More Coigach.'

But Izzy isn't looking at the view. Her eyes are open but unseeing. She looks, if she looks anywhere, into the space between the clouds and the land, where the sun has just fallen. Her soul reaches out in a wordless prayer to ask *Is my son, my first born, still alive*?

As the day empties of its light, she hears nothing to persuade her that he isn't.

× × ×

Once inside the care home Leah's mood changes. Sarah comes out of the office and takes her in hand. She's carrying a uniform, but seeing Leah she dives back in and comes out with a smaller size.

'Females change here.'

It's a small room with lockers and no privacy. Sarah stays with her, tells her it's hot working in the home so she needs to strip to her underwear before putting the uniform on. Leah does as she's told. She finds a locker with its key still in the door, locks it and takes the key.

'No jewellery except for a single ring.'

Leah lifts up her hands to show her fingers are empty.

'Great. You look the part.'

Leah glances at herself in the mirror. The uniform does nothing for her.

'Now you need to follow me, observe, learn.' Sarah hands her a phone. 'Not for calls. We record everything we do. I'll show you how. We'll start with Room 2. Always refer to the room number when on the radios, use names when you are face to face.'

'Who's in Room 2?'

'Neil.'

Sarah knocks and Leah follows her in.

An old man is lying in bed.

'Morning Neil.'

The man mumbles something.

'Are you getting up today?'

Leah listens to Sarah's tone. It's respectful and cheerful.

'What's there to get up for?' At least that's what Leah thinks Neil says.

'It's a nice day. The sun's shining.'

The man swings his legs out. Leah can see that he's wet the bed.

'I've brought you a new friend, Neil. This is Leah.'

It's time to begin. 'Hello Neil. I'm Leah. Let's get you up and dressed.'

Neil stares at her. She thinks he says, 'I don't like new people.'

'You'll like me.'

He stares at her again. 'Can you sing?'

She nods. 'What do you want to sing?'

Sarah is watching them. Neil begins. 'Oh, what a beautiful morning.' He's note perfect.

Leah joins in.

Sarah waits until Neil forgets the next words. 'Come on, Neil, let's freshen you up.' She hands him his frame and Neil walks towards the toilet.

'Each room has its own en suite,' Sarah explains. 'There's always a pack of gloves and wipes. You'll spend all day pulling gloves on and off.'

Sarah stands Neil in front of the toilet, deftly removes his pants, then wipes him down and dries him. All the time he's talking to her and she's answering. She puts fresh pants on him, then bags the wet ones and ties up the bag. She takes the gloves off and bins them.

As soon as that's done his mood brightens. He grips his frame and says to Leah, 'Do you dance?' He does a few wiggles as if he's inviting her to dance with him. For a moment she's overcome with the pathos and the pity of it.

'Look at you,' says Sarah as he heads for the door. 'You can't go out like that. Which shirt will it be today?'

'Shall I deal with the bed?' Leah asks.

'Housekeeping will do that while Neil has breakfast.'

She's putting a shirt on for the old man. 'Now watch, Leah. You put one arm in and then the other. Only when both arms are in do you pull the shirt up and slip it over his shoulder like this, you see? He has to hold onto the frame with both hands while you dress him. He has to feel safe. You can't go bending his arm up his back.'

'Now breakfast,' Sarah announces when he's ready.

'Bye Leah,' Neil says as he frames his way to the door. 'I'll hold you to that dance.'

The rest of the day is a blur, informed at its very centre by the growing realisation that she belongs here. She admires the pride and perseverance in the old people. Some are grateful, some demand and criticise, but both attitudes are a way of individuals saying *I'm still here. I'm still me.* Second childhood isn't only pathetic, it can also be funny. One of the carers has uncontrollable black hair. She didn't have time to sort it out this morning and gets comments from the residents. 'What do you think of my hair?' she asks Eric. He looks at it and announces, 'It's positively dynamic.'

There's something else in the home too. As Leah follows Sarah into room after room, she comes to realise that it isn't just an act. The friendships between individual carers and residents are real, and perhaps the least complicated in any of their lives. It's a world of touch and flirtation, where each is safe.

At teatime, when Leah's beginning to tire, she sees Wendell again. He's stayed in his room all day, but now he makes his entrance. She happens to see him reach the lounge door and she spots the way he pulls himself together, straightening his back and keeping his face still. Even from where Leah's watching she can see the effort involved. He walks in, head held high. He's wearing a shirt and a tie. The shirt is brightly coloured and tones with his cardigan which looks clean on. His trousers are neat and have creases. He wears shoes that lace up which must, the new Leah thinks, be a faff for the carers. Everything about him says *I shouldn't be here. I don't belong.* As he crosses the space to an empty chair he's an isolated spark of defiance in a sea of acceptance.

The others greet him as he slowly, regally, passes them.

'Hello Wendell. Come to join us?'

'Come for tea and cake?'

'Wendell, you do look smart.'

He smiles.

Once seated, he hooks his stick neatly over the chair arm and folds his hands in his lap.

Sarah is by Leah's side. 'Will you tell me about Wendell?' Leah asks.

'He's himself. You can't josh him or have a laugh with him. You've seen his room. Everything has its place and must be in it. It's like he's afraid of something, but for the life of me I don't know what.'

'No photographs,' Leah says. 'I've only just realised.'

'He has no family. I once tried to talk to him about that, but he closed me down.'

'Visitors?'

'None.'

'What was his job?'

'We don't know.'

A loner, Leah thinks, like me but not like me. She leaves Sarah for the first time that day and crosses the room to sit beside him. She senses that he's wary, that he doesn't trust anyone. He seems to be waiting for her to speak, but she doesn't. She'll play it his way. She smiles at him and then ignores him. If there's one thing she's really good at, it's silence.

As Leah maintains her silence she can feel Wendell relaxing.

9

Chloe and Danny have reached Juozas's house. Chloe works at the lock while Danny watches. The door moves in its frame and then opens. A smell, long cooped up in this airless building, rushes past them to get outside. Chloe leaves the front door open and steps over a colourful pile of fast food adverts. Danny bends down to search for any real mail, but is stopped.

'We touch nothing unless we have to,' Chloe snaps. 'Here.' She offers him a pair of surgical gloves. 'Put these on. They'll know the door has been opened. They'll know someone's been in. But they mustn't be able to prove it's us.'

Danny sniffs the air in the way Leah might. He recognises the odour: it's what his house smells like. He wonders again who it was who broke in through his back window. He follows Chloe as she makes a search. The front door leads into a corridor. Other doors open from it, and there's a staircase on the right. All the doors are shut except the one at the end, which is open just enough to let in natural daylight. Chloe's walking slowly, head down, going towards the open door. Instinctively, Danny looks up. That's when he screams at her to stop.

She turns to him. 'What?'

'Above your head.'

Now she sees it. Balanced on top of the door, ready to fall if the door is pushed open, is an object that looks like a sword with an ornate brass handle. It's been placed there ready to drop on anyone who enters the room.

'Soap bubbles,' Danny reminds her. 'Microphones that turned into loud speakers. He knew we'd come looking for him. He's booby-trapped the house.'

Danny is taller than Chloe, so he reaches up and carefully removes the sword. There's not enough light to see what he's doing, but he can tell the blade is newly sharpened. As he gently pulls the sword away it resists him, and he wonders why. He balances the sword back on the door frame and holds it in place as he carefully opens the door.

Chloe goes in first. Danny follows. The room is absolutely as it should be. A window, a table, settees, a television, an open fireplace, some ornaments, several pictures, a crucifix, speakers, a CD/DVD player.

They're wary now, hardly speaking, moving slowly and looking around them.

Danny turns back to the door. The sword is attached to a wire. The wire is in plain sight and no attempt has been made to hide it. It leads to the back of the CD player. Danny touches Chloe on the shoulder and points it out to her. 'Do we need a specialist team in here?'

At that moment a gust of wind flings the front door wide open and moves the inside door. The sword falls and there's a noise that freezes their blood. It's laughter, a strange maniacal cackle on full volume that fills the house. Chloe sees the CD player is now on and switches it off. The laughter stops.

'He's a joker,' Chloe says. 'He's a bloody joker.'

'Not entirely.'

Danny is examining the sword. Chloe comes over to stand beside him. The sword is unusual. It has a round bobble on the end of the brass handle and the hand grip has four rounded indentations. The hand guard is curved down at each end. The blade is double sided. It's heavy but usable and very sharp.

Danny removes his glove and gently feels the blade with his thumb, then quickly pulls his hand away. 'It's lethal. The wire on the handle would have made it fall blade first.' He smiles at her. 'Say thank you.'

She doesn't. She's frowning again. 'It's a child's trick coated in a grown man's venom.'

'If he knew we were coming he won't have left anything for us to find, will he? I suspect any further search will be a waste of time,' Danny says. Then he adds, 'Perhaps we aren't the only ones he's afraid of. Perhaps the reception was there in case someone else came looking.'

Chloe has detached the sword from the wire and is swishing it through the air. 'Do you need a permit for a weapon like this?'

Danny is working his phone. He wants to check if his guess is right. He punches in *Is there such a thing as a special Lithuanian sword*? It takes him to Wikipedia, and there on the coat of arms of the Commune of Grunwald is a pair of identical swords.

He shows it to Chloe. 'These are part of Lithuanian history.'

He reads: *The battle of Grunwald was part of the Great War fought during 1409–1411 between a Polish-Lithuanian coalition led by King Władysław II and Grand Duke Vytautas (Alexander) on one side and the Teutonic Order aided by West European knights and led by Grand Master Ulrich von Jungingen on the other side. It was a decisive battle of the war and one of the largest in medieval Europe.*

Then he skips on before gasping, 'Listen to this.'

As both sides were preparing for the battle in the morning of 15 July 1410, two heralds carrying two unsheathed swords were announced to King Władysław II. According to the chronicle, they bore the coats of arms of their respective masters: a black eagle in a golden field of King Sigismund of the Romans, and a red griffin in a silver field of the Duke of Pomorania The heralds had been sent by the grand master to Władysław II and Vytautas, but since the latter was busy making his troops ready for the battle, it was only the king, accompanied by his closest aides, who received the envoys. The heralds spoke in German:

'Your Majesty! The Grand Master Ulryk sends you and your brother (...) through us, the deputies standing here, two swords for help so that you, with him and his army, may delay less and may fight more boldly than you have shown, and also that you will not continue hiding and staying in the forest and groves, and will not postpone the battle. And if you believe that you have too little space to form your ranks, the Prussian master Ulryk, to entice you to battle, will withdraw from the plain which he took for his army, as far as you want, or you may instead choose any field of battle so that you do not postpone the battle any longer.'

'In other words, the swords were an invitation to fight. Did Vidar know this? Does he expect us to find it out? Is he issuing us with such an invitation?'

'Weird,' Chloe says, 'but of a piece with what we know.' Then she adds, 'So where's the other sword?'

Danny doesn't follow.

'I want to know what sort of contest I'm in,' she tells him. 'If Vidar is literal, then there will be another sword. Two swords were the invitation, not one.'

They search the house for the next two hours, warily opening cupboards and drawers. They climb into the loft. They check the rubbish in the shed and the garage and find nothing.

At the end of it they are dusty and sweating.

'Perhaps he only has one sword.'

'Or it's his father's sword, used by the partisans to kill Soviets and nothing to do with a battle invitation.'

They go outside. It's late and they are booked into the nearest Premier Lodge. Chloe drives there. Danny wonders what the protocols are for agents staying over. They register. The Premier Lodge is next to a Harvester Inn. He'll eat there. He doesn't think he can ask her to eat with him; that might not be appropriate. In any case, he isn't attracted. He wonders if his meal will be on expenses.

'What time in the morning?' he asks her. She's the boss.

'On assignments we usually eat together,' she tells him. 'But first, I need a shower. Shall we meet over the road in an hour?'

'Okay.'

He picks up his rucksack and looks for the lift.

× × ×

The old city of Cordoba is smaller than Julia expected. On her first walk out to explore she finds the Hotel Mezquita without actively searching for it. It's evening, dark and warm. She walks on without breaking her stride, heading for the river. She wasn't searching for his hotel and she isn't searching for him, she reminds herself. She's come to see the river and the glow of orange lights on honey-coloured buildings that her guidebook recommends. She needs to shake off the car journey and the dullness of her hotel room. Her plan for the evening includes a drink somewhere with a view and then dinner.

She looks at her watch. Last night in Seville, at about the same time, he barged into her evening drink and then left suddenly as soon as he had finished his beer. She paid for that beer. As she approaches the river, the road in front of her is steepening. It will be an effort to walk down there and then all the way back up. As chance has brought her close to his hotel, perhaps it's the perfect opportunity for him to repay her. After all, he did invite her. 'You'll find me in the Hotel Mezquita', Zakk said. Well, here she is.

She checks her phone. There's still nothing from the Company. What the hell are they playing at?

She retraces her steps, keeping to the shadows. It would be too humiliating if he were watching from his window. When she reaches the entrance she walks straight in. The woman on reception lifts her head as if to ask what business she has being there. Julia's seen the sign for the bar and simply points her finger. This hotel is old, much better than hers. It has character.

And there he is. He's drinking at the hotel bar. He's on his own, sipping a cocktail amongst the ancient woodwork. There's just him and the barman.

She walks over, points at Zakk's drink and says to the barman, 'Can I have one of those?'

'Room number?' the barman asks.

'What's our room number?'

Zakk is grinning. There's no other word that will do

for the almost puppy-like look that suffuses his face. He digs in his pocket to check on the paper tab. '221,' he says.

The barman takes his time over the cocktail. Julia, who is on fire with her own daring, doesn't know how he can remain so professionally uncurious.

'How was your day?' she asks Zakk.

'Near perfect,' he tells her. 'I love this place. I went down to the river as soon as I got here. There's this long bridge that crosses it and the view back is terrific. I didn't go into the Mezquita. I thought we'd save that for tomorrow.'

Snap. It's arranged. She feels like a teenager.

Her drink is pushed towards her. A cocktail costs more than a beer. She'll owe him, but it seems there may be more than one chance to pay him back and stay in front. She takes her first sip. She didn't really want another meal on her own, did she? She's heard of and read quite a lot about holiday flings. If not now, when?

× × ×

Chloe and Danny are eating, largely in silence. She's ordered pasta, he a steak. There's a bottle of red wine on the table. Danny is amused. He's finding the professional relationship so unusual. The bottle tells the whole story. They help themselves when their glasses are empty. She ordered it without reference to him. Both refused to taste it. Now it's just there on the table along with the silence.

So Danny asks himself the male question. If Chloe wasn't his colleague, would he fancy her? No, is his immediate answer. She's so uptight. She's one of those women who are their jobs. The stern look never leaves her face. The long black hair which was loose when he first met her has, ever since, been yanked back into a pony tail which sharpens her features. She acts as if she's still angry with him. His offence is that he stopped Mindsett becoming Prime Minister. Today the announcement has been made. There will be no new powers for the intelligence services. Prime Minister Stella Stelling has spoken.

'It would have been worse under Mindsett,' Danny tells Chloe.

She looks up from her pasta.

'What would?'

'Your Service.'

'What are you talking about?'

'He'd have let you snoop, yes, but he'd have cut your independence.'

'How?'

'By sacking anyone who told him what he didn't want to hear.'

'You can't know that.'

'Look at Trump. He believes the Russians over his own intelligence services. He axes any intelligence officer who challenges him. Result: the services are weakened. Is that what you want?'

'You can have both,' she counters. 'I want to be able to read WhatsApp messages. I want to be able to interrogate an iphone. How can I protect people if I don't know what's going on?'

'Can't you already? I always presumed that you would employ hackers to do that for you. Are you really telling me that you never hack, and that there aren't ways you can get the companies to access key groups for you?'

Chloe is silent.

'And no, I don't think you can have both.'

Danny pours himself another glass of wine.

'What I don't understand is how you … ' he corrects

himself '... how we know who is worth hacking and who isn't. There must be so many messages that don't matter, so much chaff for a few hidden grains of wheat. I think if I had something that was secret I'd hide it in plain sight. I might publish it in print in an obscure journal that people buy but never bother to read. Perhaps I'd hide it in a poetry magazine.'

'And where would you hide a sword?'

'In something that was already shaped like a cross.'

That's when Chloe smiles. 'Bingo. Eat up. We're going back to the house.'

She sees him look at the wine bottle.

'I know,' she says, 'but I need to check.'

Danny signs for the meal. They leave the bottle unfinished on the table.

They reach the house. Chloe works the lock. They don't switch lights on, but Chloe leads the way into the lounge.

'Look,' she says.

Danny sees the crucifix. The dimensions are right.

'Careful. Vidar is a joker.'

'And I don't think he can be religious, not with his record.'

Chloe reaches up and unhooks the cross. She pauses but nothing happens. There is no maniacal laughter, no reaction. She turns the cross over. It's built around the sword. 'That's probably how he smuggled it in,' Chloe explains.

Danny sees the message. It's written along the blade. *Pagauk mane, jei gali.*

He interrogates his phone. *Catch me if you can.*

Chloe holds the cross like a trophy. 'We'll take this with us. Now, let's get out before the neighbours become suspicious.'

× × ×

Cordoba in the evening is lit up. The old buildings glow. From the other side of the river, when Julia and Zakk look back, they see the walls of the city and of the ancient Mezquita turned orange and standing proud. It's as if the relative darkness of the modern Cordoba has allowed these buildings to regain their ancient authority. What Zakk and Julia see is stone: worn stone, warm stone, stone shaped by chisels, stone marked by time. In front of them is a statement written by the builders and those who employed them, a statement that has lasted, and been given the reverence that is often accorded to what has survived. The river is more ancient still, its dark waters crested with reflected light.

Julia and Zakk stand on the solidity of a causeway. They lean separately on the warm bridge. They've shared cocktails, then eaten dinner together. He paid for the drinks, she for the dinner. They've talked surprisingly easily. They've felt relaxed with each other.

'It's beautiful,' Zakk says.

'Your hotel or mine?' Julia asks him. Although she feels the risk of everything that is to come, she's determined to stay in control.

× × ×

Back at the Premier Lodge Chloe and Danny carry the large crucifix past the astonished receptionist. They go into Danny's room and place the item on the bed, face downwards.

'So there was a second sword.' Chloe states this factually, without betraying any sense of the excitement that Danny feels. 'Vidar knew the story and somehow he got hold of two swords. It's a complete invitation to battle. So he's a planner as well as a joker. His jokes are not spur of the moment. They are central to who he is and what he is about.'

Danny reaches for the sword handle and it comes away easily from the crucifix scabbard. He examines the writing on the blade, then turns it over. There's something else written on the reverse of the sword blade, this time in English. *I believed.*

Chloe has the outsized crucifix in her hand. The cross is elaborately carved out of wood. A three-petalled clover has been added at either end of the cross piece and at the end of the central pole. There's also a halo effect around the join. It's as if a sun is shining from behind the cross, and its arrow-like rays are pulsing into the universe. There is no Christ, no suffering body with head sunken in pain.

'What do you make of that?' Chloe asks.

'Not much. Shall I photograph it? I presume we're going to replace it in the morning.'

He props the cross on his pillow against the wall and takes several photographs. 'Do you want to take it with you, or shall I keep it here?'

'I don't know about you, but I want a drink. Do you think the restaurant is still open?'

They leave the crucifix where it is.

They meet for breakfast the next morning. Danny orders the works because he's still hungry from his interrupted meal the night before. Chloe has muesli and coffee. The excitement of the previous day has evaporated. They have two swords. The swords are an invitation, but to what? And what does Vidar have that is so detrimental to the UK that it's worth spending time and money tracking him down?

'What's the next move, Col?'

She's shortened his name. 'We go to Vilnius, don't we? That's if the Service thinks it's worthwhile.'

'They'll need convincing. What will we find there?'

Danny balances half a sausage and a crescent of cooked tomato on his fork and holds it just short of his mouth. 'The man,' he suggests.

Chloe waits for more as the sausage and tomato fragment disappear.

'Whatever he did when he was over there, he doesn't want us to know. He must have had to write reports and those reports were filed. Then he stole them from the archive. Don't you think that's odd?'

'Extremely. Because the files would be anodyne. He'd hardly include anything that was self-incriminating. He couldn't be certain that no one would read them. I presume his interrogators read them and found nothing there.'

Danny frowns. 'Unless …' He starts, then pauses. The thought was there a moment ago but it's gone.

'Unless what?' Chloe has finished her coffee and calls the waitress over to order some more.

Danny remembers. 'Unless Vidar recorded something that was innocent at the time but later became incriminating.'

'He was there for years. The file must be considerable.'

'Perhaps it's not just one thing but several things. Much safer to steal the whole file than find time during a burglary to locate and extract single pages,' Danny suggests.

'The Service will never wear it. We're meant to be following a paper trail.'

'Which we can't do because we've run out of paper.'

The fresh coffee has arrived. Chloe helps herself.

'When I was allocated you to train and work with,

Col, I confess I objected.'

'Why was that?'

'I thought you'd be insufferable. I thought you'd think you knew it all.'

'And now?'

'You're doing okay.'

'I was on the streets,' Danny reminded her. 'I've finished someone's cold cup of coffee.'

10

Leah has been trained. Twelve hour shifts have become her new routine. If she's working nights she arrives home at 8.30am and has breakfast with Martin. Then, at 9am, he leaves for the bookshop and she goes to bed. She has no trouble getting to sleep. Staying asleep on a warm summer's day is harder. If she's back on duty at 8pm, Martin sees it as his job to get a meal before Leah goes to work. She has shape to her weeks and days off to look forward to.

Everything about the home intrigues her. The carers come from a variety of backgrounds. Two are from overseas. The others are local: different ages, often with similar stories. Like her, they achieved very little at school. They have children and/or partners. The two most recent arrivals are different. Both are in their early twenties and graduates who could find nothing else in the way of work. One specialised in occupational therapy; the other graduated in creative writing. The carers are a welded group. Because it takes two of them to lift a resident, and this happens often, there are many opportunities to feel part of a team.

And they've accepted Leah. She talks with them all. Actually, it's the residents who have finally made her fluent. The need to cheer them up and chat to them has loosened her tongue. Listening to the other carers has made her much less self-conscious. She has learnt to mimic their easy chatter, and picked up on the tone they use that preserves the dignity of these older people at the same time as it engages their childlike state. Not every resident is easy or accepting of their lot. In the early days she was in awe of the way the carers used subtle differences in the way they approached individuals. She remembers when Theresa May labelled care worker an unskilled job, but there is nothing unskilled happening around her.

The most unexpected thing of all is that there is love in the home. She sometimes wonders if the residents and the carers serve the needs in each other: to love and be loved. There is nothing perfunctory about the interchanges or purely professional about the way her colleagues dress, tidy, encourage, lift and occasionally calm their charges. The residents' families become of secondary importance rather than a vital prop. The emotional life of old people is richer than she could have guessed it to be.

For Leah, the heart of the home is Room 10 and its enigmatic inhabitant, Wendell. The other carers shun him. When the call goes out that help is required in Room 10 and the team is on its break, no one jumps up. So she does. Daytime work in the home is non-stop, but in Wendell's room time slows, perhaps for him too.

She knocks on his door and walks in. His room is different from anyone else's. There are no photographs of family, no ornaments or mementoes of his eighty-eight years. Other residents have brought items from home such as a small bookcase or a favourite chair. Wendell has brought only himself. Most residents have brought paintings to decorate their walls. Wendell keeps the pictures of swans and geese in their golden frames that were part of a job lot bought by the home to decorate the place. Something about the room reminds Leah of the Church of the Living Saints.

What Wendell has brought with him are his clothes. The wearing, washing, ironing regime of a home is geared to make everything easy, so the residents wear outfits that are the simplest to put on and take off. Shoes are always slippers and the colours tend to be drab. Not for Wendell. His wardrobe is full of colourful shirts, bright checks and stripes. He has a range of ties and bow ties that he fastens himself. For trousers he prefers cream, a colour no one else wears because it shows every stain. His ankles are swollen, but he buys new beige socks and cuts them himself so that they fit. He never goes out of his room without wearing a pair of polished brogues, fully laced.

He's a small man, not much taller than Leah. He walks with a stick. He has a small round face and his hair is neither white nor brown but somewhere in between. He shaves himself and recharges his own razor. It's always to be found in the top drawer of his cabinet. Leah has learnt his age and nothing else about him.

'Hello Wendell. What can I do to help?'

He never answers questions, but he has a way of signalling, which is a guessing game for the carers. When they get the answer right he nods.

Today it's obvious what he's rung for. He points to his shoe. Leah knows that putting on his shoes is an effort, only just within his physical abilities. She sees that one sock is on inside out so the shoe won't fit properly. If it was another resident she might make light of it and say, 'Did you get in a muddle? I can sort that.' But Wendell won't be joshed in that way. Leah knows he has worked on his sock and shoe until he is exhausted and has pressed the bell only as a last resort.

'It's a nice day isn't it, Wendell? You want to go outside, don't you, and you want to look your best.'

She removes the shoe and the sock which she flicks inside out. Wendell's foot is cold to the touch. She replaces the sock and laces his shoes, making sure the bows are symmetrical.

'There. Do you want help getting up?'

He shakes his head. She thinks he is entirely 'with it'. It's in the way he watches her, in the occasional grimaces and frowns, in the way he manages, just as she once did, without words. She knew the moment she walked in that he was glad it was her and not one of the others, but his face never changed.

She's intrigued. She does want to know more. 'I didn't talk for years,' she tells him. 'From the age of nine to the age of thirty-four I never said a word to anyone.'

He stays in his chair. She knows he won't get up until she goes out of the room because of the effort involved and the possibility it might take him several attempts. She looks at him and knows he's listening. 'You've found what I found, haven't you, that words are unnecessary.'

His eyes are grey with dark flecks. Everything about Wendell is controlled and calm, but his eyes are always alert. They're watching her now. Normally she would do another job while talking, empty a waste paper basket or check the bathroom, but not in Room 10.

'Do you also find that words get in the way of watching? I did. When I didn't speak, people left me alone. I could live inside my head.'

She'll stop there. That's enough about herself. She'll know next time if he wants to hear more. She looks at him and doesn't think he's offended by what she's said so far.

'You look very smart,' she tells him, 'ready for anything.' Then, because he knows they have to make notes and keep a record, she adds, 'I won't put that in the book.'

There's no thank you, not even a smile, but perhaps there's some sort of recognition in his intelligent eyes.

She leaves him sitting in the chair. Later she catches sight of him walking across the lawn wearing his hat, moving slowly and rhythmically, heading for the seat they leave out for him. It faces away from the home so that he can look out across the fields and the river up to the hills.

× × ×

Julia wakes at first light. She blinks and looks around her. It isn't her room. Then she remembers. It's his room. Of course it is. He's lying beside her and she suspects he's deeply asleep. The bedroom curtains are thin gauze and the room is full of light. She props herself up on one elbow and examines him.

He's no longer young. Around his eyes and down the side of his face there are thin creases, almost like cracks in his skin, which are spreading and widening. Where his eyes meet the edge of his skull the lines are already deep. His sideboards are white. The skin on his nose has perhaps seen too many hot sunny days. Even when he's sleeping his forehead does not smooth itself out completely.

We are similar in age, she thinks. We are neither of us in the first or even the second flush. So what does what happened last night mean to him and mean to me? Was it a one-night stand, a getting back into the saddle for only the second time since my marriage ended?

She finishes her perusal of the man whose bed she shared for the night. She stayed. That surprises her. The arrangement was that his hotel was nearer, and afterwards she would go back to hers where all her stuff was already unpacked. It was her choice, her control. Why, then, had she stayed?

He's fast asleep. She could dress quietly and abandon him. He doesn't know where she's staying, so she could leave meeting again to chance. There's only Granada left on her itinerary.

But she stays where she is. She's tempted to reach out and gently stroke his temples, like a mother might a sleeping child. She's happy just to watch him. How can that be? There are so many reasons why she should get up and leave him there: she's paid for breakfast at her hotel; if she leaves now only the night staff will see her go; she needs a shower and clean clothes; there aren't that many hours before she needs to be on the road to Granada, and she has yet to go round the Mezquita which was the whole purpose of coming to Cordoba.

Then there's the most powerful reason of all: what has just happened isn't and can't be serious. She knows nothing about him. She could never take him home and introduce him to the family. There are only four days left before the end of the fortnight, and she must focus on her own future. She checks her watch. It's 5.30am, time to be away. It will be wonderfully daring for a woman of her age and competence to steal from a lover's bed and walk through the city in the early morning light.

Still she doesn't move. But then another reason to leave flashes in her head: she's losing control by staying. If he wakes he'll know he has a hold over her. So she slips out of bed quietly, retrieves her underwear and puts it back on, finds the rest of her clothes and dresses. Before she opens the door she turns back to look at him. He's still asleep, but the cover has slipped and he's lying naked on the bed. The sight of him nude and unaroused makes him seem vulnerable. Now she is the voyeur and he is her victim.

There's a pen and paper on the desk top. She could leave him a note.

She picks up the biro and writes *11am at the Mezquita*. He'll find it or he won't. It's an invitation or it isn't. She creeps to the door and opens it. Then she closes it behind her as softly as possible, but the click is still loud enough to wake the corridor.

She walks down the stairs instead of taking the lift. There's no one at the reception desk. She steps into sunshine that is already warm. A few people are around. A water cart crawls past her as it sluices the gutter. A baker's shop hums and exudes that wonderful smell of fresh bread. Her hair must look a mess, but no one gives her a second glance.

The route to her hotel takes her by the river. The water isn't green as in Seville. Its flow is faster, and at this hour of the morning herons and egrets line its bank. At the crossroads she starts to climb the hill, leaning into her step. She feels alive. She feels whole. As she climbs, keeping the ancient wall on her left-hand side, she can't escape the thought that something important has happened.

When she crosses the square her phone pings. Yesterday she would have looked at once. Yesterday she'd have checked her phone the moment she woke. Today she needs to sneak back into her own hotel and take a shower. She leaves the phone in her handbag and quickens her pace.

× × ×

Chloe and Danny land in Vilnius. Emily from the embassy is there to meet them. She has a car waiting. They register at the hotel, put luggage in their rooms, then join her across the road for coffee.

Emily has a man with her. She introduces him as Nojus. He's lean and dapper, dressed in a linen suit. His hair is pure white. Danny guesses he's in his seventies.

Nojus shakes hands. He does so with a little bow.

'I wanted you to meet Nojus,' Emily explains, 'because to us at the embassy he is Mr Lithuania. By profession he is an English teacher, but he lived through the Soviet times and he knows the Žemaitis family. He's even met the member of the family you are particularly interested in.'

'I have met Juozas, and interestingly his father, Antanas, is back in the headlines,' Nojus states. His voice is deeper than they expect. It commands attention.

Chloe and Danny look at each other.

'Why?'

'Antanas is a hero of the partisan movement. He fought the Russians in 1939 after the notorious Ribbentrop/Molotov: Nazi/Russia pact that handed my independent country to the Russians. After the Nazis had been defeated he fought the Soviets again in 1945.'

'A brave man,' Chloe suggests.

'Oh yes, he was brave,' Nojus confirms. 'If you want to see how brave you should visit the KGB museum. It's where he was held and where he was executed. Both father and son were held there at different times. I'm willing to bet that isn't recorded in any file you have seen about Juozas.'

Chloe's eyes flash a warning to Danny. He is clearly not to confirm this. She steers the conversation away from what they know to what Nojus might be able to tell them.

'So why is he back in the headlines?'

'Antanas was a patriot. Antanas was a hero. Both statements are true, but when the Nazis invaded Russia in June 1941 Lithuania fell into Nazi hands. That is a time we like to forget. These days we like our heroes to be pure. These days we have forgotten that it is hard to be right the whole time. The accusation is that Antanas collaborated with the Nazis, that Antanas helped round up Jews to be sent to the gas chambers. So to our old people, for whom the Soviets were the real enemy, he is a hero, but to the young, who have been taught about the Holocaust, and who were born after the Soviets left, he is a villain.'

'What do you think, Nojus?' Danny asks.

He smiles at them in his urbane manner. 'I think everyone's first duty is to survive,' he says.

'Where's the museum? We should go there,' Danny suggests.

Chloe nods.

'If you would like me as your guide I'll pick you up at your hotel at 9.30am. I'll show you the museum. These days it is called the KGB museum, but during the war it was also the Gestapo interrogation centre. The two services swapped over but kept the same equipment and some of the same prisoners. I should warn you it isn't an easy place to visit.'

'Will it help us understand Juozas?'

'He was there for a fortnight.'

From the outside the building is of its age and looks like an office block, which it was.

'The bureaucrats worked upstairs,' Nojus explains. 'The interrogation centre is downstairs. Most of the important things happened in the basement. The local joke was that the basement had an excellent view because you could see Siberia from there.'

He leads them in and they walk down the steps. Nojus points out the two holding cells on the right. 'This is where people were first incarcerated,' he tells them. 'There's no light and no room to sit. Imagine listening to the noises.'

The corridors are narrow. Green paint gives a sense of oppression. Individual light bulbs hang from the ceiling. For captives and interrogators alike there was no daylight.

Nojus walks them through. They go into cells. They stare at the water torture room where inmates were continually doused in freezing water until they couldn't stand any longer. When this happened they fell against the sharp stone walls so that their blood ran down. In winter the walls were often frozen, so to walk in was to see old blood even before they felt the pain.

Danny and Chloe visit the execution room. To those about to be shot the room would look empty; the man with the gun was always hidden behind the door. They walk out into the courtyard where lorries collected the bodies and took them to mass graves that are still being discovered.

Father and son were both held here, father in the grimmest days, son in the more relaxed times when the cells had beds and the place had the air of a mental hospital. The father was shot here. The son walked out of the front door and continued spying for the British. There are so many questions.

Nojus takes them to a café. They choose to sit outside even though the day is chilly. Anything to be in the fresh air.

'Antanas Žemaitis was held there for two months before

he was shot,' Nojus informs them. 'Those who were held with him report that he was almost foolishly brave. He spent days in the water room. As far as we know he refused to talk; most importantly he refused to reveal the names of his fellow partisans and the whereabouts of his wife and child. He encapsulated the defiance this country has worshipped.'

'How many talked?' Danny asks.

Nojus's head lifts. 'That is an impolite question, one that people of my age never ask. To be under foreign occupation is to be filled with guilt. We who lived through those times did what we had to do in order to survive.'

Were you in there, Danny wonders.

'I'll paint another picture for you,' Nojus continues. 'Think of Antanas, bull brave and freezing, doused in icy water and refusing to talk. Think of the Soviet guards who have to stand and watch, with paper and pens ready to take down his confession. The guards are willing the victim to talk, since the water that freezes the victim is making them shiver too. The victim's hatred is purified by his suffering. Now think of the officers in the clean fresh rooms of the upper floors. Do they want to spend their working days hearing screams? They too are afraid because Beria, the head of their Service, is a psychopath. And Beria is afraid of his boss, Stalin, terrified that he will be the next victim of Stalin's purges. At the top of the pile is Stalin himself, and he is afraid of anyone and everyone, so he never stops killing. What you have walked round were the bricks and mortar of a deadly game in which the perpetrators were also victims.'

'And Juozas, why was he able to walk out into the sunlight?' Chloe asks.

'Of course, I don't know. Only Juozas himself knows

that.'

'What's your guess?' Chloe persists.

Nojus beams at her. 'I don't guess, young lady. I live with what is around me.'

'What's next?' Chloe asks.

'Would you like to meet Juozas's cousin?'

'Is she willing to meet us?'

'Yes. She lives not far from here. It is a nice day. We can walk.'

11

Just how many idiots are out there, James wonders. It feels to him as if the legend of Pandora's Box has been given a modern twist and the age of rationalism is finally over. These days every nutter has the right to express their view, and every view, however silly or offensive, demands serious consideration. It seems to James that *I think therefore I am* has been replaced by *I emote therefore I speak*. In his self-incarceration he watches with awe and dismay as Donald Trump, President of the United States, asserts the rights of a five year old in a priapic male body to have temper tantrums and repeat, as if gospel, whatever rumour has been circulating in the nursery. He wonders whether he and Jud would have won if they had attacked truth itself and demolished facts. Had they been too conventional? It worries him.

His heart envies the success of those who have abandoned any sense of logic or moral integrity even as his brain tells him that it will end badly, that facts will refuse to be ignored, that they will have their crushing revenge.

His phone rings. This time he picks it up with dread. As soon as he hears the voice on the other end of the line he knows he should have ignored it.

'Look, I'm sorry about calling you a tosser and all that. It was in the heat of the moment.'

'What do you want, Jud?'

'We won, didn't we?'

'If you mean did we win the ballot of members, then yes we did.'

'So I should be Prime Minister. That's the law.'

'No it isn't.' James switches into explanation mode. 'It isn't a matter of law, it's a matter of convention. The Palace invites whoever has most chance of forming a government by commanding a majority in the House. Normally that is the same as the person who wins the ballot of members …'

Jud interrupts. Three sentences is, after all, his normal attention span. 'And I won, so can we challenge Stella becoming Prime Minister in law?'

James sighs. To be, at heart, a rational person amongst such idiocy is trying.

'Let me get this right, Jud. You want to take your Party to court to demand that MPs and Party members, who are still breathing sighs of relief that you are not Prime Minister, should embarrass Her Majesty by saying that they messed up the recommendation and have decided they love you after all.'

'Exactly. You always were quick on the uptake. Can we win?'

'Jud, I'm not a lawyer but, given your self-induced notoriety, I would say there is less than no chance at all.'

Jud needs time to work out that sentence. 'Are you sure?'

'The key phrase is *command a majority in the House.*'

'I could do that. They don't hate me.'

'No Jud, they don't hate you. If they hated you that would be alright. Instead of hating you they despise you, which is much worse. They loathe and detest you because you took them in and made fools of them.' James pauses because he's not sure Jud is getting the message. 'Let me put it like this, Jud. Your MPs would rather vote for one of the cockroaches that occasionally scuttle across the floor of the tea room than vote for you.'

'I take it that's a no.'

'It is.'

There's silence.

'Then I'll phone Annabelle Pitts-Tucker and see what she says.'

'You do that.'

James puts down the phone and looks for Game of Thrones on Netflix. With so little happening in his life he's begun binging on box sets.

× × ×

Inesa Žemaitis turns out to be a little old lady with long grey hair rather precariously balanced on the top of her head. She's plump and round-shouldered, but her head is held high and her face beams at them. She speaks no English and Nojus has to translate.

'Three visitors and two of them from England. How exciting,' she tells them. 'I'm left on my own so often that any visitor is welcome.'

Danny is having a tough day. Until he walked down into the KGB interrogation centre, being in the intelligence services was a game, a preoccupation, a way of earning money and building a new persona. The claustrophobia of the building appalled him. Everything Nojus has said is giving him a fresh perspective.

'So who are you?' Inesa asks Danny.

'Juozas is missing,' Chloe explains. 'We need to find him before he does something silly.'

'Poor Juozas. We always were a headstrong family. It never got us very far. Antanas became a hero. They put a plaque up in his memory. Now it's been torn down.'

'Did Juozas come to see you when he was over here?'

'Yes. I got the impression he was here to find out as much as he could about his father.' Inesa pauses. 'I remember him in this very room, pacing round, telling me he was so proud of what Antanas had achieved. We were the same age but, because he hadn't lived through what we lived through, he seemed so much younger.'

'Did he come just the once?'

'No, at first he came every day. He wanted to know so much: names, addresses, friends of his father who had survived, all that. He wanted to meet them, hear about his hero father from the lips of those who had known him.'

'And did he meet them?'

'Yes. I fed him names and addresses slowly. I did that because I liked having him here and needed to keep luring him back.'

Danny breaks in. 'Before all that, did he tell you precisely why he was in Vilnius?'

'He said he was fighting his father's battles, spying on the Soviets for the British.' She stops. 'I never knew if that was true.'

Chloe ignores the implied question. She needs to check what she's just heard.

'He told you he was spying for us?'

'Yes,' Inesa confirms, 'more than once. It was his boast, and I feared for the Žemaitis in him. My family always needed to stand out from the rest. Is it true that he was a British spy?'

Danny keeps his face straight. He is staggered when Chloe nods.

'Oh, I might have misjudged him then. He talked about his father so much that I wondered he had time for anything else.'

Nojus interrupts his own translating. 'It was a dangerous thing to say and a dangerous thing to hear.' He explains what he's just said to Inesa in Lithuanian. She nods.

'I never passed it on,' she says.

'When you'd answered his questions, did he keep visiting you?'

A shadow passes over Inesa's face and she momentarily closes both eyes. It tells Danny the answer to his question before it's translated.

'He stopped coming to see me.'

Danny notices the frown. It's as if she's wondering whether to tell them something.

'No one comes to see me,' she explains. 'My family have died or left. The young fled to Europe to make money after the banks collapsed following Independence. In this country you can tell your age by how many people have stopped coming to see you.'

'There was something else you nearly said about Juozas.' Chloe pushes her luck. 'If it might help us find him, save him from himself …'

This time Nojus's translation seems over-long. 'There were rumours about boys,' Inesa finally admits. 'About boys and young men.'

'And do you think he found out what he needed to

about his dad, about Antanas?'

'I think he must have. I had other names, but he stopped asking questions and stopped coming, so he must have.'

They leave soon afterwards. They promise to let her know if they find her cousin. They promise to look after him. They promise anything to get away.

Nojus has other things to do. He leaves them and they thank him profusely.

The moment he's gone Chloe says, 'I need a drink. I need a sandwich.'

Danny points to a bar across the road.

It's five in the afternoon, too early for a proper meal. The bar is far from empty. Danny orders two large lagers, bread, butter and olives. The heat has gone out of what has anyway been a cold day so they sit in a corner inside.

At first they drink and eat. Then Chloe wipes her mouth and pushes her plate away. 'Are we any further forward? I have to account for this trip.'

Danny is still being trained. 'Perhaps we're a little further forward. I'm getting a picture of a proud man, proud of his family and his father, overconfident too. He was clearly fascinated by his dad and charged off to meet people who might have known him.'

Chloe shakes her head. 'It doesn't fit, does it? This was Vidar's first assignment. He was in enemy territory. Yes, it was post Stalin, but the KGB were still functioning and that place was horrific. Why was he being so incautious? He should have been too frightened to have liaisons, but he clearly wasn't.'

'He found something out and he stopped going back to Inesa. He stopped asking.'

'The file tells the story of a brave, resourceful man who

was passing back excellent information to HQ. We know the information was good because it was collaborated by defectors. Yet his cousin tells of a man spending his time going round searching for the dad he never knew. The two stories don't marry together.'

'They might,' Danny suggests. 'Inesa would give him links to the partisans. What if the partisans were his sources of information and the search for Antanas was a red herring? He went to his cousin to begin with. Through his family name he found a network loyal to Antanas and persuaded them to be loyal to him. After Inesa had fed him contacts he must have found such a good source of further information that he never went back to her.'

'Or did he find out about his dad's Nazi collaboration? Did he come to Lithuania to trace his father but found this squalid secret, that the martyred hero was in fact a collaborator in the worst crime of the last century? If he hero-worshipped his dad, what would be do with that knowledge? How might it change him?'

'They warned us about this in training,' Chloe tells Danny, 'that there are always several hypotheses that can meet any set of facts.'

'And how do you tell which is the right hypothesis?'

'You collect more facts.'

Danny stands up. 'Are we meeting up for dinner?' he asks.

Chloe has a half-rueful smile. 'I haven't drunk enough yet to get rid of the images of torture from this morning. When I have, you can rush back to the hotel. Meanwhile, it's my round and you're going nowhere.'

× × ×

Occasionally, when Leah is on nights, Martin stays at his flat. In the long summer evenings Izzy gets restless. She knows Martin and Leah are concerned for her, but they ask too many questions and so restrict her freedom. Ever since she returned from Scotland she has toyed with the idea of going back to the cult on her own. There must be more that Katherine can tell her about her son.

Tonight, without any clear idea of what she will do when she gets there, Izzy sets off. It's one of those magical nights in early June, so still that the country seems to be holding its breath. A myriad of greens entrance on both sides of the road. Some are tinged with gold from the low sun. The roads are empty, and she gets to Leeds in good time. She parks outside the cult and, seeing that the door is open, she steps inside.

The memory of being here before is as vivid as the new leaves. The corridors look the same, the walls carry the same messages, but the atmosphere has changed. It's not the foreboding place it once was. She listens but can hear no one moving. The hum has gone. It feels like walking into a school just after the staff and students have left for the summer break.

She knows where Katherine's room is. It's down the corridor, the last door on the right. This is where Katherine led them when Martin and Leah were with her. This is where Katherine finally produced the file with the photo of her real son. But first, as the door into the grounds is open, she'll explore, look for what Hilary warned her about.

It's near twilight as she steps into the deep greens of this forbidden land. She follows the wall round. Hilary told her to look for a patch of ground in the corner. Keeping the wall on her right she notices that in one spot there are tall bushes in a curve, but the wall itself forms a right angle so there is a hidden space. Behind the bushes she can see light glinting off the razor wire. The bushes are thin, recently planted. She pushes her way through and finds a corner of hard packed earth screened from the rest of the grounds. And the wall has plaques, several of them. It's too dark to read them, but she counts nine plaques of different sizes. They seem to record dates, not names. It's spooky standing in that spot, with hard earth and goodness knows what else under her feet. She pushes her way back through the bushes.

Katherine is standing in front of her. 'What do you think you're doing?'

'Trespassing,' Izzy replies. 'With a little bit of archaeology on the side. Why are the memorials hidden?'

Katherine shakes her head. 'What do you want?'

'More information.'

In growing darkness Izzy can't make out Katherine's expression, but she hears the change of tone. 'Look, it's awkward. It's my retreat night. Any moment now I'm due to be locked into the chapel. I have a night of penance and prayer in front of me. Why don't you come back tomorrow?'

'And will you help me if I do?'

'I'll do my best.'

'What time?'

'2pm, after I've slept.'

'Okay.'

Katherine sees Izzy out of the door, then rushes to prepare. Izzy watches her go and, because there is no one about, re-enters and makes her way into the chapel.

She doesn't have long to wait.

A procession is making its way towards her. Katherine is at its head. She's dressed in white and holding a lighted candle. Her hands are clasped round it and her face is bowed.

When the procession reaches the chapel only Katherine steps inside. Izzy holds her breath but no one follows Katherine in. A young woman with red hair produces a key and chants:

This is your night of penance, of prayer and fasting
when God's Woman prostrates herself before the Lord.
No food or drink shall pass your lips until dawn.
May God bless you and answer all our prayers.

Izzy sees Katherine move away from the door towards the altar. The door is shut behind both of them and each hears the key turn.

Izzy sits and waits.

Katherine places the lighted candle on the altar and kneels. Then she prostrates herself on the floor and stretches out her arms, fingers pointing away from her.

It surprises Izzy that Katherine's obeisance seems real. She lies still and Izzy can hear the murmur of her prayers. That Katherine might genuinely believe in God has never entered Izzy's head. This is both surprising and disturbing. She feels like a voyeur, a kind of spiritual peeping Tom.

She could have come back tomorrow, but Katherine has lied to them in the past and, if there are no more files and no more photographs, Katherine herself is Izzy's last chance to find out anything more about what happened to her son. This way she has Katherine to herself for a whole night, until the candle burns down, dawn comes, and the key turns in the lock again. She has to make this count.

As quietly as she can she stands up and walks towards the altar. The floor is solid so her feet make no noise. When she's within two metres of the praying Katherine, she speaks.

‘While you’re down there,’ she says sharply, ‘say one for me too.’

12

Darkness falls later in Vilnius. It's still light when Chloe and Danny walk out into the long Baltic twilight. They are no further forward. They've spent the evening drinking, eating and worrying the case until they're exhausted. The bar was crowded even at this time of night, and it's a relief to be crossing the chilly square in this strange half-light.

Chloe drunk is no less professional than Chloe sober. They've talked nothing but the case. Chloe's drunk beer and shorts until she's unsteady on her feet, but her face has the same buttoned look it always has. Danny is feeling the drink. His younger self might have flirted, just to check if that was expected. This new Danny is more cautious. They walk towards the hotel, collect their room keys, and arrange a time to meet in the morning.

Chloe goes upstairs somewhat unsteadily. Danny walks outside again. There was a bench in the square. He'll sit there until his head settles. He enjoys the monochrome world, the pattern of greys and blacks made by buildings and the square itself. He looks at his watch. It's midnight, but they are so far north that it still isn't completely dark.

Across the square is a large ornate church with several domes, each one topped with a short stone spire. Someone else is out this late. Danny has to squint through the gloom. Standing in front of the church door is a tall, painfully thin figure wearing a gilet. He's beckoning Danny over.

Danny stands and moves forward. The figure appears to be holding up a bottle and two shot glasses.

Danny stares. It has to be Ivor. What the hell is he doing here? Ivor continues to gesture, so Danny crosses the square slowly to meet him. As he walks, two thoughts are uppermost in his mind: how will he explain this to Chloe, and the last thing he needs now is any more vodka.

'Hello Danny,' Ivor says.

× × ×

Leah is back on nights. She stands outside Wendell's room. The rule is that the night staff have to check on the residents every two hours. Many of the residents are used to care staff walking into their rooms at night, but Wendell isn't.

Listening outside the door Leah hears him cry out. He must be dreaming, she thinks. She listens again, but the room is silent. She opens the door and steps inside.

But Wendell isn't in bed. He's standing at the window, staring into the darkness. He doesn't even turn when Leah walks in and speaks.

'I thought I heard a cry,' Leah says. 'I thought you might be having a nightmare.'

Wendell ignores her. He's standing very still, staring out at something. Leah doesn't know what. She sees darkness and trees through the window. She sees that

Wendell is shaking.

'I came in to see if you were alright.'

Leah has long suspected that Wendell's hearing is good, so he must have heard what she said. She won't repeat the statement but simply wait for a response. Finally, he turns and she sees he's angry.

'A dream,' she suggests. 'You must have been having a dream.'

Wendell is shaking his head and seems to be whispering to himself. His voice is too soft for her to make out, but she thinks he might have said, 'Ghosts, more ghosts.'

In a place where the early stages of dementia are common, Wendell's behaviour is not unusual. Stepping outside later, however, for a breath of air on a hot night, Leah sees something odd: a grey mass shaped like a man is moving against the black of a pine trunk. Whoever it is doesn't want to be seen. The man steps away and vanishes. Because she's holding her radio and can summon help if she needs to, Leah goes to investigate. But there's nothing to see and nothing to hear, except a car without its lights on moving away from the walkers' car park.

× × ×

'No vodka,' Danny insists, but Ivor is already sloshing transparent liquid into the glasses. Danny takes one and follows Ivor into the church. He's always done what Ivor told him. Why change now?

'Should we be drinking in here?' Danny asks.

'In great days of Soviet Empire religion was banned so good comrades turned this into liquor store.'

Ivor leads Danny into a pew where they sit and look at the altar.

'Ivor, why are you here?'

'I told you when we last spoke they either shoot me or use me. Simple choice. Perhaps not permanent choice, but for now they use me.'

'They?'

'Call them the Initials. KGB, SVR, FSB, GRU, FSO. You have the MIs, we have the Initials.'

'We?'

'I loved London, Danny; you must believe that. Or rather, I loved the idea of London, what London used to be.'

'But you never went through with your application for asylum.'

'True.'

Danny hasn't touched his vodka. Ivor is already on a second glass.

'True,' Ivor muses. 'A misused word – true. Not a useful word I find.'

'I asked my employers about you,' Danny tells the church and the crucifix behind the altar. 'I asked them because I wanted to help you, but you put yourself beyond my help.'

'Also true.'

Danny waits for an explanation.

Ivor scowls. 'I'm a clever man. I have skills. You never had to apply to your country for asylum through proper channels, did you?'

Danny shakes his head.

'They expect you to beg, to crawl to them. They treat you with contempt. I am a proud man.'

'Yesterday you were terrified of Borstov. Today you're working for him.'

'Same thing when you think about it, Danny.' Ivor takes another swig. 'I met a man once, Ukranian.

Between 1939 and 1945 he fought in four different armies. What question do you think I ask him?'

This time Danny stays silent.

'You, Danny, would have asked him why. I know that because you are the pure in heart. You would only fight for what you are prepared to die for.'

Danny nods.

'Wrong question. I ask right question. I ask him which was the best army to fight for.'

Danny waits.

'And he said, 'Yugoslavian because they gave you most weekends off from the fighting.''

I shouldn't be here, Danny thinks. I shouldn't be here. This is not the Ivor I knew.

Ivor is still talking. 'This man, he compared armies like you do supermarkets, this one for pay, that one for weapons, Yugoslavian for time off.'

There is a long silence.

Then, 'This not joke, Danny. He was military age. He wanted to survive, didn't want to be slave worker and starve. How do you survive? Simple: join an army. In modern wars army is the safest place.'

He turns and stares at Danny as if he is both drawn to him and at the same time repulsed by what he sees.

'We can't be nothing, Danny. We have to live somewhere real and be something real. You know that; that's why you join the MIs. I too have to be somewhere real and I do not have your choices. London was not real for me. Russia is my country. Russia as it is, not as I want it to be.'

Danny is tired; he doesn't want this self-pity. 'What do you want with me, Ivor?'

'To have a drink.'

'I'm not drinking Ivor. I've been drinking all night and I've had enough.'

'Okay. I come clean. You are asking questions about Juozas Žemaitis. We too are interested in Juozas. I wondered if we could share information.'

'Your Initials held him, tortured him and let him go.' Danny pronounces these as if they are certainties. 'I presume you let him go because he made you promises.'

Ivor shakes his head. 'Worse than that, Danny, I've read the file. We never realised who he really was. He spun a story that his name was passed to us because of his father and the settling of old scores: left/right splits among his father's partisan friends. We believed him. His language was so good we took him on as translator. He was on our payroll, but only for translating.'

'So why are you interested in him? He made a fool of your Service. It's a long time ago.'

'Soap bubbles and speakers hidden in the wall. The Juozas pranks are famous in Russia. They have become a code for rebellion on social media. My new masters have no sense of humour. They take themselves very seriously. They never laugh. Juozas made Soviet heroes into laughing stock. If he'd shot them all we'd have understood and merely noted it in the files. But to be the butt of his jokes ….'

'How interested in him are you?'

'The Skripals, Litvinenko, remember what happened to them and the others? Juozas is on a list. We have a new Czar, a new Emperor. He needs some clothes. He needs to show his power.'

So far Danny thinks he has done alright. Ivor has told him much he needs to know and Danny's given nothing away. His head is clearing. He takes a sip of vodka. 'When we were in London, Ivor, which game or games were you playing?'

Ivor says nothing.

'Then I'll tell you. Plan A was to use Jud Mindsett to get fast track asylum. Plan B was to use me to impress your Russian master, wasn't it? I showed you the photographs of Borstov and Mindsett. You pretended to back them up, but who were you sending them to? Were you warning those who were already your masters? Is that why they photographed me? Harry knew who you were, didn't he?'

'Only a fool has just one plan, Danny.'

'You were good,' Danny tells him. 'You had me fooled.'

'Other selves, Danny. You should know all about that. The Ivor you knew was genuine. He hated, still hates, what's happening in his country and in the world, but he has a more pragmatic twin: the Ivor you see in front of you. In London I was at a crossroads. You scuppered my plan A when Stella Stelling won. I had to fall back on plan B.'

'What do you want?'

'I didn't betray you, Danny. I had opportunity.'

'And now?'

'I need the file, the one Juozas has, the one that recounts his victories against the Soviets. What I really need is it not to be published, not ever. Juozas can keep what's left of his life. I just need you to tell me, out of our friendship, if you find the file you destroy it. Do I have your word?'

'I'm being trained, Ivor. I have a partner. What do I do about her?'

'I did help you, Danny. I told you to back photos up. Why would I do that if I was only playing for the other side?'

Danny nods, accepting the truth of what Ivor has said.

'So do I have your word?'

'My task is to find Juozas,' Danny explains. 'No one has said very much about the file. And I, of course, don't know what my partner's task is.' It's on the tip of his tongue to ask what's in the file, but he mustn't betray what he doesn't know.

'Mine is to make sure that the file is never published. This way we can both be successes.'

Ivor takes a long look at Danny and sees he is uncomfortable. Before he lets him go he must offer a justification of sorts for who he is now. 'As we are in a church, so let me quote the Bible, Danny pure in heart. In the Sermon on the Mount, Jesus said *Blessed are the pure in heart, for they shall see God*. These days the words need changing. I say, Blessed are the pure in heart, for they live in a lucky time.'

As they leave the church Ivor and Danny shake hands, then go their separate ways.

13

Katherine sits up suddenly. Izzy stands over her. 'I couldn't wait until tomorrow, Katherine, when you may or may not have seen me. I need to know now. I am your penance.'

'My penance is set by God. Go away.'

'I can't, Katherine. We're locked in together. We're locked in for the whole night, unless this whole thing is a charade and you have a key.'

Katherine shakes her head.

'I thought not. Look, I'll go silent once you've told me everything I need to know. I promise you that. I'll hide when they release you, and I'll sneak out. But I have to know. Do your penance to me first and then I'll let you do your penance to God.'

'I've told you everything.'

'Not the paperwork stuff. I want the things that are in your memory.'

'What things?'

'Let's begin with the Barrs. Who were they?'

'I don't remember.'

'I called my son Patrick. When I left him with you he became Patrick Barr. Presumably the Barrs adopted him?'

'I was a child myself when that happened. There were more Saints then. I was just growing up.'

'Think, Katherine. Think what you were told. You were older than my son. I need to know what happened.'

There's a long silence. The chapel is dark. The only light comes from the single candle. Like a Rembrandt painting it lights up two women in a pool of colour. The room is airless and has no windows, so there is no breeze. The candle flame is vertical and constant, so the area of light and the line where it ends never flicker. One of the women is sitting, one is standing. The seated woman is wearing white. Her dark hair is loose and covers her shoulders. The standing woman is older. She's dressed in bright colours. Her hair is dyed to make her look younger.

Suddenly the older woman crouches down and puts her face very close to the younger woman's face. The candlelight is golden on both their skins.

'This is a face to face, Katherine, but no one is taking notes. Nothing will be written down. I need you to feel free to talk. I'd like to bet that you've never opened your heart to another woman. Would darkness make it easier?'

She leans over and snuffs out the candle. The darkness isn't quite instant. There's an afterimage in both their minds, not of the candle but of the other's face. These linger for a long time, then go out.

'So let's talk,' the older woman says, not quite knowing what she's doing. 'Let's talk in this darkness. It'll be easier because we can't see each other. We can't pick up on sudden changes of expression. Darkness is where you have to tell the truth.'

The younger woman is silent.

'I'll start,' the older woman announces. 'I'll tell you about Gary. You've never been married, have you? Gary was my second escape. My first was when I handed Patrick over to your Church. I handed my baby over and walked out of here a free woman, but there was a hole somewhere inside me. I went to university and bumped into Gary. Gary was a doer. I spotted that at once. I thought he was the man who would protect me and make me rich. It was fun at first, but the hole was still there. I tried to fill it with children, with Julia and James, Leah and Danny. The house got noisier. There was no silence to mourn the child I'd given away. Gary worked day and night. I childminded. But the hole inside me only grew. I wasn't a good parent. It was my fault Leah stopped talking. James and Julia were terrible bullies.' She pauses. 'And the truth is that Gary made me feel lonely. The truth is that he didn't need me or any of us.' Izzy stops there and waits.

The darkness in this place is like the darkness in a deep cave. There is an utter absence of light. However long you stayed here, your eyes would never adjust.

Another voice starts and it's different: younger, full of unhappiness, so hesitant that each gap might be a full stop.

'He picked me out when I was twelve… made a fuss of me … I don't know exactly when it started. There were always hands … when you're a child those hands touch heads … go round shoulders. My mother had died. I don't know what of, and he was God's Man. I felt lucky, I suppose. He picked me. He gave me the kind of privileges everyone wanted. I used to go to his room. He called me …'

The voice stops. The silence is as loud as the darkness is complete.

'… he called me his poppet. I used to hug him when

he gave me cakes or let me stay up late. And his hands would creep down my back.'

The older voice joins in. 'And you told nobody?'

'There was nothing to tell, and then suddenly it was too late to talk about it.'

'Because he was touching you between your legs.'

'Yes.' The younger voice is sibilant in the darkness.

'And you felt guilty about that? Not him, you?'

Darkness and the same word repeated.

'Yes.'

The older voice waits, keeps the words marshalled and silent.

'He said I was his temptation.'

Words can get lost in daylight, in activity. Darkness expands them, gives them resonance.

'When Gary had an affair, he told me it was because I wasn't sexy enough.'

Silence. Then a disembodied younger voice. 'They couldn't have children.'

'Who?'

'The Barrs. They were heartbroken about that, because it meant that God had rejected them. They were given your baby.'

The temptation is to ask something else immediately. The older woman resists.

'You know, I came alive when Gary died. I shouldn't say that, but that's what darkness is for. And it was only when I came alive that I realised a part of me had been dead for such a long time.'

'And did it come back to life? That part of you?' The younger voice is more urgent now.

'I'm different now, if that's what you mean.'

Silence. They each know they have time.

'God's Man killed a part of me that could have been innocent. There, I've said it.'

'And it's never come alive again?'

'No. It's funny, isn't it,' the young voice adds, 'the way we want the opposite of the last thing that happened to us.'

'In what way?'

'I thought power might assuage his abuse of me. I wanted power.'

The older woman risks a direct question. 'But it hasn't?'

'No.'

'Fancy abusing a young girl and heaping all the guilt of it onto her. You must have hated him.'

'Not then. The hate came later.'

'I'm sorry that happened to you.' The older woman speaks the words before she's decided to voice them.

Now there's another sound in the chapel. Izzy hears it and the attempt to stifle it. She stretches out her hand to Katherine. She does this so gently she can feel the warmth of the woman before her fingers come into contact.

Another hand reaches out of the blackness to grasp hers.

In the dark, silent stillness of that space, now there is touch. The hands clasp and hold.

The stifled noise increases. Katherine is crying. Izzy moves closer, wraps the younger woman in her arms, and rocks her gently as if she were a child.

'There, there.'

But there are hurts that can't be so simply assuaged. What happened to Katherine is still vivid and has been acknowledged for the first time. The tears won't be stopped.

In the darkness there is the warmth of touch and tears, of cheek against cheek. They stay like that a long time.

'Where have you looked for him?' Katherine finally asks.

Izzy tells the story, including being mugged.

'Not the streets,' Katherine says. 'Patrick was tough. He stood up for himself. If he slept rough at first, he won't have stayed living like that for very long. He was, and I'm sure he still is, a survivor.'

× × ×

It's been a long night. Leah catches the bus home and feels sorry that Martin won't be there, that he stayed over at the flat. She wonders whether to go to the bookshop but she needs to sleep. She's exhausted.

Leah gets home around 9am. She opens the door and hears noises. Two women are talking. One is Izzy, the other voice she recognises but can't place. Surprised, she walks straight through to the kitchen and is astonished to find Katherine sitting at the table.

'Hello Leah.'

'I brought her home with me,' Izzy says. 'She needed a break. And you look as if you need breakfast.'

Leah stares at the woman who threatened and attacked her.

'You're shocked to see me. You must be tired. Please sit down, Leah.'

Leah sits. She wants Martin to be here to witness this.

'Your mother tells me you're working.'

'Why are you here?' Leah asks.

Katherine doesn't answer. Izzy does. 'Because I invited her.'

'You have a lovely house. No wonder Patrick coveted it.'

'Was that his real name?'

Katherine nods. 'It's a common name amongst us.'

Tiredness is eating Leah. She's concerned for Wendell,

worried about the mystery man outside the home, and now this. Ground has never been stable for Leah. She walks on the surface of an established planet, but for her the earth is prone to shaking. Sink holes keep opening.

'Here,' Izzy says, handing her toast and coffee.

This Katherine is different, unbelievably different. She looks as tired as Leah feels, but there is something exultant about her as well. Leah's silent self could have simply watched, listened and eaten, could have worried at the change until she found a name for it. Now she needs a reason for not speaking. Quickly Leah butters toast and spoons on marmalade, then sinks her teeth into the mixture.

She's aware as she eats that Katherine is observing her. She's aware that her mother has a secret to tell, that something has happened between them. She's full of fury that Katherine is here, calmly drinking coffee at her table and speaking to her as if Katherine is the adult and Leah is the child. She finds herself terribly conflicted: she's racked with curiosity but determined not to ask questions.

She finishes one piece of toast and reaches for another. She remembers everything: the hug which Katherine hated; the conversation at the bedside of a dying man; the confrontation at the gate; the way Katherine looked into the sinkhole as if to check that her fiancé really was dead before she simply walked away. Leah takes a drink of coffee and abandons the toast. She can't resist any longer.

'Okay, what's happened?'

Katherine looks to Izzy and leaves it for her to explain.

'We talked. That's what happened. I went to the cult and found Katherine alone. We talked all night. I think I now know everything there is to know about my Patrick. I think I may have been looking for him in the wrong places.'

'Your real half-brother, Patrick, stood out from the others, Leah. I was older, but you couldn't help noticing him. He had a spark, he was a performer, he was also tough. I've told your mum that if he slept rough at first, he'd soon have picked himself up and made something of his life. My guess is that he's still alive and thriving.' Katherine pauses. 'I'm sorry, Leah.'

Leah wants to know more: how? why? But tiredness is calling her.

'You must excuse me, Katherine. I'm just off a twelve hour shift. I need to sleep.'

She walks out of the kitchen and heads upstairs.

× × ×

Chloe is already down in the breakfast room and has helped herself from the buffet when Danny arrives. Her eyes swivel at him as if she has questions. He grabs coffee and a cooked breakfast, then sits opposite her.

'Who did you meet last night?' Chloe asks. 'My room's at the front. I saw you as I closed the curtains.'

'Ivor.'

'Who's Ivor?'

'I don't really know. I knew him in London. At that time I thought he was an asylum seeker. Now he appears to be working for the opposition.'

Chloe frowns. 'The Russians?'

'Yes.'

'What did you talk about?'

'Life, betrayal and Juozas Žemaitis.'

'Why Juozas Žemaitis?

'They want him too.'

'Tell me, Col.'

Danny tells her, leaving out the arrangement about the file.

Chloe's frown deepens.

'So what does Ivor get?'

'The Russians are really bothered about the contents of that file. According to Ivor, it recounts Juozas's victories against the Soviets. They'd like to kill Juozas Žemaitis. He made a fool of them. In their eyes that's unforgivable. Apparently, his name is a code used by all the malcontents who can't stand the present Russian regime. His jokes have made him a hero.'

'Shit,' says Chloe. 'He disappeared not because he was frightened of us, but because he was frightened of them. The sword was for them. He's gone to ground because he doesn't want to be the next headline. I need another coffee.'

'How's your head?'

'Tolerable.'

When she returns from the coffee machine she's still frowning. 'What did you give in return, Danny? I really need to know.'

'In information terms, nothing he didn't already know. He knew about the arrest. His version is that Juozas blagged his way out and the Russians never knew he was spying for the British. They even hired him as a translator.'

Chloe continues to look at him.

'I think Ivor may be under the illusion that if we find Juozas first, we will destroy the Lithuanian file.'

'What do you mean? Tell me precisely, Colm.'

'I told him that our task was to find the man. I added that I didn't know precisely what your instructions were. I implied that we were not overfussed about the file.'

'Next question, Colm. Is Ivor a rookie?'

'I don't know. He may have been working for them

when I knew him in London. He was also seeking to blackmail Jud Mindsett into giving him asylum. I think he always has two plans, perhaps more.'

Chloe looks around her. 'Our flight is at 3pm. We need to think. If Ivor is a rookie, it's okay. The file can't be so vital if both sides give the job to a trainee. If he's an established officer, then we might be outmatched. How did he know you were here?'

Danny thinks of his phone. It's the same one Harry gave him. Was Ivor always tracking him?

'In London, before the election, he did have access to my phone.'

'I should have checked. Hand it over.'

Danny does so. Chloe is a blur of fingers, then the fingers pause. 'Shit, he's no rookie.'

'Did you find something? Have you removed it?'

'I've left it there. We can use that. Most of what we do is innocent. If we need to, we can send your phone on a separate journey.'

'I'm sorry,' Danny tells her.

'It's my fault, Col. I should have checked.'

'So he knows we went to the house?'

Chloe nods.

'Has he heard everything we've said?'

'It's a tracker, not a microphone.'

Danny is intrigued. 'Is this how the game works? Everything you plant can be turned against you, like in tennis? Advantage us, advantage them?'

'We'd better walk while we talk. There's a riddle in all this, one I still don't understand.'

14

Another hotel, another country, another breakfast.

Julia is alone. After showering she looked at her phone. There was an urgent message. With three days left before the end of the fortnight they have sent her the twerp's accusation and his detailed statement. Has she any comments she'd like to make? Of course she has. Luckily, it's still early enough to draft a response before her 11am tryst.

Julia, needing coffee, was first down to breakfast. Now she sits at a table where she reads and sips. At first it's a whinge document, full of slights and accounts of times when she was (she might admit this) occasionally too forceful with Twerp. He builds a case of having to work with someone who consistently belittled him. Then she comes to the core of the accusation. He writes that she demanded he finish a piece of work by the morning (which was true), so he stayed late to finish it. He claims that she stayed to catch up with other work (which was certainly not true). She skims the graphic description of her assault (what films has he been watching? where did he borrow this from?). She almost admires his honourable defence of his virtue as he pushed her away as politely as possible, then fled the building. She loves the section where he considered resigning until his flatmate persuaded him to make a complaint. Most of all, she loves the date. He's taken the risk of putting a date on his work of fiction. She's in no doubt it's the date she insisted on him finishing the piece of work, but it's also the date of her hair appointment. A quick check on her mobile phone confirms this. Her hairdresser will confirm it too. She can even produce the salon log as evidence. On the way back from the hairdresser she phoned her mother. That call is logged too. She has him where she wants him. He'll have to resign.

She checks that the twerp's statement is signed, and wonders if she should say what has to be said in just six words: He's lying. I can prove it. She could flesh it out with *How many witnesses do you want*? She'd like to add *How can someone work in a Human Resources department when they have such little regard for detailed accuracy*? This won't be a he said/she said argument. She's in the clear. This calls for a second croissant.

As she gets up she sees Zakk. He's at the entrance to the dining room and in conversation with the girl who takes room numbers. She goes over.

'Did you forget, darling?' she says to Zakk. 'Have we been in so many hotels recently that you muddled the number?'

'Room 46,' she says to the girl.

She sees that Zakk is amused. She leads him to her table, points out the queue for the coffee machine, then collects her croissant and decides to have jam with it. A weight has fallen from her shoulders now that she knows she is absolutely and completely in the clear. She's determined to enjoy this moment.

She sits down again and watches Zakk. He's decisive and quick at the coffee machine. He doesn't need to stand and read instructions. She likes that about him.

'You walked out on me,' he says when he sits down. 'That's a traditional male role and you usurped it.'

'The world's changing. Get over it.'

'You didn't even leave a note.'

'What sort of note? What were you expecting? And I did leave a note: to meet at the Mezquita at 11am if you wanted to.'

'I never saw it.'

'Men,' Julia pronounced, 'are hopeless at looking for things.'

'But I did find the sleeve for your hotel key. That's how I knew where you were staying.'

He produces it from his jacket pocket. 'I may keep this as a souvenir.'

She laughs. She can see the girl at the door in conversation with the manager. The girl is pointing at them.

'Whoops, we may be in trouble. They know I made a single booking. They may want me to pay for your breakfast, or even for last night as well. How's your Spanish?'

He shakes his head. 'You ruthlessly left me in my room at my hotel when you walked out on me. You deal with it.'

Julia gets up and heads for the door. Zakk watches her at work. Before long, disapproving frowns are replaced by nods of sympathy and then by laughter.

Julia returns to the table.

'What did you say to them?'

'I said I was a psychiatrist and you were a client of mine. I told them you had delusions which I needed to play along with. I also offered to pay for your breakfast.'

'Really?'

'The paying for your breakfast is true.'

Zakk is looking at her. 'I don't know if I should say this, but you are different this morning.'

'And you were going to take the credit, were you?'

'Modesty forbids.'

An image of him naked and asleep comes to mind. 'I've had some good news,' she tells him.

He wants to know more.

'I'm on gardening leave,' she explains. 'A junior colleague made allegations against me. This morning they sent me his statement and I can prove he's lying.'

'Can I see?'

She finds the twerp's statement on her phone and hands it over.

Zakk reads slowly, more slowly than she did. She watches as he scrolls down. When he reaches the end he hands the phone back but says nothing.

'Well?'

'It's none of my business.'

'What isn't?'

'It's your problem.'

He's right. She should shut up now, take the phone back and talk about something else. But his lack of response niggles her and threatens to derail her good mood.

'What do you think?'

He was leaning forward over his food. Now he sits upright. 'I feel sorry for him.'

'What!'

'Read it again,' he says. 'Read it as a stranger might. I

know he's lying. I know that, even without the evidence you can produce.'

He goes to get another coffee. She takes the phone back and starts to read the statement. She tries to blank out any sense of herself and concentrate on the twerp, but finds she is offended all over again.

She's frowning when Zakk returns to the table.

She looks up. The problem is that she cares what he thinks. And she mustn't ask him to explain. She ducks her head and reads it through a third time.

This time she sees what Zakk means. This time she understands. The twerp… she'd better call him Stuart from now on… was always out of his depth. She reads what he's actually written. Yes, he made mistakes, but she had no sympathy. On this reading she senses his unhappiness, his wish to please her and her rejection of him, again and again. This time she sees the pathetic nature of his accusation. This time she understands how limited he is. After all, to date a false accusation is a terrible risk that only a very limited person would make. He was needy and all she did was get angry. Is that how Stuart sees her? Is that how they all see her? This new image of herself threatens to overwhelm her. She finishes reading and looks up.

'Did you appoint him?' Zakk asks.

She nods.

'Then you've only yourself to blame. There's nothing worse than putting someone into a job they can't handle.'

She's on holiday. She need never see Zakk again. She can fly to England asap, take her job back, insist Stuart's not sacked, and give him a different manager. That way there'll be no lasting damage done.

'I feel sorry for you too,' Zakk says. 'To have that hanging over you must have been horrible. No wonder you had that turn in the square.'

'They've left it late,' Julia explains. 'I need to reply.'

'How long will you need?'

'An hour, maybe two.'

'Right,' Zakk says. 'Plans? Are you going to Granada next?'

'Yes.'

'Where are you staying?'

'Somewhere in the town itself.'

'Cancel that. I've taken a double room in the Hotel Americana. You'll like it there. It's like hotels used to be. Can I suggest we meet at the Mezquita at noon? That way you have time to write your reply.'

'Are you sure?' she asks, feeling that her control is slipping and not, for the moment at least, being at all upset.

'Sure enough, yes.'

'I'll meet you at twelve.'

× × ×

'I'll drive you back,' Izzy says to Katherine.

Breakfast is long over, but Katherine has stayed, drinking coffee as an excuse. The two women have reached an understanding. There is nothing more that Katherine can teach Izzy about Patrick.

'Are you sure that's okay? You must be exhausted.'

'It'll hit me later on and tomorrow, but I'll be fine.'

'I've got to get back,' Katherine explains. 'Since God's Man and Patrick died, I am the place. I am the queen bee everything revolves around. I'm needed.'

They walk to the car. 'What will you do when you get there?' Izzy asks.

Katherine grimaces. 'I don't know. Last night was

extraordinary. The amazing thing for me is that last night was what a face to face is meant to be. But faces, mine included, can lie with extraordinary facility.'

'That's why I snuffed the candle out.'

There's silence. Early June rushes past them. The May blossom is over. The tree leaves are settling into their uniform green.

'I suppose I'll go on being God's Woman. Neither I nor they know anything else. I can't just close the place down. There are financial considerations, and my people don't understand how wonderful the real world can be.'

'Will you tell them what really happened last night?'

'No. As far as they're concerned, they let me out of the chapel at first light. You scooted when no one was looking. They left me to sleep, but I joined you instead. No one will have disturbed me. They'll think I'm still sleeping.'

'And in yourself?'

'Ahh,' Katherine says. 'I have to forgive what Matthew Holmes' father did to me. I have a lot to discover about who I am. I suppose we all do that at some time: ask questions about ourselves. But I have to ask those questions in the context of who everyone else thinks I am.'

As she drives back after dropping Katherine, Izzy is amazed by what she has done. When she reached out to hug Katherine in that velvet darkness, when their hands met and she felt the tears on Katherine's face, something happened between them. She found herself rocking the woman who locked her into the car boot and who was complicit in foisting the other Patrick on the family. She rocked her as if she were a child. They talked right through that short summer night. Izzy already knows that this was the most intimate conversation she has ever had and will probably ever have in her life.

And out of it emerged a picture of her son, of her Patrick. He was the boy who challenged, the liveliest member of the church, the one who went his own way, the one whose voice rang out clearly in the chapel and changed from treble to tenor when he grew up. Above all, she's learnt that he is a survivor, and she knows that at least until he left the cult he kept Patrick as his first name and Barr was his surname. She has a definite search in front of her.

And the gift Katherine gave her was the knowledge that, if she finds him, he won't be the waif and stray, the drug addict or the alcoholic. He'll be himself, an equal. The weight of her own guilt has shifted. She feels clear-headed and re-energised, but when she gets home she needs to sleep.

× × ×

Julia has finished her statement. She's feeling humble. Zakk and Stuart (she'll never denigrate him as the twerp again) have shone a light on how she can appear to others. She's glad Stuart didn't charge her with workplace bullying, because in that he might have had a case. In her statement she admits that she could have managed him better, but makes the point clearly that what he alleged never happened, and she can prove it. When the statement is ready she reads it through for a final time and presses send.

It's 11.30am. She packs, pays and leaves her case with the concierge.

She arrives at the Mezquita early and has time to read her guidebook while she waits. It was a mosque, then it was converted to a cathedral, not smashed down and rebuilt. At the present time, when the crusader wars between

Christianity and Islam are threatening again, this seems extraordinary. He's late. She reads further. The original Moorish architect, whose name she can't pronounce, used old Roman and early Christian pillars. If they were too long he sank them. If they were too short he built columns on top. So it has always been a hybrid and these stones have worshipped many deities.

'Face deep in that book again,' Zakk says.

She snaps it shut. 'You're late.'

'Not very.' He smiles.

They aren't as relaxed as they were at breakfast. Julia has done what he suggested and cancelled her hotel. Tonight they are booked in together.

They enter through what was the ablutions courtyard and are met by a perspective demonstration piece of the columns Julia has just read about. She wants to lecture him about the origins, but she doesn't. She doesn't do this because what she sees in front of her isn't what she expected. It's so much more wonderful.

From a polished floor, columns rise all around them to meet arches which are striped with stone and red brick. It's like walking into a wood, or rather a grove of date palms. Julia doesn't search for the plan in her guidebook; instead she looks. No wonder the Christians didn't tear it down. Pillars of stone, pillars with ionic caps, pillars of marble; a plantation of straight trunks and shade from their decorated branches. It's like no space she has ever been in. It calms. It reveres. She's aware of Zakk at her side, of his wonderment as they walk almost in step through this calcified forest.

She sees him turn in a full circle and shake his head.

'I don't normally like churches,' he confides to her. 'I tend to avoid them whenever possible. But this!'

They omit the Christian centre of the building by instinct and walk round the edges.

If the side doors were all open, as they would have been before the Christian era, the sense of being in a grove would have been complete. In midsummer this would have been a cool oasis with the running water of prayer.

'You know, I wouldn't have come in here if you hadn't suggested it,' Zakk tells her.

'What would you have done instead?'

'Walked the streets, sat outside a café, stared at the river, poked my head into shops.'

They've reached the Muslim heart of the building and it's exceptional. Now the arches are elaborate, coloured in red, blue and gold, with a flowing Arabic script running through the decoration.

'Why,' he asks her, 'does a religion that once created all this beauty now specialise in carnage?'

She turns and looks at him. 'You're not just a pretty face, are you?'

'Don't try to work me out,' he warns her. 'I don't understand myself sometimes.'

Ditto, she thinks, but doesn't say it. When I first met this man in Ronda, I knew exactly who I was and what I wanted. Now …

They are on the point of leaving. She swivels round and takes in the whole size and wonder of the place, then steps outside from the mystery of shadow into the glare of bright sunlight.

15

Danny and Chloe are back in London. They are sitting in the same room in the Service HQ. Chloe explains that no one has their own office anymore, except those who work on the fifth floor. Everyone else hot desks and books rooms for meetings as they need them. This room is theirs for the day.

They are sitting in front of a whiteboard. On it are the key dates and what they know about Juozas Žemaitis, alias Baldr, alias Vidar.

1931	born Vilnius, Lithuania
1939	age 8 Soviets take over
1941	age 10 Hitler invades Lithuania
1941	father a Nazi sympathiser helps round up Jews
1944	age 13 Soviets reconquer, father in partisans
1947	age 16 father captured, interrogated, shot
1947	family flees to England
1953	age 22 joins Service

1955 age 24 played back into Lithuania
1955 contacts father's partisan colleagues
1955 discovers father's Nazi past
? interrogated, blags his way out, no report
1963 age 32 returns to London, offered promotion
1963 turns promotion down to avoid transfer?
1969 age 38 promoted, i/c Lithuania, Estonia and Latvia
1969 rumour: running private war
1970 age 39 changes code name to Vidar
1987 age 56 soap and speaker scandals
1991 age 60 retires from Service
2017 age 86 disappears

Chloe and Danny stare at the board. Something is hidden in that record. They need to discover it before they can understand the man and perhaps work out what might be in the file he stole.

'Okay, let's add what we've discovered,' Chloe suggests. 'Juozas returned to Lithuania worshipping his father. According to his cousin, Antanas was his idol. He made contact with his father's partisan comrades and provided excellent intelligence for us. Then he discovered another side to his father's reputation and another side to the partisans. They betrayed him, but he talked his way out of that horrific place. Very significantly, he didn't report his interrogation. Why was that?'

'Because he'd have been recalled,' Danny suggests.

'I agree. So he stayed where he was. The intelligence remained good. After ten years he was offered promotion but he turned it down.'

'Is that common?' Danny asks.

'Extremely rare. So why did he do it?'

'Same reason. Promotion would have given him a

desk job or another posting. Something in Lithuania was keeping him there.'

'Agreed. What are the possibilities?'

Danny counts them off. 'A woman, a man, a boy.' He pauses, then he adds, 'A cause perhaps?'

'His masters were concerned . He was interrogated in London but, because he was a one man band, in a country no one really cared about, either they couldn't find the right questions or he gave all the right answers.'

Chloe adds, 'For them he must have been a dream to manage.'

Danny chips in. 'Presumably the posting could have been anywhere in the world: USA, England, Russia, places that matter?'

'But places where he'd be part of a team. When they next offered him promotion, widening his brief but leaving him in charge, he accepted,'

'Because it left him where he was. Our hypothesis has to be that whatever held him there was still holding him.'

'Then it started to go wrong. There were scandals. He seemed to be assisting the partisans, feeding them information.'

'And he changed his code name. That upset his masters. He insisted on being known as Vidar instead of Baldr. Why?'

Chloe suddenly brightens. 'What if we put some other dates into his record, dates of external events? I didn't tell you I studied modern history at uni, Col.' She grabs the marker pen and approaches the chart. '1968, before everything began to go wrong for Juozas, the Prague Spring happened. Czechoslovakia rebelled against Soviet rule and the western powers did nothing. What if that affected him? What if his cause was passionately anti-Soviet and he believed the West was as passionately anti as he was? If that was so, he'd feel betrayed.'

Danny listens, wishes he knew this stuff.

Chloe muses. 'Betrayed for the second time. The first betrayal was his own father.'

'True. Any other dates, Chloe?'

'December 1965, Roger Hollis retired as the head of the intelligence services. In *Spycatcher*, Peter Wright claimed that Roger Hollis was a Russian spy. Did Juozas know that? It was our worst period, cock-ups everywhere. Is that why he turned down promotion, because he wanted to stay out of London?'

'So he took greater risks.' Danny sees the pattern. 'He took matters into his own hands. If the West wouldn't fight the Soviets, then he would. Hence he used the partisans as his private army.'

'Stop,' says Chloe. 'This historian in me thinks there's too much conjecture and not enough fact. If the Prague Spring upset him, why didn't the Hungarian uprising fifteen years earlier have the same effect? I suggest we make notes of what we think we know so far and leave it there for the moment. Not least because we're about to run into a major problem. If he was so patriotic, if he was nothing more than an old fashioned nationalist who hated the Soviets with a passion, why did he never go back to Lithuania when it became free from Soviet power in 1991? Why didn't he celebrate?'

× × ×

When Leah returns to the care home, she senses that the atmosphere has changed. She is warned in the morning handover about a new resident. He's called Bill, the night staff tell her. He's in Room 2. Gladys died last week, and the care home rule is one out, one in, in order to maximise income.

'What's he like?'

'Strange,' Sarah tells her. 'We think he's foreign. He walks with a stick we're not altogether sure he needs, and he snoops around the place. He's not liked. He upsets the residents, especially Wendell.'

'Wendell hasn't come out of his room since Bill arrived,' Lisa tells her.

Leah wants to know more, but handovers take long enough without extra questions.

It isn't long before she bumps into the newcomer. He's a menacing size, and even though he's stooped with age and leaning on his stick he towers over Leah. He has dyed black hair which is down to his shoulders. He carries a black leather bag slung diagonally across his chest. It looks heavy. He fondles the bag, clutching it to him.

Leah watches as he swings into the room and makes straight for Wendell's seat, the one in the corner which allows him to watch all the comings and goings.

She's thinks Bill's aware of her looking at him. She sees in his eyes a flash that is almost, but can't be, one of recognition.

She goes over. 'Hello, I'm Leah,' she says.

He looks at her again. It's quite an appraisal.

'You're new and your name's Bill. Have I got that right?'

'Near enough.'

Leah sits down next to him. His hands go straight to the bag as he twitches it away from her. She remembers Helen telling her that new residents must be made welcome.

'Where do you come from?' Leah asks.

'None of your business. And I'm not deaf,' he adds, 'unlike most of these others.'

Leah tries another tack. She lowers her voice, 'Do you have family living locally?'

'No, no family at all. I'm the last of a line.' It's said more as a boast than a statement of self-pity. 'There'll be no visitors for me.'

He glares at her as if he's daring her to be sympathetic.

'I don't need people.' It's said loudly. The other residents, unless they are profoundly deaf, all hear the comment.

By now Leah has built up a whole lexicon of comments for use when caring for the elderly. She sees at once that none of these is appropriate.

'Everyone needs people, even when they say they don't.' She says this quietly so that he hears but no one else does. 'Especially when they say they don't.'

She makes a mental note that Bill is fully 'with it' and needs to be faced down. 'I must get on though. I'll see you later.'

As she walks away she feels rather than sees his eyes following her out of the door.

Leah goes straight to Wendell's room. The little man is sitting on his bed and only one of his shoes is laced. The mask of being able to manage for himself, of not being like the others, is slipping.

She kneels and ties his shoelaces. 'There,' she says. 'Now you're fit to go.'

But she senses a real hesitancy about him, as if he doesn't want to leave the room. She remembers him at the window in the middle of the night and asks a direct question.

'You don't know Bill from before, do you? Is he one of your ghosts?'

Wendell closes his eyes and his chin sinks. She'll take that as a yes.

She glances out of the window. 'Look, it's a nice day.

Bill ….' She notes an almost invisible reaction to that name and stores it away. 'Bill is sitting in the lounge. Why don't you go out of the side door and sit in your normal seat in the garden?'

He brightens and makes for the corridor.

She checks his bed and makes it. His bathroom is tidy as always. Then she goes into Joan's room and encourages her to get up and get dressed. Glancing out of the window ten or fifteen minutes later she sees that Wendell is sitting in his chair, looking across the river to the distant hills. But then she spots a shadow and notices the bulk of Bill making his way across to join Wendell.

Yes, he's walking with his stick, but he's carrying that bag and a chair as easily as if he were twenty years younger. Why is he here? Why would you want to join the residents in a care home if you can still do all that for yourself?

× × ×

Danny's feeling good about himself. He's back at the heart of things doing important work. They have a case, and the unease that was there in the beginning between Chloe and himself has diminished. They are becoming a team. He has made the leap he wanted. If he carries on like this he will become a fully paid member of the intelligence services. Will that be enough? Can he then come in from the cold?

In spite of all that confidence, something nags at him. It's seeped out of the Juozas/Vidar case. It's a sense of being alone.

Ivor was his friend. Ivor was his confidant, but not anymore. They are now on opposite sides. There's a streak of purity in Danny that Ivor doesn't have. It was that purity that led him to talk to Stella, that same purity that made him go to The Guardian. The case of Juozas, alias Vidar, worries him. He senses a kinship. Juozas has the same streak within him. Loyalty to his father morphed into loyalty to the country of his birth. He refused promotion in order to stay loyal, but if they are right in their conjectures, he suffered a second betrayal after the failure of the Prague Spring. By the time that happened it was too late to change jobs and walk away. He was then the same age Danny is now and, to Danny, keeping and holding his new job is important, so long as he doesn't have to compromise too much. If it doesn't work out, will he ever get another throw of the dice?

Danny remembers a promise he made to Shaun, the rough sleeper who mentored him on the streets. That promise had to do with being genuine, with loyalty. Shaun had said to him *I helped you because I thought you were genuine. Don't disappoint me. I need to believe that out there somewhere, someone is genuine.*

It's an echo of the way Danny feels now.

I'm working my way back he'd replied. *If I ever get there, I'll come and find you.*

He has reached that point. He needs to find Shaun, make good on his promise.

He knows where to look and sets off.

But he's reluctant. Shaun is an addict. When Danny sought Shaun's help in the past, the bargain was always sealed with cans of extra strong lager.

As he walks, Danny picks at the language they both used in that last exchange. That gibe about being genuine. What did it mean? Shaun is surrounded by genuine rough sleepers. If anything, it was Danny who was always the fraud. You can't be a genuine rough sleeper and have an unclaimed lottery ticket in the house you've abandoned.

And he, Danny, had made a very ambiguous promise. *I'll come and find you.* Not *I'll come and take you off the streets, set you up in a house and look after you for the rest of your life.* What can he give Shaun that isn't drinkable? What do you do to help the man who is in love with the kind of oblivion strong lager provides?

His footsteps slow. He's heading towards Shaun's patch, but he needs to be absolutely clear about what he will say and do when he finds him.

× × ×

Chloe lets the man she must professionally call Colm go before she follows him. In her head she uses his real name, Danny, not his nom de guerre. She tells herself that tailing him is to keep her hand in, but she's interested in this companion who says absolutely nothing about himself. With everyone else she has ever worked with there has been some conversation about the day to day lives they lead. With Danny there has been nothing. Personally, she's intrigued. Those who say nothing about themselves often have something to hide. Professionally, she's worried about his relationship with Ivor. Did Danny make him a promise? If so, he's unemployable. Or did Danny extract vital information and give nothing in return? Chloe lives in a world of continuous questions.

This case will soon be over. The Juozas/Vidar file will be closed. Then she'll have a recommendation to make. Michael made it absolutely clear to her that there must be no special treatment of Danny. He's only to be hired if he's good enough.

She keeps out of sight. It's vital that Danny doesn't sense he's being followed. But then, why should he? He's got his head down, is going somewhere, and London pavements provide plenty of cover. If he does see her it must seem like a coincidence.

He was going somewhere at speed. Now he's slowed down. He looks, she thinks, like a man who's uncertain. He's slowed so much that people he's already passed are now passing him. Chloe stays back as Danny comes to a stop. He can't have guessed he's being followed; he's had his head down all the way. There's too much noise and fuss in central London to allow a sixth sense to operate.

She watches him take a step to the side so he can lean against a shop window and no longer block the pavement. He has his back to her. His left hand is on the window glass. He isn't slumped; rather, he looks coiled. Any moment now she expects Danny to push himself away from the window and click back into the fast, weaving pace she followed before.

He doesn't. He stays there. Chloe glances at her watch. Four minutes go by before the hand pats the window and the pace starts again. She can match his speed; she keeps herself fit. He's moving easily again as if he's made his mind up about something, but then several streets later he slows and looks about him. Is he lost? No, he can't be. He passes street signs and never glances at them. She guesses that he knows the area. He's acting as if he's searching, but whatever he's looking for is at ground level. His head turns constantly as he checks both sides of the road.

Then he stops again. He appears to have found what he's looking for. And he hesitates as if he isn't certain about what he'll do next.

Chloe ducks into a doorway in case he comes back her way. She has a clear field of view. She sees Danny walk across the road and crouch down beside a rough sleeper who seems to be dozing. Danny looks around and then prods the sleeper awake. What's he doing? It isn't obvious that the two know each other. The sleeper comes awake slowly. Danny has notes in his hand and he seems to be offering these to the young man.

Danny's saying something Chloe desperately wants to hear. She senses a certain reluctance about the rough sleeper, but when he takes the notes she spots the slick way he hides them.

Rough trade. What other possibility is there? That's why Danny has told her nothing about his life, has never shown the slightest interest in her. If so, it's the end of his career. Gay men form an important chapter in the history of the Service she belongs to, but it isn't a glorious one. She thinks of Philby, Burgess and MacLean; adds Blunt, Keeper of the Queen's Pictures. But as far as she knows, they never indulged in rough trade.

It fits. It makes sense of the hesitancy.

The historian in her wants to check. The rough sleeper is standing up now and picking up his things. If she's careful she can place herself in the right spot for a coincidental meeting.

She considers their options. Danny will be taking the man he's bought to somewhere private. There are no public toilets nearby, but there is an overgrown churchyard. She crosses the road. The two men are talking. Chloe stands by the lychgate as they walk towards her.

16

Martin should be getting his accounts together ready for the annual audit. It's a task he hates. Around him are bank statements and a myriad of scruffy pieces of paper. In front of him is his computer and an Excel spreadsheet he doesn't fully understand and only uses once a year. Because he's uncertain, he's created a copy of last year's results and changed the file name. He's in the process of substituting this year's figures for last year's. They are about the same.

Lots of thoughts are going through Martin's mind as he works. He worries about whether the town might raise business rates. He wonders if he's pricing his books a little on the low side. A second-hand book is always a bargain. The kind of people who buy second-hand books rarely quibble about the price. He recognises he would sell more of his valuable books if he had an online presence, but he doesn't want the fuss. Besides, because he's keeping his head above water, he can postpone that decision for another year. He knows he needs a new van and a new computer. He wonders if his accountant will allow him either or both of those luxuries offset against tax. The thought that never occurs to him is that he could have sold Stella Stelling's letters and Howard's journal for enough money to cover both purchases.

And through all these thoughts the image of Leah is never far from his mind. He knows he loves her, but the problem is one of equality. When they first met they were equals. That dalliance between a mute girl and himself was so simple and straightforward compared with now. It was one of mutual needs, mutually satisfied. After the rape, Leah became the supplicant and Martin the provider of money, transport and support. Leah came to him for help and he helped. That all changed again the moment he saw where she lived. One day she will be a wealthy woman. The figures in front of him remind him remorselessly that he will never be a wealthy man. He knows the details of the Goulden will. Even as he helped the family fight to keep control of their fortune, he feared that fortune might divide him from the woman he loves. The irony is that, if the cult had taken the Gouldens' money, Leah the care worker would be well matched with a second-hand bookseller.

What is wealth, he wonders. Leah did nothing to create the fortune she will eventually share. She hasn't changed her habits or the way she dresses. She has never made him feel uncomfortable about the disparity between them. Come to think of it, she has never reimbursed him for the expenses of that Scotland trip, and he can see in the figures in front of him that he has spent more on fuel than last year.

He stops working and saves what he has done so far.

You're drifting, he tells himself. You need to stop drifting. Perhaps it's time to make a move.

× × ×

The shadows in the London churchyard are deep where Chloe waits. She's under a yew tree, peering from the gloom into the sunshine on the street. She watches Danny as he approaches. She sees the strain on his face and gets ready to confront him. This isn't going to be pleasant. She's grown used to him now. He was an okay drinking companion in Vilnius. He works hard. He's relentless. He has ideas. He's very good looking and muscular; she's noticed that much. But she knows nothing else about him. Once she challenges him he'll know she followed him, but why not? He's being trained and evaluated. Following is a skill she needs to practise and, if he's to be any good to the Service, he needs to constantly check if he's being followed. She hasn't actually told him that her recommendation will be vital to his future employment, but she suspects he's worked that out.

Danny and the young man are talking as they walk towards her. The young man is looking up at Danny. The relationship between them doesn't look like a transaction. But it's odd, and money changed hands. She needs to know. She steps out in front of them.

'What the hell….'

That was going to be her line. Danny is clearly surprised to see her, but there is no guilt in him, just a quizzical look.

'Hello,' says Shaun, 'are you the woman he's working for now?'

'My name's Chloe.' She holds out her hand.

Danny does the introductions.

Chloe takes the hand that's now offered. It looks clean enough. The grip is friendly, but it's taking all her self-control to shake hands with a homeless man.

'I'm his mate,' Shaun explains. 'He was never one of us. He said he'd come looking for me when he made it.'

She quickly realises Shaun is half-cut. She can smell it on his breath.

Shaun beams at her. 'You're looking for someone who's gone missing, aren't you?'

Chloe nods.

'Danny, what did you say his name was?'

'I didn't,' Danny explains, 'but he calls himself Vidar.'

'Norse God of Revenge,' Shaun says.

Danny frowns.

'Norse God of Revenge,' Shaun repeats.

'Is that who Vidar was?'

'Of course. You see, I know stuff. We did those stories in primary school. I know about Vidar and also Baldr, Thor, Odin and Loki.'

Danny's recovering from his surprise at seeing Chloe. 'You followed me?' It's both a question and an explanation.

'Yes,' she says.

'Why?' He senses her unease.

'Curiosity, and to keep my hand in.'

'If you want to know something about me, why don't you ask?'

She tries to be all official. 'Look, I am responsible for you. I have to make an evaluation.'

He stands in front of her and shakes his head. He's grinning at her, and his grin is both endearing and reprehensible. It lights up his face. He's a very handsome man.

'Look, I've got to look after Shaun now,' Danny says.

'I'll see you on Monday as we planned. Ask your questions then. Come on, Shaun.'

Reluctantly, Shaun follows Danny. As he does, Chloe distinctly hears him say, 'She's fierce, but she's a bit of alright. Have you tried it on with her?'

'Shh,' says Danny. 'First, I need to sober you up.'

× × ×

Izzy has slept well. She's having Sunday breakfast with Martin. Leah is on duty at the care home. Outside it's pouring with June rain. The trees are heavily in leaf and the wind pushes and tugs at them like kids playfighting.

There's a fresh percolator of coffee and Izzy, who's been busy with a frying pan, is carrying a plate of blueberry pancakes. The Observer has been unwrapped and its sections are scattered across the table.

'Here,' Izzy says, 'help yourself.'

Martin grabs a handful. They are still warm and squishy. 'Lovely,' he murmurs with a full mouth. He's just reading Andrew Rawnsley's column which is always the one he goes for first.

The euphoria of Izzy's talk with Katherine has not yet worn off. She's feeling buoyed. In all probability Patrick is alive and well. The chances are that he's still calling himself Patrick Barr. He won't know about Izzy, but he might know that he was adopted and be curious about his birth mother. He's at the age when men go searching for their roots or start to construct family trees. He might even come looking for her.

'Martin?'

Martin looks up. Once he sees the intensity of Izzy's expression he folds the paper and waits.

'How can I put myself out there?'

The question doesn't surprise him. He's used to Leah's mother by now and the need to interpret.

'You mean if Patrick comes looking for you?'

'Yes.'

Martin likes to encourage her in her search for her son. Izzy optimistic is so much easier to live with than Izzy self-pitying.

'I think the options are these. Now you think he's not on the streets, look in all the normal places. Check there's no Patrick Barr on Twitter, then search Wikipedia and Facebook.'

'How do I do that?'

Martin tries not to sigh. The pancakes were a bribe. Leah's mother is manipulative.

'I forgot. You don't do computers and the internet.'

Izzy has that helpless look again. Martin needs to think fast if his Sunday, the only free day he has in the week, isn't to be wheedled from him.

'I can give you an hour,' he tells her. 'I'll show you what you have to do, but then you need to set yourself up with the right tools. You need a computer or a smart phone. You need to update the wifi and you need to be patient.'

'When?' she says. Her eagerness is palpable.

'In half an hour.'

Her face falls and he relents.

'Okay, now.'

Martin takes his time with Izzy, but even so he knows she isn't understanding what he tells her. His computer's slowness doesn't help. He shows Leah's mother his bookshop site on Facebook, explains about signing in and how people post things about themselves. Then he shows her how to look for individuals. He explains about searching and introduces her to the magnifying glass icon. He makes her type in Patrick Barr. There are several of them. He shows her how she can open up each one and check the details, such as age and where they live. He himself opens up several of the Patrick Barrs, but none of them is right. He tries to get her to understand about platforms, but knows she imagines these are like the ones at railway stations. He shows her Twitter. She's heard of that because of Trump. Facebook is one platform, Twitter is another. He tells her she can do the same search with Twitter as with Facebook, or she can simply Google a name. He types in his own name on Google, scrolls down to find himself there, and shows her. When the hour is up he knows Izzy wants to carry on, but he shakes his head. 'I have books to sort. I have my washing to do. It can take days to search for a human being,' he tells her. 'You need to do this for yourself.'

She's grateful but disappointed when he closes the laptop lid.

'Buy one of your own,' he tells her.

'Does Leah know about computers?'

'She's learning,'

'Then will you, one day soon, take me shopping?'

'Tomorrow lunchtime,' he promises. 'Be at the shop when I close at noon.'

'Thanks, Martin.'

He heads for freedom. As he reaches the door she calls him back.

'I know I shouldn't ask this, but are you and Leah definite now?'

Martin smiles and shrugs his shoulders.

× × ×

In the care home Leah knocks on Wendell's door. There's only an hour to go until lunch and he's not appeared. She knocks and walks straight in.

Wendell is in bed. 'Hello Wendell,' Leah says, as brightly as possible as she opens the curtains.

He blinks at her.

'You'll feel better if you get up. It's Sunday. It's roast chicken and a glass of wine. I'll help you.'

He lifts his head from the pillow and she can see he's wearing his shirt but not his tie. She pulls back the covers. Under the duvet he's dressed except for his shoes. She fixes her smile in place. She can tell he's embarrassed. 'You get up and I'll help you.'

The tie is on the floor. Leah picks it up and ties it for him. Then she puts his shoes on and laces them. He's deteriorating, she thinks. Soon he'll be beyond such niceties, but now they still matter.

'All fixed,' Leah says. For the first time her brightness, that optimism Helen insists on, nearly deserts her. Wendell is so crestfallen at his own ineptitude.

She wants to hug him, but he'd hate that. She wants to say, 'You belong here. You need help. You'll soon need more of it. It's downhill all the way from here,' but of course she doesn't. She carries the mirror over so he can check how he looks.

He peers and nods.

As he makes for the door she does say, 'And stay away from the new man. Find a chair with someone already sitting on either side.'

A ghost of a smile. Was it even there?

When Leah walks through the lounge half an hour later the scene is almost comical. Half the room is crowded with not a single space left. Wendell did find a chair and he is in with the throng, looking much happier. Alone in the other corner is Bill and his black bag. It reminds her of a David Attenborough documentary where the small fish cower away from the shark. The room is almost silent. Then Helen walks in and speaks to Bill. He follows her out and the room relaxes. Lisa emerges and stands next to Leah.

'I've never known anything like it,' Lisa tells her. 'No one has ever dominated this place the way he does.'

Lunch is ready and they are soon busy with frames and wheelchairs. As she helps settle and serve, Leah is aware that everyone is looking towards the door. There's one place left. When plates are cleared away for pudding the place is still empty, and at the end of the meal it remains unoccupied.

But Bill is in the lounge. He's had his meal in there and, instead of the one glass of wine they have each been offered, he has the bottle.

Later that evening, when Izzy goes through to watch television and leaves Martin and Leah together, Leah tries to explain the effect Bill has on the others.

'He frightens them. He makes them all uneasy. It's not what he says as much as the sheer bulk of him. The others think he's acting old age rather than genuinely needing care.'

'You like them, don't you, your old people?'

'Yes, I do. Does that surprise you?'

'No. I'm glad you're enjoying your work. I had your mum to myself today.'

'What was that like?'

'She made me pancakes. They were a bribe. I showed

her how to look for people on the internet. When I shut the shop for lunch tomorrow I'm taking her to buy her own computer.'

Leah reaches out a hand and rests it on Martin's wrist.

'You're a good man. Thank you.'

'She asked me a question,' he says. 'I couldn't answer it.'

Martin feels the hand tense but carries on. 'She asked if we were definite.'

'What did you say?' Leah's hand is still on Martin's wrist but it's relaxed.

'I smiled and shrugged.'

'It's none of her business.' Leah says this with certainty, then adds, 'Are we?'

'I suspect we're drifting that way. I'm content to drift if that's what you want to know.'

Leah says nothing, but her hand closes round his wrist. Martin glances at her. She's looking straight ahead, a half smile on her lips.

He reaches forward. There's still some wine left after their meal. He divides it between their glasses.

'To drifting,' he suggests.

'To drifting,' she echoes, and downs the wine in her glass.

The kitchen is a mess. Empty roast trays and saucepans crowd round the sink. Their plates are pushed to the middle of the table. Surfaces need to be wiped. Cupboard doors are open. The wine bottle needs recycling.

'Well, that's that,' Leah says. 'I'll wash. You dry.'

× × ×

Wendell is back in his room when the door opens without anyone knocking first. Bill walks in without his stick and closes the door behind him. He has a torch with him which he shines in Wendell's face.

'I couldn't sleep,' Bill says, 'so I didn't see why you should.'

Wendell says nothing.

'You can't speak, can you? Too bad, because I can. And I've got a lot to say to you.'

Wendell reaches for the red button to call for help, but Bill gets there first. 'That's not very friendly, Wendell. I only want a chat.'

Wendell has no alternative but to listen.

'We're two of a kind, aren't we? I see it in the way you dress. We've both lived a long time, and what we need hasn't always been legal, has it? Even when it became legal we remained social pariahs. Then Aids came along and took our friends. We survived all that, didn't we, and at last it became truly alright to be what we both are. But it was too late for us, wasn't it? By that time the urge was leaving us.'

'Sad that, isn't it? Sad that the others in this home probably still hold all the prejudices we've fought against all our lives. Sad that we never truly escaped the stigma. Were you ever locked up for it? No. Me neither. But we're locked up now, aren't we? No parole and only death as a way out.'

Wendell says nothing, shows no sign that he's been listening.

Bill is clearly bored by his own one-sided conversation. He gets up and then, because he is still holding it, he lets go of the emergency button which swings away from him and just misses Wendell's head.

'Your name's not right, is it? We've met before, only once if I remember rightly. I'm good at names but I can't remember a Wendell. Goodnight.'

Then Bill turns and goes, walking quickly with no sign of a limp. When he's out of the room Wendell sinks down onto the bed.

If he had a case he'd start packing, but even if he had one he couldn't carry it. And where would he go? He sits on the bed and cries for the young man he once was and the choices he never had.

× × ×

James's phone rings.

'James Goulden here.'

'We are the SDS.'

'Who?'

'The SDS.'

'I'm sorry, I don't understand the acronym.'

'We are the Statues Defence Society.'

'Okay, got that. How can I help?'

'We want you to head our recruitment drive.'

At last, thinks James. This sounds a solid proposition. Statues are a good thing. They are part of British history. They help set the national character. James doesn't understand yet why they need protection, but he presumes this is a society like the Preservation of Rural England or English Heritage.

'Where can I find out about you?'

'Why don't you come to one of our meetings?'

'I could probably do that. Where and when?'

'This afternoon at Winston Churchill's statue in Westminster, 2pm.'

'I'll be there.'

James arrives early outside the House of Commons and walks into Parliament Square. The statue of the warrior Prime Minister manages to dominate the square in much the same way as the warrior himself dominated the Commons in the 1940s. It's not just the bulk emphasised by the coat; it's the step forward and the sense of thrust that produces the statue's authority. Standing in front of it, James feels its power. At the very least you wouldn't want to collide with it or have it topple on top of you.

So why does it need protecting? Surely the man in the coat could still deal with any opposition. He only has to raise his walking stick, which already looks more like a weapon than a prop. Tourists are walking round. It's Churchill they stop for. It's Churchill who gets the selfie. Is James on a wild goose chase? Has he been had? There are no middle class earnest souls standing waiting for something to happen. Instead, characters James regards as unsavoury are beginning to make their way from whichever pub they have been drinking in and moving into the square. They are quintessentially English. Their uniform is work jeans and sweatshirts. Their hair is short. There is a roughness about them and a cockiness that comes from the sense of having comrades around them. An examination of their knuckles shows teeth marks. The odd ear looks chewed. A certain loudness comes into the square with them. It is as if their volume control is a function of their numbers, turned up as more and more of them appear.

The one whose jeans are ironed and have creases, whose sweatshirt looks clean-on that morning, is at the front and heading James's way. What must he look like to them, smartly dressed as he is with that signature head of ringleted hair? He makes a mental note to get it cut. He stands his ground. He'll be the rock this tide of bouncers and security men break round, but they will not sweep him away.

The clean-cut man has reached him. 'You came. I wasn't sure you would. My name's William Baton.'

'I know who you are.' James tries to hide his distaste. He shakes the hand that's offered and feels his knuckles being crushed.

The movement in front of him changes names as often as a conman. They have been Blackshirts, the National Front, the British National Party, the English Defence League. Like struggling schools and dodgy companies, the names change but the personnel stay the same. James is kicking himself. He should have been wise to the word Defence. Defence and Protection are very different things.

They are all round him now. He can't just turn and go. He can't stay silent either. 'So, who are you defending this statue against?' he asks.

'That comes later,' William Baton explains, 'when the word gets around. They only attack it because we defend it.'

'Is Churchill one of your heroes?'

'Course he is. He's the real British Hero. He saved us from the Germans.'

'Don't you mean the Nazis?' James enquires.

'Ahh, that's a bit of a sore point with us, 'cos many of us are Nazis. That's why we say the Germans.'

Shit, how much more of this can he stand? James changes the subject. 'What happens now?' he asks.

'We wait for the film crews. Then I make a speech about defending British values. The lads cheer and by then the Anti-Nazis will have arrived and the punch-up begins. It's all organised. You'll be able to watch it on the news tonight. I expect you've missed being on the tele.'

James looks at the faces that are arranged round him in a phalanx. This is a time when he must either be true to his intelligence or not. He takes a deep breath and readies himself.

'So, let me get this right,' he begins, speaking slowly. 'You are here to defend a statue that no one has attacked.'

They nod.

'You are secretly Nazis…'

They nod again.

'… but you are here to defend the statue of the man who did more than anyone else to make sure that the Nazis lost in 1945….'

One face in the crowd seems perplexed. The others nod enthusiastically. No one has thumped him yet, so James goes on.

'… and who, in our darkest hour, ensured that the straight-arm salutes never caught on in the UK?'

Some cheer and give a Nazi salute. 'Dead right,' says William Baton, who doesn't. During James's attack on him, William's smile has never wavered. 'I knew you were clever, Mr Goulden. Now turn and smile for the cameras. They've already picked you out.' He indicates the filming crews that are in position. 'You've served your purpose.'

'What purpose?'

'You're mainstream. That's where we want to be. The more we are photographed with toffs and tossers like you, the more people will take us seriously. Think of the rumours this will generate. Now be a good boy and smile again before we let you go.'

James feels hands holding him from behind. He really has no option.

'And by the way,' William Baton adds, as the cameras turn their lenses on the approaching Anti-Nazi League, 'I do understand logic and consistency, but it's such an old fashioned, middle class trope that we've abandoned it.'

× × ×

The Hotel Americana is as much a relic as the Alhambra itself. To reach their room Julia and Zakk have to walk through the dining area and climb an iron spiral staircase with only enough room for one person and one small case at a time. The staircase creaks and shifts but stays in place. At the top there are two rooms. Theirs is at the front above a shadowed, dusty courtyard where diners are crammed in out of the heat.

'No escape,' Zakk says, as he turns the key and steps aside so she can walk in first.

The room is tired. Paintings and furnishings belong to the last century. But the en suite is clean and the bed isn't too hard.

'Okay?' he asks.

She nods. 'Different.'

What is she doing? In a fit of remorse over her handling of Stuart, aka the twerp, she's allowed a man she knows very little about to inveigle her into cancelling what she is sure would have been a perfectly good hotel room with all mod cons and furnishings - for this.

'I like different,' he says.

She sits on the bed. It squeaks. How embarrassing.

'It's the Ziggy Stardust in me.'

She's aware that he's watching her closely, that he too is uncertain about being with her, that this is also a risk for him. She remembers the first night she spent in a similarly run-down hotel with the man who became her husband. At that time there had been voices in her head that said yes and others that said *definitely not*. The *definitely nots*, she remembers, were louder, but she hadn't listened. She'd thought she'd be able to drown them out over time. It was funny how those voices had persisted for years, getting louder, until they were all she heard. That's why she and her first husband had called it a day. She could have saved so much money and the paperwork if only she'd listened.

This time the *definitely nots* are silent. Are they biding their time? She thinks of her younger sister, Leah the listener. Leah would know, wouldn't she? But Leah isn't even certain about Martin, and they've been together for a long time now. So Leah would be no help to her.

Hang on, she tells herself. This is a holiday fling. The sex is fun. We both have separate flights to catch which will land at separate destinations. Enjoy it for what it is.

She pats the bed. 'Come and sit beside me,' she commands.

He does so. They kiss. The feel of his lips and their taste are still new to her, but already familiar. Their combined weight seems to have silenced the bed.

'I need my dinner,' he says.

They climb back down the stairs and find a table.

'Proximity to food, tick.'

Menus are brought quickly. They order a bottle of wine.

The food is good. Then they walk out into a soft warm evening and peer down into Granada. The sky is clear but pink at the edges where it touches the buildings and the trees.

'I love this place,' Zakk announces.

She's standing a little way from him, looking over the excavation.

'You said.'

He leans with his back to the wall. 'I told you I love the country, but for me this place is its epitome.' He laughs at himself. She likes that about him.

'Let's walk,' she says.

They turn right and go into the Palacios Nazaríes. 'That's what I've come for.' Zakk points to a pantiled roof, just about the dullest thing in the scene. To their right is a round palace. To their left is a gateway through an ancient wall. What Zakk points to looks like the attic of a modern house.

'I don't understand,' she says.

'Outsides and insides,' he tells her. 'Wait until you see the interior.'

'What is it?' she asks him. 'Tell me now.'

'It's the Alhambra, built by the Moors when their time as rulers was already over. It's the perfect antidote to mortality.'

She doesn't want talk of mortality. Zakk looks younger in this half-light, and she feels younger when she's with him. She grabs his hand. 'Come on. I want to see what's on the other side of that arch.'

17

Danny makes sure he's early that Monday morning. It's high time he had it out with Chloe. What was she doing following him? The point of following is to not be seen, so why step out and confront them? Danny has a terrible suspicion about that, which had better not be true.

He sees her coming along the corridor and ducks his head as if he's reading the file. The moment she walks into the room he takes up the conversation from where they left off. He's no longer laughing.

'What do you want to ask me, Chloe? What was going through that dirty mind of yours last Friday afternoon?'

'Concern,' she said. 'Concern for you.'

She's looking as if she didn't sleep well last night. She's looking guilty … and something else. She doesn't sit, so he stands up too.

'You followed me the moment I left work. You watched me as I searched for Shaun. Then you deliberately confronted us. Why?'

'I thought…'

'Spit it out.'

'I don't know you, Col. I hardly know anything about you.'

He can tell she's both furious and ashamed.

'Then read my file.'

'I followed you to keep my hand in. I followed you because I have to write a report. And I must say you were cavalier. Anyone who works in this building is suspect. You walked and never looked behind you. Now you work for us ….' She corrects herself. 'For as long as you work for us, you must be aware that you are a potential target, not an ordinary citizen.'

'You didn't trust me.'

'Of course not.' She shouts this at him. 'No one in this building ever really trusts anyone else. Even you must have heard about Burgess, Maclean, Philby and Blunt. I've told you about the suspicions around Hollis.'

'But it was worse than that, wasn't it?' Danny isn't about to back down. 'This isn't about me not watching my back. This is about what you thought I was up to. Spit it out, Chloe. Let's see what your nasty little mind was thinking.'

'What was I supposed to think? You were stressed. Everything about you, the way you just stopped in the middle of the street. Then you went searching for a rough sleeper and held a wad of notes in front of his face. What the hell was I supposed to think? Get off your high horse, Colm, and face the realities of the job I'm training you to do. What would you have thought in my position?'

She has a point, so Danny sits down and explains.

'I was a rough sleeper too. I walked out of my previous life because I wanted to change. I lived on the streets and Shaun helped me, showed me the ropes. I beat up several men who were attacking him, broke the leg of one of them in two places. At the time of the leadership hustings, because they knew I could handle myself, MI5 hired me as a deep watcher and used my street persona. When I left the streets I promised Shaun I'd go back and look for him. You caught me keeping my promise.'

'Where is Shaun now?'

'Drying out. That's the condition I made. If I'm to help him, he has to manage without the booze. He has to do that while he's still on the streets and then I'll help him.'

Chloe sits as if she's winded. 'You're a good man, Col.'

And she looks interested in him at last, not as boss, not as trainer, but as one human to another.

'Will that get me fired? This job, this chance of interesting work, matters to me.'

Chloe speaks slowly. 'This building is full of weird, twisted people. You're not like them. I'll have to keep that a secret if I'm to recommend you.' She smiles at him. 'I'm sorry.'

'Okay.' Danny accepts her apology, then adds, 'By the way, for the sake of your report, so you get all your facts straight, I'm not gay.'

Chloe nods.

'But Juozas was. And another thing, now we've settled our differences. Shaun was right. Vidar is the name of the Norse God of Revenge.'

Danny turns to the file and checks the dates. 'So after the failure of the West to support the Prague Spring, he changed his code name to a word that means revenge. Revenge against whom, the Soviets for invading, or the West for not intervening?'

'Or both. Think of what Juozas did next. He started to work with the partisans against the Soviets, feeding them information he'd gathered from other sources. He also took risks in his private life.'

'Who is Baldr?' Danny asks, re-examining their chart. 'Shaun said he was another Norse God.'

Chloe searches on her mobile phone. There's a note of excitement in her voice. 'Baldr is the Norse God of Purity.'

They are both excited. 'You did say, didn't you, that agents choose their own code names?' Danny checks.

Chloe nods. 'Just like you did, Colm.'

'So the first code name Juozas chose explains what he was feeling when he was first sent to Lithuania. We know he loved his father. Even at the time of his first betrayal, when he found out his dad was a Nazi sympathiser, he didn't change his code name.'

'Can we presume then, that his purity remained in spite of his father? In that case, his purity was anti-Soviet,' Chloe suggests.

'And loyalty to Britain, his adopted country: the purity of knowing what he was for and what he was against. It was that purity which deserted him after the Prague Spring. He's a Lithuanian Nationalist first and foremost. Simple as that.'

Chloe calls a halt. 'But we are still stuck. I agree with everything you've just said, and thank God for your friend Shaun. What he's given us helps explain why Juozas refused promotion. What it doesn't explain is why he never returned to Lithuania after Independence. Given what we think we now know, isn't that all the more surprising?'

Danny looks back at the chart. 'There are twenty-one years between him changing his code name and Independence. What happened in those twenty-one years? What the hell is in that file he stole?'

× × ×

Leah's back on duty. She walks in to find the place in a minor uproar. Sarah tells her about it. Lisa tells her about it. Helen is looking occupied as she talks to the owners in her office. The problem is Bill. Ever since he arrived he has upset staff and upset the residents. After morning briefing Leah walks into the lounge. Wendell isn't there. She goes to his room.

He's in bed. As she walks in, even though she knocked first, she's sure that he's afraid of something or someone and that his face relaxes when he sees it's her. The room is shrieking at her. Something is wrong.

She starts talking. 'Another nice day,' she tells him as she opens the curtains to let light into the room. 'You'll feel better when you get up. You've had no breakfast, have you? I can get you something. I know you don't like our new resident. Why don't I get you ready and then you can have breakfast in your room?'

She's busies herself tidying. Wendell's room isn't usually untidy, but this morning it is. She sits down by the bed. 'When I didn't talk, Mum used to play guessing games. If she thought I wanted to tell her something, she'd make a line of guesses and I nodded if she was right. I didn't use words, but I did nod and shake my head. So let's try it. I know you can nod and I guess you can shake your head.'

'Has Bill been frightening you?'

There's no nod and no shake of the head, but the eyes tell her.

'Has he been in your room?'

Wendell is expressionless, just looking at her.

'I want to help,' Leah tells him, 'but you have to let me.'

There's a slight shake of the head.

'It's something I can't help with, isn't it?'

He keeps his head still, but the tears are there. He's lying in his bed as if nothing can be done.

To be old and to feel like that.

'I do respect your privacy. You know that, don't you?' She looks at him. There's no reaction. 'Right, let's get you up and get you some breakfast.'

He doesn't shake his head. She lifts the duvet and sees he's fully dressed again. She rolls the duvet back.

'Wendell,' she says to him, 'he really frightened you, didn't he?'

The face is still. The tears are gone. His eyes are no longer looking at her; they are focussed past her.

'Come on, stand up,' she says, 'and that's an order.'

Surprisingly, he does as he's told.

× × ×

That afternoon Julia and Zakk join the queue for the Alhambra. Entrance is timed and the guards check their watches frequently. Julia has deliberately not brought her guidebook. When their time comes they walk in. It's another hot day and the scent of myrtle permeates the still air. They pick up the sound of running water before feeling the coolness it brings. Julia is aware that Zakk wants her to like this place. At first she's unsure. It's another Alcazar with the same use of space as the Seville version. She's moving quickly and he tells her to slow down and look.

She does as she's told. She watches the patterns on the flowing water. She sees that the plasterwork has its own ebb and flow. There are inscriptions she can't read because they are in Arabic. These soon become simply decorative and act like Latin chants in great music, made all the more perfect because meaning doesn't interfere. In places, corners are festooned with plaster, more elaborate than any they have yet seen. This plasterwork is reflected on the water and picks up the tiny ripples that curl the surface. This interplay adds harmony. She picks up on the rhythms as they move from one courtyard to the next. The effect on her is like that of a butterfly's wing softly brushing against her and whispering to longings she never knew she had.

He's watching her closely when they walk into the Palace of the Lions.

How could they have done this? How could they have built this perfect space when under such threat from everywhere around them? They must have known the end was coming and the Christian conquest of the South would soon be complete.

And then she understands.

It's the sense of an ending that gives life its sweetness. Zakk is close beside her. She's aware of his fading beauty, of his sheer niceness. As the building floats past her it captures the miracle of human existence and freezes it. For a short space of time the people who built this wonder would be allowed to live in it. For a shorter period of time she and Zakk will walk through it. Life is a DVD you can only play once. The Alhambra is its pause button.

Julia turns on the spot to take in all that she is seeing, but she isn't seeing it any longer. Her eyes are full of tears. She's Julia, the woman who dominates and bullies, the executive who has always prided herself on her forcefulness. Why is this happening? Has he noticed? She hopes not. Angrily, she brushes the tears away with her fingers.

Pain can make you cry, so can unhappiness, but this is different and deeply embarrassing. Can beauty also make you blub?

She's reaching for a tissue when his hand reaches out and touches her shoulder. She looks up before she dabs her eyes.

His look is one of concern, but is there also a hint of triumph? The old Julia would have shaken his hand from her shoulder. The new Julia responds to his touch. He moves her to one side to let other people pass and she lets herself be moved.

He takes the tissue from her and carefully wipes under each eye.

'Ignore them. Let them think that this is unhappiness; let them think we've had a row.'

Then he puts his arm back around her and leads her slowly through the other rooms, urging her to keep looking. She does this through further tears which only enhance the fairy tale quality of the building.

She is content to be led. All too soon they reach the end, climb the stairs, and time starts again.

'I'm sorry,' she says. 'I'm sorry. I hope that didn't ruin your visit.'

He shakes his head. 'I was jealous. That's how I felt when I first saw it.'

'Jealous of what? You've met a woman who collapsed in Ronda, and now the same woman has wept her way through your favourite building. How embarrassing!' She dabs her eyes to get rid of the last traces of her tears, blows her nose and looks straight at him.

'I'm not usually like this,' she insists.

× × ×

Before she leaves that evening Leah asks for a private word with Helen.

'Are you going to let Bill stay here?' she asks. 'He's upsetting everyone and he's terrifying Wendell.'

'What makes you say that?' Helen asks.

'This morning I found Wendell lying in bed, fully clothed and wearing his shoes. I think he'd been like that all night, wondering if he should run away. I think Bill had been in his room. I say I think because he doesn't talk, but I watched carefully when I questioned him.'

'That's not much to go on.'

'When I was on night duty before Bill arrived, someone was in the grounds. I only caught a glimpse, but soon afterwards a car drove off with no lights. I was in Wendell's room when it happened. He was standing on his bed and staring out of the window.'

'You're not the only one to contact me about our new resident. I've talked to him about the way he acts. Let's wait and see.'

'Thanks for listening to me.' Leah gets up to go.

'You're doing well here, Leah, especially with Wendell. I have you down as a real find. Do one thing for me when you're next on duty, will you?'

'What's that?'

'Get to know Bill for me. Then tell me what you think.'

× × ×

It's night-time in Granada. Julia and Zakk are in bed in the Hotel Americana. They've made love and are listening to all the noises that come through the thin walls: the bed creaks and the loo flushes as well as footsteps on last year's dead leaves in the lane outside.

It's dark in the room. Each can see the outline of the other's face. They are so close they can feel each other's breath, but their eyes are shadows and the night seems to hold them awake. Sleep will not come. Julia rolls away from Zakk and stares into the blackness of the ceiling.

'I'm sorry I made such an exhibition of myself this afternoon in your favourite building.' She waits for a reply or for his forgiveness, but there is nothing. He was wide awake a few seconds ago. She doesn't think he's gone to sleep. 'I don't know what came over me. What you said about my treatment of Stuart was true. I don't really like myself at the moment. I'm like a caterpillar who thought she was a butterfly before she looked in the mirror. Now all of me is churned up inside this shell and I don't know who I am anymore.' She stops again. Is he listening? He's very still. Somewhere in the Alhambra gardens an owl calls to another. She listens but there is no reply. She's goes on talking. 'I don't know about you either. You're kind, you're determined. There's something about you that something inside me recognises and responds to. I don't know what this is between us. I've never had an affair. When I was married I stayed faithful. Is this what an affair feels like? Perhaps you've had many affairs. If so, you can tell me.' She stops and listens again. He's either asleep or he's bored or he's simply not going to play her game. 'I like the suspense of it,' she tells the room. 'I like the not knowing. I like you.'

She stops there. The owl is calling again. Her husband used to pretend to be asleep. Part of her wants to dig Zakk in the ribs, but she doesn't. She breathes in deeply, closes her eyes, and eventually she sleeps.

× × ×

Wendell is awake. He can hear footsteps moving in the corridor outside his room, but they don't stop at his door this time. He breathes a sigh of relief. He hears another door open. Bill's taken to sleeping during the day and prowling at night, but just now he's returned to his room and Wendell can relax. Leah will be on duty tomorrow. He's looking forward to that.

He listens. A tawny owl is calling but then goes silent. The road is still at this time in the morning. Nothing untoward is going to happen tonight, so he can allow himself to sleep. He has his insurance. He has his secrets. He is not defenceless. Coming to this home was the right thing to do, in spite of Bill. His body was telling him he could no longer live alone. Being here is as safe as he can ever be. He knows he needs looking after.

× × ×

Julia wakes the next morning and finds the bed empty. Has Zakk done a runner? She looks at her watch. It's late. Perhaps he was hungry and wanted breakfast. She opens the curtains just wide enough to look through the gap and she sees him sitting down below with a pot of coffee.

She showers quickly without washing her hair and climbs down the spiral stairs to join him.

He looks up and pours her a coffee. 'Yes, no and ditto,' he says to her, and smiles.

She doesn't understand him.

'Your questions last night. Yes, I don't know what this is between us either. No, this isn't what an affair feels like. Ditto, I like you too.'

'You were listening.'

'It would have been impolite not to.'

'Okay,' she says, 'so what's next?'

He puts down his toast. 'I've really no idea.'

'Practicalities,' she says. 'I have an early flight booked for tomorrow, so today I need to drive to Malaga. The hire car is due back tonight.'

'Stuff the practicalities.'

She orders real food because she's hungry. This is too serious a conversation to play with a croissant and a cup of coffee.

'What are your arrangements?'

'Much the same as yours.'

'Don't you have a job to get back to?'

'Yes, but it can wait.'

'What are you suggesting?'

As she asks the question she finds she's totally relaxed about his answer. He is impossible. She cannot imagine, even in a year's time, taking him and introducing him to her siblings. Leah's guy, Martin, at least has a serious name. *This is Zakk. Zakk, meet James, Leah and Martin.* But nor can she imagine kissing him goodbye in a departure lounge and never seeing him again.

'I want longer with you,' he insists.

'But haven't we run out of Spain?'

'That takes a lifetime.'

'I know nothing about you,' she says.

'And all I know about you is that you bully stupid young men at work.'

He's being flippant, perhaps serious and flippant, maybe seriously flippant. It occurs to her that he does care about what she says next, so she says nothing. And this is not like her. She always sticks to her plans. Cancelling flights costs money. Any moment now she will be asked to come back to work, and she can't reply *Thanks, but I need a bit more time with my lover.*

'I just think we should give this a few more days.' He stretches his hand across and grasps hers. 'Please.'

How can she resist? The touch of him has always felt right, has always been comfortable. Now it is compelling.

She answers with her hand before she picks the right word. There are so many to choose from: okay is non-committal; cool just isn't her word; fine would be dismissive; great isn't what she feels. She settles on, 'Yes,' then adds, 'I've never done this before.'

'I have,' he tells her, 'but not for a very long time.'

She gets practical. How many days? Where do we go? I expect to be called back to work soon, so we do need to rebook flights.

'You're right,' he says. 'We're not gap-year students. My Company needs to know when I'm coming back too.'

They settle on three more days. Today they'll go back to Malaga and dump one hire car. They'll rearrange flights and set off in the other car with no hotels fixed and see where they get to.

Even as they agree this Julia has doubts. It's not the way she's ever travelled. It indicates that Zakk might not be a serious person, but it might answer her questions about him. Anyway, for the first time since she was a child, she doesn't want a holiday to end.

18

Izzy's bought her new computer. She's upgraded their broadband. She spends hours looking for her son, frequently calling on Martin to teach her about other platforms. Patrick Barr isn't on Facebook. He isn't on Twitter. There are lots of Patrick Barrs on Google, but much as she stares at the photos, she can't see the baby she gave away or the sixteen-year-old from the Living Saints photograph in any of these middle-aged faces.

'I wish I knew what he looks like now.' she tells Martin.

'There's one way you might be able to do that, but it will cost you.'

'How?'

'There's a man in London who's an expert in how we age. He produces images of what someone might look like when they are older. We see his work on news bulletins every now and then. If you show him the photograph of Patrick when he was sixteen, he'll study it and produce an image of what he might look like at fifty.'

'How do I contact him?'

'You know the answer to that. Ask Google.'

Three days later Izzy catches the London train. She has the Living Saints photo with her and an appointment in Bentinck Road. Waiting on York station she is overcome with a sense of hopefulness. She'll find Patrick and she'll find Danny. Her family will be back together. She also feels that she's coming alive again. A few weeks ago she travelled up to Scotland. Today she's going to London. She can use the internet, and its ways are becoming familiar to her.

She thinks back to what she told Katherine about Gary that night they shared together, things she'd never told herself. How horrified Julia would be with that series of revelations about the father she loved. Are our secrets at the core of who we are, she asks herself. Does Katherine feel better or worse because she unburdened herself to me?

The train comes in and people crowd on and off. Izzy finds her seat and prepares to enjoy the journey. In London she negotiates the tube. As she crosses the city she finds herself thinking, I was so controlled by Gary, so cowed by my own parents. Is it too late at sixty-eight to find out about the person I might once have been? Her face is lined, she knows, but inside she's growing younger. She's aware that parts of the body age at different rates, that the physical heart can be years older than one's chronological age. What about the emotional heart? If people can be emotionally old before their time, can they be emotionally younger? Is it too late for her?

She finds Bentinck Road and rings the bell. The transaction is quickly accomplished. The man thinks he can make something of the photograph she gives him.

He'd like more detail, but he'll do his best. She pays up front and he promises to send her both a digital and several paper copies of his projection.

She's free and she has two hours on her own in London before she catches her train home.

× × ×

It's morning briefing in the care home. Sarah has been allocated to Wendell. Leah has Bill to work with, just as Helen requested. The staff report that it's been a quiet night. Yes, Bill prowled round at first, but after midnight he settled down and went to sleep. As far as they know he's still sleeping. The night staff are eager to leave. They finish their report quickly and go. It seems like a normal changeover until Lisa walks into the room.

'What happened?' she asks.

'What do you mean?'

'Come and look.'

She takes them on a tour. Some staff photos are upside down. Each one has been carefully removed and then pinned the wrong way up. The sign outside the front door, which in all weathers says *Danger Ice*, has had an M added to it so it says *Danger MIce*. The wooden calendar indicates it's Christmas Day. Several room numbers have been switched.

'Check on Wendell,' Leah advises.

They do and he's asleep, but everything in his room is in the wrong place.

'It'll be Bill,' says Lisa. 'Over to you, Leah. I'll warn Helen. He'll have to go.'

Other residents are in uproar. The chairs and tables in the lounge have not been touched, but the two toilets downstairs have *Out of Action* signs propped against their doors.

Sarah is amused. 'It's funny. It's clever. You've got to laugh.'

Then they go into the garden and find the cat lying on its side, its back legs stretched out and its eyes closed. There are signs round its mouth of it having been sick. Lisa reaches out and touches it. It feels cold and stiff.

'It's dead,' she tells the others.

They take her word for it and remove it so the residents don't see it. They are used to hiding a death; it's what they do. They tell each other that the cat was old and too fat. It won't be worth doing an autopsy, but they wash their hands carefully. Bill didn't like the cat; it must be Bill.

Leah knocks on Bill's door and walks in. He's asleep. Nothing in his room seems to have been moved. But then, if he's responsible for the havoc in the rest of the home, his own room will have been left untouched.

Leah opens the curtains and Bill swears at her. 'What the fuck are you doing?'

'Getting you up.'

'I don't have to get up. This is my home. I can sleep as long as I like.'

'Not today.'

Leah liked the cat. Other residents liked the cat. It didn't notice they were decrepit. It ran its sides against ulcerated legs. It let bony fingers sink into its fur.

Bill grabs the duvet. 'Fuck off,' he yells.

Leah grabs it back and pulls. She wins the tug of war.

'Up,' she says.

'This is abuse. I'll have you sacked.'

'The cat's dead,' Leah shouts at him.

'Good,' he shouts back. 'I don't like cats.'

Leah pauses. If he did kill it, he wouldn't say that, would

he? He'd say, 'I'm sorry to hear that.' If he was responsible he'd cover his tracks and mute his responses. Everything he's saying is too slick, too confident, too like himself. He's just as he was yesterday and the day before that.

'I've always hated fucking cats.'

He's uncouth. He's abusive. He's without feeling. He's an angry man, physically intimidating, but is he a cat killer?

She pauses. 'Did you walk round in the night?' she asks.

She hasn't been told to interrogate him, just to get him to Helen in the office.

'Yes,' he snarls. 'I like walking round at night. It's the only time the place isn't cluttered up with nearly dead people.'

Leah is still holding the duvet. 'Helen wants to talk to you.'

He snatches at the duvet and she lets it go. 'Then Helen is going to have to fucking wait.'

She leaves him in bed and closes the door behind her. She's read lots of things in his eyes, but guilt isn't one of them.

Michael can see them. They take the lift to the top floor. They are invited to sit at his conference table. Coffee is brought in.

Chloe begins. 'We don't know where he is. We haven't recovered the file he stole.'

'But you have something to report?' Michael adjusts his glasses. He clearly has other things on his mind today and wants the meeting over quickly.

'Something to report and a crucial question to ask.'

'Go on.'

‘We suspect that Vidar began with three reasons for serving MI5: his gratitude to this country for taking him in, his love for his dead father, and his love for Lithuania. By 1970 two of these passions had been betrayed. He discovered his father was a Nazi sympathiser who helped round up Jews to be sent to the gas chambers, and he despaired of the West and of Britain in particular after they failed to support the Prague Spring. After 1970 he interfered directly in Lithuanian affairs, passing information to the partisans to assist in their struggles. He disappeared following our vote to leave the European Union as soon as it became clear that it was going to happen. That is not surprising, because the European Union has done so much for the independent Lithuania. We don’t know everything yet. Most significantly, we don’t know why he never went back to Lithuania once Independence had been achieved.’

Danny takes up the story. ‘His first code name was Baldr, Norse God of Purity. After 1970 he changed that to Vidar, Norse God of Revenge. There have been no further changes, but there is another Norse god we are interested in. Loki is the Norse Joker God. Loki is the trickster. If you think about the soap suds incident and the microphone mini speakers you might think of Loki. If you think about the booby trap that nearly injured us, you would think of Loki. We have a tentative hypothesis that between 1970 and 1991, when Lithuania became independent, Juozas suffered another betrayal, something that grated on him so badly that, although he remained a Lithuanian patriot, he would not visit his independent homeland.’

‘Good work so far.’ Michael looks at his watch.

Chloe continues. ‘There’s one other thing you should know, Sir. According to a source Colm met in Vilnius, the Russian Federation is also looking for him. Putin wants him dead because of the jokes he played against the Russians. Putin would hate the file to be published. Colm's source implied that the Russians know what's in the file. Do we? I ask this because it might help us find him.' She waits. 'Of course, given the RF involvement, you might want to hand this over to a higher grade officer.'

'Two files actually,' Michael corrects them. 'So no, I'm leaving you both on the case.' He pauses. 'The first is the Pol Pot file. It details the way the British stood by the worst mass murderer in modern times, even supported him as the true leader of Cambodia. The publication of that file would further damage this country's already tattered reputation. The second file was his, Vidar's. We don't know what's in it, but I'd guess it contains the names of high ranking people in the present independent Lithuania who collaborated with the Soviets and have airbrushed their own pasts.'

Chloe and Danny look at each other. 'Thank you, Sir. That would fit.'

'Find him if you can, before the Russians do. We don't want another Salisbury.'

'We'll do our best.'

The moment they are out of the room Chloe turns on Danny. 'That Loki stuff. You hadn't shared it with me. I should reprimand you for that, but it was brilliant.' She looks at her watch. 'Let's take an early lunch. There's a vegan place. It's not far.'

They walk out of the building.

'Tell me about Loki,' Chloe demands. 'I've seen the films.'

'Not the Marvell comic character. I meant the ancient

Norse figure. Yes, he was the trickster, but his jokes were never funny. He killed Baldr. Baldr was the pure one, the son of Odin himself. The gods were throwing darts around when Loki introduced a dart made from mistletoe. Someone else threw it and it killed Baldr, but Loki provided it. That fascinated me. Loki was the shadowy figure whose fingerprints were never on the murder weapon.'

'It fits.' Chloe nods. 'It makes Juozas a more worrying figure. I was beginning to feel sorry for him after all those betrayals. Why has he taken the Pol Pot file?'

'Did the Russians support Pol Pot? You're the historian, Chloe.'

'The other way round. The Russians and other Warsaw Pact countries helped fight the Khmer Rouge and helped rebuild Cambodia. The West supported Pol Pot.'

Danny thinks. 'So the file is the perfect example of how Britain talks about liberty and freedom at the same time that it supports appalling tyranny.'

'It's the war the world has forgotten. Loki the joker wants us to remember.'

'It should be published,' Danny asserts. 'If it's true, it should be published.'

Chloe grimaces. 'We're not the Salvation Army, Col. We play our games for advantage.'

'Then we're no better and often worse than the opposition.'

'Be careful Col, you're beginning to sound like Juozas.'

They reach the café and order.

Chloe is asserting her authority. 'What do you make of the suggestion that the other file contains the names of previous collaborators with the Soviets, who now pose as patriots and are high up in the modern Lithuanian government?' she asks. 'Is that why Juozas never went back, because he felt that Independence was tainted?'

'It's a hypothesis. It fits the very few facts we have. Imagine you are Juozas. You fight for something that really matters to you. You dismiss distractions like your father's betrayal. You have a purity about you that you won't compromise. It takes your whole working life to achieve Independence, this thing you've wanted so badly. Finally, it happens and it's disappointing, rendered impure by the very people who brought it about.'

'Are you getting to like Juozas, Col? They say when you search for someone you either love or hate them.'

'I think I'm beginning to understand him. Perhaps in some ways we're alike.'

Chloe shakes her head. 'I may have to fail you after all. You're not cynical or immoral enough to work for the Service.'

Their food comes and they eat. Danny finds the food surprisingly good given that there's no meat involved.

Over coffee Chloe shakes her head. 'For all that we now know, we're actually no further forward. We have to find him, and find him before they do. Where do we look?'

'And what do we look for? We have no photograph, which is odd. There should be a photograph in the file, shouldn't there?'

Chloe nods.

'And there's no physical description.'

'He clearly doesn't want to be found.'

'And when we do find him we need to be careful. He's dangerous.'

× × ×

Driving her hire car to Malaga, Julia is thoughtful. The roads are empty. The Sat Nav, in spite of all her attempts, refuses to speak anything except Spanish, but the rolling maps are clear enough. Neat plantations stretch on either side of the road. It looks like a prosperous countryside. Every now and then she drives through or sees on the hillside another white painted village, its houses brilliant in the strong sunshine.

The human mind is such an odd thing. She attempts as she drives to ponder her problem, but her thoughts are lawless, unfettered by time. Images from her past come and go as the car maintains its speed: hanging Leah over the sinkhole; the way Dad loved her; standing at the altar and already knowing her marriage won't last; laying down the law to the Board about how Human Resources should be handled. Woven into these memories, a weft to their rational warp, are more recent events: Zakk's ability to laugh at her; his body asleep; the way she cried; the sense of belonging when she's with him. These too come and go, unmarshalled. Occasionally she restates the question *Is this a holiday fling or something more*? Then she finds she is merely listing what she already knows and cannot reach a conclusion. Part of her is on the present holiday, part is concerned about the future, wondering what this will feel like when she looks back on it. Zakk is somewhere on the same road, perhaps thinking similar thoughts.

Then Julia remembers a particular blue dress. She'd seen it in a shop. She wanted it but didn't have the money. It must have been when she was still at school. She begged Mum to buy it for her. She wouldn't. Then she begged Dad and he caved in. The money was handed to her and she worried all night that the dress would have been sold. The next day she rushed to the shop and the dress was still there. When she tried it on it didn't fit. She went home without it and returned the money. She remembers the way her parents laughed at her. Is Zakk another blue dress?

Be sensible, she tells herself. Enjoy these days and then go back to being who you always were and what you always did. Leopards and spots. Leopards and spots.

19

If not Bill, who?

But for everyone else the answer is clear. It has to be Bill. They list the evidence against him. He prowls round at night. He hated the cat and had been seen kicking it away. He frightens them. They think he's a phoney because he can walk without a stick. He swears. Agnes sums him up when she says to anyone who comes within earshot, 'He's just a nasty man.'

Leah sticks to her brief from Helen. She is trying to get to know Bill. When he eventually comes out of his room and goes to sit outside, she goes to sit beside him.

She asks him about himself.

He tells her to fuck off.

She asks him what's making him so angry.

He tells her to fuck off again.

She talks about herself and he tells her to shut up.

That's when she gives up and goes to see Helen.

'I don't think it was Bill who killed the cat,' she tells

her. She goes on to explain what she thinks Bill is and what she thinks he isn't. She repeats his rudeness, word for word. Finally, she describes his reaction to her accusation about the cat.

'He still has to go,' Helen says. 'He's upsetting everyone. He has to go.'

'Even if he's innocent?' Leah asks.

'I was going to ask him to leave even before last night's events,' Helen explains. 'This is their home.' She gestures towards the lounge. 'They have a right not to be continually upset.'

Leah sits in silence.

Helen reinforces her point. 'You told me he'd been in Wendell's room. You told me he was frightening Wendell.'

'I did.' Leah has to agree. 'The home was a nicer place before he came,' she admits.

I'm new here, Leah reminds herself. Helen knows what she's doing.

'When will this happen?' Leah asks.

'As soon as we can find him alternative accommodation.'

Leah walks out into the sunshine. It's lunchtime and that means all hands on deck. Residents need moving, toileting, seating. She lets herself be swept up in the activity. Agnes is unhappy with her seat and wants to sit somewhere else. That means moving a parked wheelchair and two frames just to extract her.

When they are all slurping soup Leah has time to look around. Wendell is sitting upright in the corner. He's smartly dressed and such a contrast to Bill, the over-large, long-haired man who's always been too big to belong. Wendell will be happy if Bill leaves. At least that's something.

She stands back and leans against the wall. It is a kind of family, this gathering, and it has enough problems of joints and incapacity without the aggressive bulk of Bill. She'll let it go. It's none of her business, and perhaps it was Bill after all. If so, once he's gone there will be no repetition.

That evening she talks to Martin and describes what happened.

'Why the cat?' Martin asks. 'The rest is funny and clever and must have taken someone time. If nothing else had happened we'd be laughing. But killing the cat is cruel and vindictive. Was it the same person? Is Bill ever funny? I mean, clever funny?'

'No. He's aggressive, unhappy, uncouth and he hates cats.'

'Not the person to turn staff photos upside down, alter the calendar to Christmas Day?'

'No.'

'What did the night staff say?'

'They never noticed. It was Lisa who spotted it. Night staff can grab some sleep in the middle of the night. It's been known.'

Martin grimaces. 'It doesn't make sense, whichever way you look at it. You've got someone altering things in a funny way in the night, someone who knows the place. It takes time. It needs planning and dexterity. This person also needs to know when the night staff will be asleep. Is that the same person who poisons the cat? If so, why?'

Leah shrugs.

'Does Bill have access to poison?'

'How on earth would I know?'

Martin laughs at himself for asking such a stupid question. 'Okay. I asked that because I wouldn't know how to poison a cat. Would you?'

Leah shakes her head. 'Perhaps it died of natural

causes,' she suggests.

'In that case, you have a joker and not a murderer.'

'Well, Bill doesn't strike me as a joker.'

Martin laughs again. 'In that case it almost certainly wasn't Bill.'

He's right, and one look at his thoughtful face tells her he isn't finished. She waits.

'But if the cat was poisoned, the result of that poisoning will be that Bill leaves the home pronto, won't it?'

'Enough of your Sherlock Holmes act,' Leah insists. 'I'll talk to Bill tomorrow.'

Martin goes silent.

'I do have something else to say.'

She waits again.

He's hesitant. 'It's about the other night, about our drifting.'

'What?'

'Well, I thought I ought to make our drifting official. So I bought you this.'

In his hand is a jeweller's box.

'I bought it sale or return. You can always choose your own.'

Leah looks at what is in his hand, looks at him, takes in the high forehead and the tufts of hair, the lack of pride in his appearance, the utter unsexiness of the man who wants to marry her.

'I don't do romantic,' he explains, 'but I thought in your case I should make the effort, so I went to the shop and bought you this.'

He flicks the catch. Inside the box is a gold ring with four rubies.

She stares at it, then takes the box from him to have a closer look.

'The setting is Art Deco. It's second-hand, like my books,' he explains. 'But second-hand is how I lived my life until I met you, until you decided to take on the world. As I say, you can take it back and choose you own if you'd rather.'

'Why would I do that?' She takes the ring out of the box and is about to slip it on her finger when she stops herself.

'Shouldn't you be on one knee?' she asks.

His brow furrows. 'That's not really us, is it?'

'No,' she says. 'No. Julia would insist on a proper proposal. James would come bearing flowers and champagne. Danny, I don't know. He had…' she hastily corrects herself '… has a sense of doing things properly. But you're right, it's not us.'

She holds her finger out and slips the ring on. It fits. It looks okay.

'Thank you,' she says. 'It's lovely.' She holds it up to the light and to the window. 'The house approves,' she announces. 'Diamonds are such a modern habit.'

She comes over and kisses him. 'Every time I think I know you completely, you surprise me. I hope you'll always do that.' Then she adds, 'Does that mean I can plan a wedding?'

'Yes,' he says.

'Any stipulations?'

'As small as possible.'

× × ×

The picture arrives through the post. Izzy picks up the reinforced envelope with its DO NOT BEND sticker on the side. She takes it to the kitchen, locates the sharpest knife and slits the tag. The package inside is wrapped. She slides it out and unwraps it. There are four photographs. She picks up the first of these and stands under the kitchen window to examine the image.

It's the head and shoulders of a middle-aged man. His hair is thinning. His eyes are lined in the corners. It's uncanny. It's Patrick's father, the folk singer, grown older.

Izzy wanders out into the sunshine to look at it more closely. She can see his father's cheek structure and chin in Patrick, but nothing of herself, which is disappointing. The eyes are cold, but then they have to be. It's an identikit picture, not a portrait.

Will it do the job? It's enough of an individual portrait for her purposes. It looks realistic. Now she has three pictures of her son: as a baby, at sixteen and at fifty. She puts down the black and white artist's impression and examines the others. They are in colour. One is a straightforward colour version of the black and white image. In the next photograph Patrick is wearing glasses, and in the final portrait he's wearing a hat.

Still carrying the new images she goes up to her room. She collects the two framed pictures of the baby and the sixteen-year-old, then brings them all downstairs. She sits at the table where her family have so often sat and studies the sequence. She can almost feel her long lost son coming nearer. Having the new images makes him seem real.

There's a note from the artist. *These are the best I can do. I hope you find him.*

Leah and Martin are both at work. When Martin gets back she'll ask him to load the new images and redo the search site. She's rich. She can spend money on this, but to advertise would be to invite charlatans to apply. They still have a lot of work to do.

She makes herself a coffee, bothering to use a cafetière in honour of the occasion, and sits with the images of her son. She remembers all too clearly the man who let her down all those years ago, and ponders the way her life might have been different if only he'd stuck by her.

Another thought crosses her mind, put there perhaps by the over-strong coffee. Searching for Patrick is her life now. Leah doesn't need her. Danny will come home in his own good time. When she's found Patrick, what will she do then?

× × ×

It's all happened so quickly for Leah. From being indolent, her life is now full and parcelled out in segments of intense work and intense leisure. Today is a working day. She's wearing her new ring, thinking that no one will have time to notice, but all the girls do. She thinks they pity her because it's second-hand and there's no diamond.

'What if the other woman who wore it was unhappy?' Lisa asks. 'It might bring you bad luck.'

'It's unusual,' Sarah says. 'Did he get down on one knee, do the thing properly?'

She has to embellish. They want a drama from her, the description of a rite of passage. She fears if she explains how low-key the whole thing was they will despair of her. It was a mistake to wear it, but dishonest not to. Now they want to talk weddings and she has nothing to say on that subject either.

Bill is sitting by himself outside, staring out over the landscape. She goes over and sits beside him. He's subdued. He doesn't immediately tell her to fuck off.

It's mid-morning. She asks him if he wants her to bring him a drink.

'Coffee,' he says.

She goes and fetches it with a couple of biscuits on a plate. She thinks she'd make a good waitress.

On instinct she sits down beside him on the bench.

'Do you want to talk?' she asks. With Wendell it isn't possible, but with Bill it might be interesting.

'Suppose.'

She shows him her ring. They have to talk about something.

He deigns to look at it but says nothing.

'Were you ever married, Bill?'

'No.' It's said decisively. 'I was tempted,' he adds, 'but it would have been a lie.' He looks away into the distance. 'I don't lie.'

They sit in silence.

'They want me out of here,' he tells her.

'Well, you don't like it much here, do you?' she says, as brightly as she can.

'I've never liked it much anywhere.'

She lets the sadness of that sink in.

'They'll find you somewhere else.'

He snorts. 'The trouble with somewhere else is that it might be worse.'

Her radio buzzes. They need someone in Room 8 urgently. She says she'll go. She tells Bill she'll come back as soon as she can.

'No, you won't.'

She hesitates, then goes, leaving him staring out across the fields.

In Room 8 Agnes has fallen. Leah needs help to lift her up. They don't think anything is broken but they need to check. An ambulance is called for and Leah will have to go to hospital with her. Before the ambulance arrives she rushes over to where Bill is still sitting.

He is about to expostulate, but she doesn't have time to be sworn at. The ambulance is already making its way up the drive.

'Agnes has fallen and I have to go to hospital with her, but I came back as soon as I could just as I promised, Bill. I'll look in on you as soon as I get back. Okay?'

He seems mollified.

'See you later,' he says.

Leah gets back at 4.30pm. Agnes is alright, bruised but has no broken bones. As soon as she has handed Agnes over to Sarah she goes looking for Bill.

He's not in the lounge and not in his room. Has he already been transferred? Then she spots him. He's still sitting outside, but he's moved further away, out of sight of the home. She walks over to him. Her shift is nearly finished and she should be at a handover meeting, but she sees this as important.

'You took your fucking time,' he says.

She points to where the ambulance is still unloading Agnes. 'I came as quickly as I could. Now, talk to me.'

He's turned his enormous head to look at her. 'You said you'd come back and find me and you did. Not many do that.'

She waits.

'Not many have ever done that.'

She waits again, then takes a risk. 'I don't think you killed the cat,' she says.

'Too fucking right I didn't.'

'Who did?' she asks.

He pauses. 'I have to get to know you better before I tell you that.'

'You know, though, don't you?'

The large head with its dyed black hair shifts from perusing her to looking out across the fields.

'I don't know. I can guess.'

'Tell me about yourself,' she says. In a home with so much dementia, it's a treat to talk to someone who can hear what she says and has all his faculties.

'Too enormous, too outspoken, too perverted.'

His head is turned away from her. It's as if he's telling the horizon and the sycamore these truths about himself.

'I've never fitted in.'

'I know that feeling,' she tells him.

The head comes round quickly. 'You can't.'

'I didn't speak for nearly twenty years.'

'Why not?'

'To borrow your favourite word, I simply thought, fuck them.'

He bellows with laughter.

'Them?' he asks.

'My family: my sister and one of my brothers who bullied me, and my dad who never had time for me.'

'Oh God,' he says. 'What a pair. You who never spoke and me who never shut up.'

'I'm gay,' he adds, 'in answer to your earlier question. That's why marriage would have been a lie.'

There's another long pause.

'But you fit in now, now that you speak?' Bill's question is urgent.

'More or less.'

He looks at her again. 'You're small and pretty and you're wearing an engagement ring you can't leave alone. Even if I'd shut up and been charming, I'd still have been enormous and gay or enormously gay.'

'And you feel sorry for yourself.'

'Didn't you? I mean, when you weren't talking?'

She thinks about it. 'No I didn't. At least, I don't think I did.'

Lisa is making her way across the lawn. 'Leah,' she says, 'we need you at the meeting.'

'Time for some camouflage,' Bill whispers. 'Fucking run along now,' he shouts at full volume.

'I don't know how you put up with him,' Lisa says. 'He's just rude.' She says this loudly enough for Bill to hear.

Leah daren't turn round, but she does hear the snort. It reminds her of Julia.

When Leah gets home Izzy shows her the artist's impressions. Leah lifts the first carefully and examines it. 'He's handsome,' she says. 'It's a bit spooky, isn't it, having such a good picture of a man we've never met.'

'He looks like his dad,' Izzy says.

Izzy spots the ring on her daughter's finger. 'When?' she asks.

'The other night. Do you approve?'

'I like Martin. I like having him around the place. You suit each other. Have you told the others?'

'No. Should I?'

'We're hardly a family anymore, are we?' Izzy says. 'Julia is on holiday in Spain. A postcard came today. Danny has disappeared, and James won't show his face until he has something to brag about.'

'What do you think has happened to Danny?' Leah asks.

'I don't know. He'd lost his oomph, hadn't he? That last morning he was here he looked out of sorts.'

'He'll come back when he's ready,' Leah asserts.

'I wish I was so sure. Anyway, congratulations on your engagement.'

20

‘I’m a hopeless case,’ Shaun explains.

Danny wants to shakes him in exasperation.

‘It’s summer. Sleeping outside isn’t too bad at this time of year. I mean, who’d want to be inside in weather like this?’

They’re in the high street sitting on a bench.

‘I told you a long time ago that the drink had got me.’

‘I didn’t want to believe you,’ Danny replies. ‘You’re still a young man.’

‘Just look,’ Shaun says, ‘look and remember. They …’ he points at the people walking past… ‘are going somewhere, meeting someone, wrapped up in their own lives.’

A middle-aged man in a hurry and with a certain swagger goes by. ‘Look at him. He’s a leader,’ Shaun pronounces.

He’s followed by a woman of colour in a smart suit with her hair fiercely tied back. ‘She knows who she is and exactly where she’s going.’

An old man with a stick, shoulders bent, head down, passes them slowly. ‘He’s been somebody too, and he remembers.' They watch the old man walking, pausing to get his breath, determined.

A Muslim, bearded and robed, walking slowly, crosses the road. 'He has a place,' Shaun points out. 'He has Allah and a social position.'

Then Shaun turns to look at Danny. 'You too. You're somebody. Look at the way you sit. Look at the woman you're working with.'

There is a short silence. 'Now look at me. Really look at me,' Shaun insists. 'Turn your head.'

Danny does as he's told and sees the dirty face and the unkempt hair, the red edges to both of Shaun's eyes.

'I looked like that once,' Danny says.

Shaun shakes his head. 'You never did, you just got a bit dirty on the outside. You played at degradation.'

Danny knows he's right.

'You were always a fake. I'm the real thing.'

Danny makes his pitch. 'I can help. There are places where you could dry out. I could find you accommodation, find you a job. You can change. Anybody can.'

'What then?'

'What do you mean, Shaun?'

'When I'm sober and clean and nicely dressed, what then?'

'You find a job, a house, a partner. You go to AA meetings.'

Shaun reaches out and pats Danny on the shoulder. 'I'd like to help you feel better about not being me, Danny. I really would.'

'I don't understand you.'

'You're a do-gooder, my friend, and do-gooders are really needy people. They come to beg from us, only it's not money they want, it's a smile, a thank you, something to give them valediction. I sometimes think those of us who live on the streets ought to have stamps or stickers so we can give everyone who helps us or even talks to us a gold star.'

'I don't want a gold star.'

'You do, my friend. You promised to find me. You kept your promise. Gold star for you.'

Danny stays where he is. He thinks of the lottery ticket, wonders if he could cash it and give Shaun an income. He is no longer as frightened as he was of that enormous sum.

Shaun wants Danny to really understand. 'Look, I'm not bipolar. I don't have a personality disorder. I'm not autistic. I'm not sure I have anything anyone can cure me of. I'm just like this.' He turns his dirty face towards Danny again, reaches into his bag and takes out a can. 'I'm not sure I'm even unhappy.'

Danny gets up to go. He feels in his pocket for his wallet, takes out some notes and hands them over.

'Thanks. I should give you another gold star, only I've lost my stamp.' Shaun pockets the money and then points across the road. 'Your friend is waiting for you.'

Danny swivels, expecting to see Chloe, but the tall, painfully thin figure in the gilet is unmistakable.

× × ×

Izzy has dropped Patrick from her searches. She's using the surname Barr, sometimes accompanied by his date of birth. Her search is worldwide, and worldwide there are thousands of Barrs. It's endless, painstaking work. She quickly learns that she has to be systematic, noting down details about each individual she looks at so she doesn't keep going back to someone she's already dismissed. The list grows because it isn't in any particular order. Martin teaches her about Excel and gives her some simple column headings so she can add to and reorganise her lists in sequence.

Outside it's close to the longest day and good weather. She finds herself stuck indoors, her eyes fixed on the screen, getting nowhere. Nothing she does is foolproof. Lots of people, herself included, are not on Tik Tok, Instagram, Facebook, Twitter. She begins to limit her searching time, but the house feels empty when Leah and Martin are at work.

What keeps her going is that just occasionally she feels she is getting close. There was a Barr of the same age in New Zealand, with the same birthday, but his face was the wrong shape. Each time she gets close she feels the thrill of the search. Another click, another name. This could be the one. But at the back of her mind is the fear that Patrick changed his name completely when he fled from the cult, that he made himself a new identity, and therefore the whole basis of her search might be invalid.

She tries to imagine what she would have done in his shoes. She knows the cult keeps tabs on ex members. At sixteen, young people are pure in their hatreds. Her son must have got through the first bewildering days and started a new life. Her other son, Danny Goulden, can't be using his real name. He must have created a new identity for himself by now. What if Patrick isn't Patrick and isn't Barr? Then she has no chance, and because he has no knowledge of her existence he cannot come looking for her.

She puts the artist's impression in a frame alongside the other photographs, comforts herself with stories of successful searches, of people who have reappeared after more than thirty years, and wonders what she might do with the rest of her life.

× × ×

Leah knocks on Helen's door.

Just to get this far has taken a mini battle with herself. It's none of her business. The others dislike Bill intensely and he feeds their dislike. The home would be happier without him. He's an absolutely hopeless cause.

But she has a bond with Bill. They've exchanged secrets and she's convinced he wasn't the person who switched the photos and poisoned the cat. She's satisfied that her purpose in coming to see Helen is simply to warn her that when Bill leaves they may still have a problem. She isn't here to ask for clemency and reconsidering.

When Helen opens the door Leah asks if she has five minutes. Helen nods and invites her to sit down. For a while they chat about how Leah is finding the job. Leah says she loves it and is really happy working at the home. Helen says they are very pleased with her. When that conversation has run its course, Leah says what she came to say.

'I've been spending a little more time with Bill,' she begins. 'I ignored the swearing and got him talking. There's a human being underneath the bad language.'

Helen interrupts. 'Are you suggesting we let him stay?'

'No, that's your decision. You have far more experience than I have in such matters.'

'What are you suggesting then?'

Helen's tone is not exactly encouraging, but Leah carries on. 'Bill's his own worst enemy. He hates his shape, his size and his sexuality. He never fits in, never has. He's outspoken and clumsy, incapable of hiding his feelings.'

Helen nods. 'I didn't know about the sexuality, but the rest fits with what I think. Go on.'

'Whoever rearranged the photographs and changed the date to Christmas Day was subtle and funny. Has Bill got that sense of humour? Whoever killed the cat used poison. Where does Bill get poison from? Has he that kind of knowledge?'

She stops. Has she said enough? Helen's looking thoughtful.

'Were you a detective in a former life?'

'I was for a while in this life. I did once have a crime to solve.'

Helen sits and thinks. Then she picks up some letters and passes them over to Leah. 'I don't expect or want you to read those, but every one of the letters in your hand is from a resident's family member saying how Bill has upset the home and needs to go. Why should the residents put up with Bill?'

'I never said they should.'

'I know,' Helen says. 'I was hoping you would. I hate having to ask residents to leave.'

Very slowly Leah says, 'My problem is that I feel sorry for him.'

'Why?' Now there's an eagerness to Helen's question.

'For the reasons I've outlined. He's the wrong size, far too big, and that frightens people. He's gay, and I suspect he's suffered for that, perhaps at the hands of the police. He told me he could have married, but that would have been a lie.'

Helen doesn't seem convinced.

'And he does have some good points. He's honest, absolutely straight in what he says, even to the point of rudeness. And he's got a nice laugh.'

'You got him laughing!'

'I did.' Leah blushes. 'I told him I hadn't talked for twenty years. He asked me why not and I borrowed his language.' She hesitates. 'I actually said, 'Because I thought, fuck them.' Sorry. It's a word I don't normally use.'

'Tell me more.'

'He told me I was the only person who'd kept their word. That seemed to mean a lot to him. It was when I had to leave him abruptly to go to hospital with Agnes. I told him I'd come back to find him and, even though it was hours later, I did.'

'Leah, can we settle him?'

Leah laughs. 'Why are you asking me? I'm new here.'

'Answer the question.'

'I suppose I think we should try.'

'Good. If I remind these letter-writers that the process of settling in is difficult, and that we need to give Bill more time, will you help me settle him?'

'Yes, but what about Wendell?'

'I'm making you key worker for both of them. Okay?'

'Okay.'

Leah is about to leave when she turns and says to Helen, 'Just one other thing. Bill swears he didn't kill the cat and I think I believe him. If he didn't, someone else did. Someone who knew Bill would be blamed.'

'I know,' Helen says. 'I'd worked that out. I'm glad you like it here, Leah. You're doing well.'

× × ×

Julia's gardening leave is coming to an end, signalled by three emails that have pinged into her phone within ten minutes of each other. The Company has emailed that she has been cleared of all the charges levelled against her. In a separate email, the Board has endorsed her exoneration. In a third, she's been offered a phased return in line with the policy she herself wrote. In this email she is politely requested to inform Human Resources when and how she intends to come back to work. Did she write that? Has it been lifted straight from her policy? It seems far too open-ended.

Of course she'll go back to work, and go back full time. There'll be none of this namby-pamby phased re-introduction for her. Meanwhile, she'll demand a copy of the statement that will be put out to all staff about her suspension. She needs to check that it is both sufficiently exonerating and grovelling.

Her fingers and thumbs work quickly constructing her response. She has a last day with Zakk and she wants to be done with this before he wakes up. She completes her reply, checks spelling and grammar, reads it one last time in case predictive text is being particularly vindictive, then sends it.

No hesitation. She's back to her decisive self, in control again, and she relishes the feeling.

The snap of the phone case closing wakes Zakk.

'Our last day together,' he says.

Good, Julia says to herself. If that's what he's thinking, so much the better. It's been great, but it's now firmly identified, labelled and pinned in the category headed Holiday Romance. There will be no scene when they part, no tears at the departure gate. Her flight leaves first, which is good. She'll be back at work the day after tomorrow.

'Or not,' Zakk adds.

'What do you mean?' Did she ask that flatly enough?

The important thing when you part from someone is to do it with dignity. She thinks of the way stags walk side by side in order to weigh each other up before they fight, because antlers are dangerous and the challenger only wants to fight if he has a chance of winning. In the contest between Zakk and herself, the important thing is to make sure she is the more casual and to seem the less needy.

'There's always an *or not*,' Zakk insists.

'Executions,' she counters, 'income tax, going bald.'

He frowns at her. 'The thing about last days together is to not have them,' he pronounces.

'We can't change the flights again.'

How will they remember this scene? The bed is ruffled, untidy. He's still under the duvet, grinning at her. She's wearing knickers and is perched on the edge of the bed, towering over him. She wishes she was fully dressed, but she needs to shower and wash her hair. She decides she'll take control.

'I need a shower,' she says. 'Do you want to use the en suite first?'

'No you don't,' he counters.

'Don't what?'

'Don't get all practical and purposeful when I have something important to say to you.'

OMG. Is he going to make a declaration? Where's the view? Where are the drinks they should have sipped first? There will be views this evening when they sit together and watch the sun go down. That would be much better timing for a proposal, because then she could gently refuse him, go to sleep, and leave early to catch the plane. Then there wouldn't be time for recriminations. Now is not the right time, right place, right venue or even close to the right circumstances.

'Have you something to say to me?' she asks.

He smiles at her. 'It can wait.' He gets out of bed and walks to the en suite.

She watches his bottom as he reaches the door. She doesn't have many bottoms to compare it with, but it's not too fat or too muscular. Nor is it, she has to admit, a young man's bottom.

He's almost through the door when he announces, 'In fact, I might not say it at all.' Then the door closes, and she can hear him laughing at his own joke.

She springs off the bed and searches in her case. There's not much that she hasn't worn, but she finds one clean and only slightly creased outfit. It'll do.

While she is showering, Julia imagines the opposite of what she intends will happen. She visualises them agreeing to meet for weekends, phoning each other, texting, worrying about why the other hasn't replied and if the signal is down. Then the next step: each other's family. *Mum, this is Zakk. James, this is Zakk.* Or even before that: *James, I want you to meet my boyfriend. I'm going to bring him down for the weekend. He's called Zakk.* Couldn't he be called something else? Does he have a middle name? She doesn't know. Flip that for when she meets his family. Zakk is now doing the talking. *Mum, this is Julia.* She can't imagine being looked over by a seventy-year-old mother, whose eyes tell you she is wondering if some other man's cast-off is good enough for her son.

One last day, one day more, then away. And when she's home, might she risk dating again? She'd forgotten how fascinating men can be. When she's dumped Zakk, will she still be satisfied? Will she be happy when she goes back to living alone?

21

Danny turns, following Shaun's outstretched finger. He spots Ivor on the other side of the road, standing in the shade of a London plane tree. First Vilnius, now here. Danny waves Ivor over, but he doesn't move.

'Stay there, Shaun. I haven't finished with you.'

'I'm not going anywhere. I've got my tinny.' Shaun holds the can up as if it is the winning argument.

Danny crosses the road. Ivor is waiting, but he's withdrawn further into the shadow. Could he be dangerous? Danny doesn't think so. Could he have someone with him who is dangerous? It's a possibility.

Danny's alive again. He's a player. He loves the surprises in his new work, that daily frisson of unpredictability. He joins Ivor in the shadow and knows at once that something is wrong.

It's in the way Ivor is standing. He thinks of the man who boldly followed Mindsett down Doughty Street; the man in the bar who had the world all worked out; the man whose fingers, rapidly moving over Danny's phone, copied and stored photographs faster than Danny could see what he was doing.

This Ivor is fearful. This Ivor is unnaturally still. Danny doesn't think he's drunk.

'I couldn't do it,' Ivor says.

'What?'

'What they ordered.'

'Sh!' Danny says. 'Not here, not now. We need to go somewhere safe. And,' he adds, to make things absolutely clear, 'if you come with me, I have to involve Chloe and Michael.'

Ivor nods. 'I may need their help,' he says.

'Have you anything to trade?'

'I think so.'

Danny signals to Shaun that he's not coming back. Shaun waves his lager can. Then Danny walks Ivor across London, using all the tricks he knows to make sure they are not being tracked. In Mornington Crescent tube station there's an individual who may be following them, since he also waits until the last possible moment to board the train. But when they get off two stops later there's no sign of him. Ivor, who knows London as well as Danny, allows himself to be steered and takes no part in checking for followers. It's as if something has happened to him recently, something that has drained him to the point where he doesn't care anymore.

Danny lets Ivor into his flat and hustles him upstairs.

'When did you last eat?'

'Two days.'

Danny makes him baked beans on toast, watches as he gulps it down, then makes him a coffee. They keep away from the window.

When Ivor has eaten Danny starts the interrogation. 'Was this always your plan C, Ivor?'

Ivor shakes his head. 'Plan B is crap. I had no plan C.'

He tells his story slowly. He'd thought by working for the FSB he could chill and wait his chance. He explains that they have so many spies he thought he could lose himself in the sheer volume of ambitious young men who loved the new Emperor. That way he could stay alive and his family wouldn't be troubled. But it hadn't worked out like that. They'd recalled him from Vilnius and told him they had another assignment which was perfect for him. They wanted him to infiltrate a new opposition group in Moscow and report back. His time in England, his record of subversion, was perfect cover. His computer abilities would help with communication. His thinness, when compared with the thuggish build of many of his fellow FSB members, was also perfect. He looked the part. Ivor glances up at that moment in his narrative and tells Danny, 'You can tell secret service personnel the world over, especially in poorer countries, because they are always well fed.'

They gave him inducements. There was the promise of rapid promotion if he provided them with sufficient evidence to put troublemakers inside. Sufficient, that is, for a Russian court, where the conviction rates are always over 95%. He would have freedom to travel. He would join the waiting list for a Moscow Centre flat. His parents would be left alone.

That last item worried him deeply. 'It's their way of keeping you on straight and narrow,' he explains, 'to keep you walking. You have something to look forward to in front and something behind that terrifies you, so you continue to move in the direction they want you to go.'

He knew then that he couldn't do it, that in spite of his London cynicism and professed cleverness he had reached a point where prevarication was impossible, where pragmatism no longer had any appeal.

'So I came to look for you. I came to find one of the pure in heart. I came to find you, Danny Goulden.'

Danny looks at him. Ivor parries the look and shrugs. 'You are my friend, so I put you in danger. If you are unlucky enough to live in a dictatorship, that is what friends are for.'

Sometimes Danny surprises himself. The self-centred Danny who worked out at the gym and never thought about life very deeply has disappeared. The indolence that Gary Goulden had guaranteed, through the allowance he paid his son, has vanished. 'Tell me the rest, Ivor, or I can't help you. I can't go to Michael and plead for protection just because we drank vodka together. You must have something for us. The Ivor I knew would always have had a plan C.'

'I know where Juozas is. I can take you to him.'

'Wait there.'

Danny goes into his bedroom and phones Chloe. He must presume his phone is bugged. He must presume his flat might be known to both services. When she answers he's ready with what he'll say. He only hopes she'll work it out.

'Hello gorgeous,' he says. 'Your place or mine tonight?'

He can almost hear her thinking, but she gets it. 'I can come round now if you need me that badly.'

'It's the thought of you,' he says, 'and that perfume you wear. It's driving me wild.'

'If you're that horny, should I bring a friend?'

'You've read my mind. I really fancy a threesome.'

'You're on.'

He shoves the phone in his pocket and returns to Ivor.

'Keep your head down,' he tells him. 'I'm going to check outside.'

Danny takes his phone and wallet and walks to the local shop. There's a queue at the till which suits him fine. He can see his front door from here and watch the whole street. There's nothing to worry him. He remembers the crowd that followed Borstov. It's difficult to pack streets with watchers in a foreign country. Perhaps they haven't realised that Ivor is missing, or simply have no idea where he might be. When Danny eventually reaches the till he stocks up on tinned meat pies and sausages. He adds a bottle of vodka.

Returning to his flat he saunters and takes stock. The area no longer feels abandoned in the heat. The street has changed. As he strolls along the pavement he spots three or four people in key positions. Have Ivor's mob got here already, or are the extra personnel from his Service? He lets himself into the flat and soon there is a ring on the intercom. Chloe is there 'with a friend'. He buzzes them in.

The friend is about Chloe's age with the same hard-bitten look that Chloe had when Danny first met her. She's taller than Chloe with a sharp nose and luxurious dark hair. She isn't introduced to Danny, so Danny steps back and watches.

They frisk Ivor. They do it thoroughly. He isn't armed. He's carrying no ID. He has the clothes he stands up in and nothing else. They soon let him sit down again.

They go through his narrative, this time concentrating on dates and places. Danny learns that he had a weekend's leave before his new assignment, that he went to the Crimea and walked across the front line into Ukraine, then flew to Manchester. He admits he has a tap on Danny's phone so knew where to find him.

'Will you be missed?' they ask. 'When were you due to report for your new duties?' All the time Danny watches. He sees Ivor's new meekness and wonders about it. Is he a plant or has he really had a moment of epiphany? Is this total exhaustion or superb acting? The interrogation reaches a pause point. Colm is introduced to Laura. Danny makes a round of drinks and hands Ivor a pie he's heated in the microwave.

Chloe and Danny leave Laura to guard Ivor. They go into the bedroom.

'Well?' Chloe asks.

'I can guarantee nothing, but for what it's worth I think he's frightened and exhausted, close to collapse.'

'And does he know where our friend is?'

'He says he does, but that's what I find odd. If he does know and can get to that place, confront Juozas and get hold of the files, he'll be in a stronger position with us and with the FSB. Perhaps he knows Juozas is in a place which for some reason he can't access. I haven't asked him where Juozas is, but I don't think he'll tell us yet. It's too early in the negotiation. Ivor is clever. He won't give away his only bargaining chip until he has his bargain. First, let's ask him how he knows.'

Chloe nods.

They re-join Ivor and Laura.

'Okay, Ivor, we're not going to ask where our mutual friend is just yet, because we suspect you won't tell us. But can you tell us how you traced him?'

'I followed the money,' Ivor tells them. 'I went searching behind passwords and stepped over favourite phrases to see his monthly statement. If you follow where I went, you won't get in. I swapped passwords and substituted a phrase of my own.'

Ivor is recovering. He's finished the pie.

'What do you want from us?' Laura asks him.

'Asylum. This may be a tired country with a terrible history of colonial exploitation, but it is still free and it will defend that freedom. I'd like to stay, please.'

'That's up to others. Meanwhile, we need to move you to a safe house. For that journey you have to be blindfolded. Okay?'

Ivor agrees. He's seen the vodka bottle and picks it up, but Chloe swiftly disarms him.

Laura makes a brief phone call. The buzz on the intercom is clearly a signal, because Ivor is moved downstairs fast to where a car is waiting. Laura hands him over to two men who sit either side of him on the back seat. The car moves away.

Once Ivor has gone the room relaxes.

'Good work, Col. Why did he come to you?'

'He thinks I'm the pure in heart.'

'What a shame,' Laura says. 'Chloe told me about your earlier phone call. I was quite looking forward to it.'

Danny looks at the two women sitting on his sofa finishing their coffee. Both clearly work out. Both have gleaming skin that gives off a healthy glow. Both have deliberate, focussed faces. Both are superior to him, better trained, more adapted to their calling. Chloe's friend can't be serious, can she? Nothing surprises him anymore. They are looking at him enquiringly.

'I'd be terrified,' he tells them.

× × ×

Izzy's search is getting nowhere. She feels she needs help and fresh ideas. Martin and Leah canoodle around her in the house, too wrapped up in each other and in their work to pay her real attention. She tries to help Leah plan her wedding but Leah refuses to set a date. Izzy senses that her daughter wants a quiet 'do' with none of the money and publicity her father would have insisted on. That none of her children is married is another source of dissatisfaction for Izzy. Julia, she has long despaired of. If Leah is to have children, she needs to get on with it because the clock is ticking. If not, there will be no grandchildren, unless Danny or James marries someone younger. She had hopes of Roz, but Roz and James have split up. Since the Mindsett defeat James has never contacted Izzy. She hasn't seen him since the last family conference.

Some days she looks round the house and thinks, Gary bought this place and we filled it with children. While he was alive they came and went. At Christmas and Easter the house was always full. If I can find my son, and particularly if Leah and Martin marry and have children, it can be full again.

Meanwhile it feels empty, and she hates the thought that Leah and Martin may want a place of their own. What will she do then?

She decides to contact James. She doesn't think he's working, and James might bring fresh ideas to her search. She phones him on his mobile. He doesn't pick up, so she listens to the answerphone message.

'Hello, this is James Goulden, Political Analyst and Campaigner. I'm busy creating history right now, but please leave your number and a brief message after the tone.'

Quintessential James! She waits for the bleep. It comes very quickly, so he can't have many or any messages.

'Hello, it's Mum. Can you phone me? I need some advice.'

She rings off. How long will he keep her waiting?

22

'Has Helen spoken to you?'

The care home garden is not looking its best. The enormous yew hedges need trimming. The geraniums need both watering and weeding. The view of the river is obscured through the tall summer grass. Bill is sitting as close to the iron railings as he can get. He looks at Leah as if he can't remember who she is. She sees him frown quickly and then his face relaxes. 'Where were you yesterday and the day before?' he asks.

'At home. They were my days off.'

'I don't get those,' Bill says, and clutches at his bag.

Leah tries to read his mind. It's a funny thing that humans have such expressive faces and yet you never quite know what they are thinking.

'Did Helen tell you that you have another chance? She's made me your key worker. I'm to settle you down, stop you swearing, and then you can stay.'

'Fat chance.'

It seems to Leah that Bill isn't 'with it' today, as if his brain has slowed down. He's sluggish. She wonders if he's been put on medication to control his behaviour. 'Bill, are you there? I need to talk to you.'

'Sorry,' he says. 'I didn't sleep much last night.'

He is a little red-eyed, she notices, and his shoulders are slumped. 'Why was that, Bill?'

'He was walking round all night.'

'Who was walking round all night?'

'Wendy.'

'His name's Wendell, and I'm sure he wasn't walking round all night.'

'I'm not a fucking liar.'

'Not that word, Bill. That word will get you into trouble. If someone was walking round all night, how did you know it was Wendell?'

The great head comes round. 'You were a listener. When you didn't speak you listened. I bet you can tell one person's footsteps from another.'

Leah remembers walking in darkness through the cult, listening to every noise.

'What do Wendell's feet sound like?'

'He pats his stick on the ground. It's a gentle noise. His feet are quick and timid. It's like listening to a rat with a ball tied to its tail.'

'Where was he walking?'

'I don't know. I was in my room in bed. I'd hear him go along the corridor and down the stairs. He finds those more difficult. You can hear him reaching for the next step.'

'But he usually takes the lift,' Leah objects.

'Not last night. Several times he came along the corridor and went down the stairs.'

Leah wonders at this. She heard Wendell call out in fear

and found him standing at the window in the darkness, watching shadows. Now, if Bill is being truthful, this frightened man walks round the home at night and actually goes down the stairs, risking a fall. Might Wendell have turned the photos round and poisoned the cat? She scrutinises Bill. 'He doesn't come into your room as you once went into his?'

'That was only the once. I've not been in anyone's room since.' It's interesting that Bill doesn't deny going into Wendell's room. Again, she finds him honest.

'You've had a tough life haven't you, Bill?'

His head drops. It's as if his neck has suddenly suffered from metal fatigue.

'Can we make it up to you?' she asks.

His head comes back up. It's become a spring. He shakes it and the long hair moves horizontally.

'No, I have to accept it,' he says. 'I was brought up a Catholic. I used to love going to church. I prayed that I would stop growing and I never did. I prayed that I would fancy women, but it never worked out. I loved men, lusted after men. I begged God to take this away. I offered to stay celibate and join the priesthood. He never listened, never gave me any inkling that I might have a vocation, and how could I serve a deity who had let me down so badly?'

He drops his head again. 'And now God has made me old just at the time of liberation for people like me. He's left me with the instinct but removed the physical possibilities.'

'And left you with a brain that's still as sharp and as angry as it has been all your life,' Leah adds.

'Exactly.'

'So you still believe?'

'That's another old habit I haven't quite grown out of.'

As Leah looks at Bill and pities him, she thinks again

of Theresa May's statement that caring is a low skilled job. It's not yet coffee time and she's already been nurse and cleaner, has faked enthusiasm she doesn't feel, has indulged in psychology and philosophy, then added a touch of theology into the mix. Getting to know Bill is challenging. She'd like to spend longer with him, but she's already given him all the time she has. She needs to move on.

'I'm sorry for you Bill, but there's not much either of us can do about what's happened. I've got to go now. Your time is up for this morning. I'll find you later.'

She touches his arm as she did before and he doesn't reject it. 'Your challenge, should you be prepared to accept it, is to swear at nobody until I come back.'

He promises he'll fucking try.

Leah goes to find Wendell. He's in his room.

He's up and dressed but his shoes aren't laced. She sees that at once and laces them for him without asking.

'Ready to go down?'

He nods. His eyes are rimmed with weariness. 'You didn't sleep last night, did you?' There's no reaction. 'Never mind, you can catch up later.'

He attempts to get up but she sees he's too exhausted to manage it. She puts a hand under his arm and lifts him that way. The moment he is upright he pushes her away. She steps back and he almost falls. She reaches for him again, this time by the shoulder to steady him, and holds on until he really is back in control. He's panting. His mouth is open and he's dribbling. His eyes wince as if the lids are threatening to close, but he forces them to stay open and by sheer willpower makes for the door.

'You're not right, are you?' Leah tells him. 'Shouldn't you

go back to bed? You've had a restless night, haven't you?'

He continues walking with his stick, taking small steps to reach the door.

'And you're so stubborn you won't give in,' she adds.

Leah sees that Wendell really needs a walking frame. The stick isn't giving him enough support. That can easily be arranged, but she knows he'll refuse. She calculates the distances. He has to get from his door to the lift, from the lift along the corridor to the lounge door, and from the lounge door to his chair in the corner. Does she need to let him try, because only a fall will persuade him to accept more help? His face is grey, so she suspects Bill was right, and that Wendell was up all night. Why? What was he doing?

He's not yet out of his room because he's moving so slowly. Leah stands in front of him to make him stop. 'I'll let you walk to the lift but I'll be close by.' She checks the corridor. 'No one's watching. Let's go.'

Is it courage or stupidity? She remembers Bill's description of Wendell's fluttering walk and it fits with what she is now seeing. She's been off duty for two days and, in that short time, Wendell has gone downhill.

He reaches the door, using the stick between each step. When he is outside in the public corridor he pulls his shoulders back just in case someone comes along. Leah walks beside him. She can feel his tension and his fear. They reach the lift and she supports him while they wait. His eyes are glazed. She thinks of a shaman summoning spirits. Once inside the lift he grabs the rail. He's holding on so tightly that his hands show each bone and vein with the skin crinkled and the knuckles white and yellow.

The lift reaches the ground floor. 'One last effort,' she says.

Now there are people around, but he preserves his place

in the pecking order. He is the man managing with just a stick when everyone else needs a frame or a wheelchair. Leah stays with him. Once he turns into the lounge she hangs back. Now he's in the public gaze and he must maintain this image of himself, by himself.

His chair is empty, but to reach it he mustn't trip over legs and feet.

Six metres to go. 'Hello Wendell.' People greet him as he turns the corner and lines himself up. Leah hangs right back. If he falls here he'll sway, grab a chair arm and hang on. She watches his back straighten. She can no longer see his face, but his hand gripping the stick is white.

Four metres. Compared with this, what is a run at goal, or a batsman's dive for the line as the cricket ball zeros in on the wickets? Now Wendell is pushing the stick into the carpet and keeping his arm straight. Each time he does this his elbow quivers.

A metre. He's past Agnes, whose vague gaze is seeing him home. His left hand is already on the chair arm, but there's a ruck in the carpet and suddenly his stick slips. Wendell stumbles and finds himself kneeling in front of the chair with his head in the padded seat. His right hand is stuck behind him and is still holding the stick.

Leah rushes forwards. She wants to lift him up as quickly as she can before anyone notices or comments, but she's too late.

Bill has wandered into the room at the wrong moment. His voice booms out, 'Say one for me too while you're down there, Wendy.'

Leah attempts to move Wendell, but he stays where he is.

'Come on,' she whispers, 'you so nearly made it.'

Gradually she lifts him and turns him round. He makes himself comfortable, then looks round the room as if nothing has happened. However, Leah notices how upset he really is. He may be holding his head high, but his lips are pulled tightly together, bunching the muscles at the top and bottom of his mouth.

× × ×

Chloe and Danny are at the safe house with Ivor. He's slept and is looking better.

'Sorry,' he says, 'sorry to do this to you both.'

'Juozas,' Danny says. 'Tell us where he is.'

'I can't until I have my guarantee.'

'There isn't time, Ivor. We need to find him before the Initials do. If you have traced him, they can.'

'Perhaps,' Ivor says, 'but a service where loyalty is everything doesn't foster individuality. They know my skills and yet they wanted to use me as an informer. The stupidity of these people. Time after time they get caught and they don't care; they simply deny. So unprofessional.'

'Poor Ivor,' Danny says. 'You're trapped now, aren't you, now you've come to us? If we give you asylum you can never go home.'

'Never is long time. Besides, what's to go home to? Perhaps I'm young enough and clever enough to outlive our new Emperor.'

'But it's worse than that, isn't it?' Chloe suggests. 'You're like the convicted murderer who knows he will never be freed. Such a person has only one bargaining chip: the body's whereabouts. Revealing where the victim is buried is his last chance to be in the newspapers. But the secret is useless to him. He knows full well that once he points to the spot he will be left to rot. When you tell us where Juozas is, what will you do with the rest of your life?'

She's hit his weakness. Danny sees Ivor wince.

'I can be useful to you because I'm Russian. I know the way they think. I know how the game is played. Employ me. I can find their signatures in the ether. I can help you, and you need my help. They really are out to get you, you know.'

Chloe nods, then continues. 'You'll have to walk a tightrope. Our guys will assess your skills and you'll have to outwit your assessors. Unless they discover that you know more than they do, they will not employ you. If you ever teach them as much as you really know, they will know it too and they can discard you.'

Ivor shrugs. 'This is not a single moment in time. I am self-taught. I discovered what I know. I can go on discovering. I am good. You need me.'

'We'll do what we can,' Danny assures him. 'But I have a personal question, one that matters to me.' Danny is tense. He tries to cut out the others in the room. 'When you first knew me, what really happened between us?'

'Truth?' Ivor asks.

'Truth,' Danny says. 'I'm speaking for myself only, not for the Service. I need to know if I can trust you. But they have to be here, and of course it matters to them too.'

'You want to know why I let my application for asylum lapse?'

Danny nods. 'I want to understand what happened between us. I want to know how much of you was genuine.'

'I'm Russian,' Ivor explains. 'In my country the official channels are slow. In yours too. You treat real asylum seekers so badly. Some you lock up. Some you allow to stay only if they don't work, so they can't eat and they starve. I didn't want to take the proper road. I knew about

Mindsett's mistress. I had photographs of them together. I knew he was corrupt, but I never got to meet him face to face. If I had done I would be citizen by now. In my country we have two channels and we don't confuse them. In your country also, but everyone confuses them. If I had applied through the official channels, I thought it would have been more difficult for Mindsett to help me. Besides, I didn't want the Initials to know I was seeking asylum. I had to have both my plans.'

'Because you were already working for the Initials?'

Ivor throws both arms in the air. 'I admit it, but working is too strong a word. I had developed an alias, a nom de guerre. I used that alias to feed the Initials.'

'What exactly did you tell them about me?'

'Everything they already knew.' He sighs. 'I told them about Mindsett and his mistress. I did that before Borstov met Mindsett. I told them the meeting had been observed by MI5. I told them MI5 was using rough sleepers. That's about it.'

'Is that why they photographed me?'

'Yes.'

'Did you tell them I had photographs of the meeting?'

'No.'

'Did you remove those photographs from my phone?'

'No.'

'Then who did?'

Ivor shrugs. 'I told you to back them up. You didn't do that. If I was working only for them and feeding them everything, why would I warn you?'

Danny leaves it there. He's seen something in Chloe's face. He'll ask his private questions again, but not here and not in front of Chloe. However, there is something they both need to know.

'So I was never a target of the FBS as you told me in Vilnius?'

Ivor shakes his head. 'I lied to you about that. I needed you grateful. I already thought I might need to take this step. Through you I fed MI5 the information it needed about our friend, Juozas. I also learned you had been well trained. The Danny I first met was much less wary.'

Chloe takes over.

'Let's stop playing games.' She holds up a letter. 'I have authorisation to offer you a deal. We will offer you political asylum. We will also assess your skills and see if you can be useful to us. In return you must help us to locate Juozas so that we can recover our files.'

Ivor is listening attentively. She goes on.

'And I think you already know the other cost, the cost to yourself, don't you Ivor? You will be an exile. You will be subject to our whims. You know enough to understand that the secret services have needs that change, and they play people like pawns. So I want to offer you a last chance to change your mind, Ivor. We're prepared to let you go now. You can choose to walk out of this building and go back to your other masters. You can claim you wanted to visit some girl, a last visit before you are sent to Moscow. You can make your excuses, bite the bullet, and then make sure brave young people are locked up for wanting freedom. This, they will say, is your patriotic duty. The door is unlocked and no one is holding you, but you have to choose.'

Ivor has been watching her intently. 'For me there is no choice. When they ask me to spy on my fellow Russians my options close. I thought I was the ultimate pragmatist. I thought I can work with them whatever they ask me to do. I was wrong. I've already made my choice. I will stay. I will help you.'

23

'Choose,' Zakk says. 'We have to choose.'

It's evening in Spain, their last evening together. The day has had a bitter-sweet feel to it. They've already handed in the second hire car and are now staying in Malaga, a short taxi ride from the airport. They've walked to the restaurant through holiday crowds. Their unencumbered hands came together naturally as they strolled through the heat of a June evening spent so close to the African coast.

The restaurant has inner and outer areas. They are sitting in the street under a gazebo. Lights hang down from horizontal wires and illuminate each table. The lights pick out his face and hers.

Now Zakk produces two small notebooks from one pocket and two hotel pens from the other. He hands one pad and one pen to her. He places the other set neatly in front of himself, lining up the pen against the edge of the pad.

'I'm not married,' he tells her, 'although you've never asked.' He raises his eyebrows at that. 'You're not married either, I believe.'

Julia shakes her head. The look he gives her is typical Zakk. He's enquiring as to her marital status as lightly as possible, but with real intent. He continues. 'So both of us being free, and this being our last night together, we have to choose whether to stick or twist.'

He looks at her again but she keeps her head still, giving him no clue. He reads fascination and uncertainty in her face. He swallows and goes on. 'To keep this real, to keep it absolutely truthful, we need to tell each other simultaneously what we feel, hence the pads and the pens. We must both have questions. I'm proposing that we write down the answers at the same time, pass them face down across the table, then turn them over on a count of three and read them out. Okay?'

'Who asks the questions?' Julia wants to know.

'Alternately,' Zakk suggests. 'We toss a coin for who goes first.'

He's not ready to say goodbye, Julia thinks, but he's not brave enough to make a declaration, even of the soft, opening gambit kind that lovers use. But would she rather he made a declaration? Does she crave a pre-feminist proposal?

She could refuse to play, turn him down flat because there is nothing to write. Even to agree with this methodology might be to spark hope in him. It would be kinder to stop the nonsense now and put down the pen she has already, quite unconsciously, picked up. But if that's what she really thinks, why has she pulled the pad towards her and not left it in the centre of the table?

'Okay,' she says.

The waiter appears and asks for their drink order.

'No drinks,' Julia stipulates. 'We need to do this sober.'

He winces.

'Have you got a coin?' Julia asks.

He has. He holds it up. He spins it in the air and she calls, 'Heads.'

The coin clatters on the table, slides off the edge of a knife and stays the same way up. Zakk calls it. 'Tails. I go first.'

Julia finds she is gripping the pen, waiting. He'll be ready with his question. Because he devised the game he's had time to think this out. It will be her turn next. When that time comes, what should she ask?

'Okay, first question. What do we see as each other's worst faults?' Zakk asks.

Julia thinks and writes, tears the page from the pad and turns it over. Because he asked the question, he has already finished his answer. Could he read hers as she wrote it? She must hide future answers. The pieces of paper are passed across the table. Julia calls the timing. '3 - 2 - 1 go.'

Julia reads Zakk's answer and winces. She's missed his reaction to what she wrote.

'*You have to be in control*,' she reads out.

'*You take life too lightly*,' he reads out.

They look up, nod and smile.

He screws up the piece of paper. 'You can't do that,' she says. 'You have to keep it.'

'See what I mean? I rest my case.' But Zakk unscrews the paper and flattens it with the heel of his hand.

'My question next.' Julia is now into this. 'What did you first notice about me?'

She scribbles quickly, tears and turns over, then watches as he tries to find the right words. His hand is round his pad. She can't see what he's writing.

He finishes, smiles at her, and they swop the papers.

'3 - 2 - 1 go.'

They turn the papers over. He reads first. '*Your swagger.*'

She reads, '*That silly quiff on top of your head.*'

'Okay?' he asks.

She nods. They each have two pieces of paper.

'Next question. So why are you still with me?' Zakk asks.

Julia wants to be funny, to carry on in the same vein, but something in the way he asked the question told her that would be inappropriate. He too is paused, uncertain, even though the question was his. Then both are scribbling. Both squares of paper are quickly turned over and pushed across.

'3 - 2 - 1 go.'

She reads, '*It's as if I've known you for years.*'

He reads, '*Because I've changed.*'

The waiter is hovering again. Zakk shoos him away. 'Go on', he says to Julia, 'your question.'

She feels the same way he does. 'What frightens you most about the future?' she asks.

They write more slowly. Glances are exchanged. Hesitant fingers separate the papers from the pads, then flip them over and push them across the table. The waiter is watching now, thinking *crazy Brits.*

This time they both call it. '3 - 2 - 1 go.'

Julia turns and reads his answer in silence. There is no possibility of a mistake. 'Who goes first?' she asks.

'I do.' Zakk says. He'll change the pronoun, keep his voice as relaxed as possible. 'You wrote that what frightens you most about the future is never seeing me again.'

She nods, owning that her mind is at last made up. Now she must read his words. She smiles. 'You wrote something similar,' she says. Then she stops.

'Read it,' he says. 'Read it word for word.'

She bows her head and takes a deep breath. 'You wrote that what frightens you most about the future is not having me in your life.'

'Drinks time, I think.' Zakk signals to the waiter. 'Then I have another question.'

Julia orders a tequila sunrise. Zakk has a Harvey Wallbanger.

The waiter brings menus. To his annoyance they leave these unopened.

'What was your other question?' Julia asks. She has her pen ready.

'I don't trust easily,' he says. 'It has to do with the way I was brought up. I think I love you, but I don't trust myself entirely. What do you feel about me?'

Julia puts her pen down, clicks it closed, reaches over and kisses him on the lips. 'I think I love you too,' she says. 'I don't entirely trust this new version of myself either. We need to give this serious time.'

The drinks come. In silence they discard the unnecessary frippery of cocktails: the miniature umbrellas, the orange slices and the stirring sticks. Silently, they drink to each other.

Only then do they open the menus. They are both suddenly hungry.

When Zakk isn't looking, Julia takes the opportunity to gather up all the answers, hers and his, then places them carefully in her handbag.

× × ×

Chloe is driving. Danny phoned and made the appointment. Part of him didn't want to come. It's too near home, but the thrill of the chase trumped the remote chance of running into a member of his family.

When Ivor told them where Juozas was hiding they both laughed. It was, after all, so like him. Now they understood why Ivor could hardly have managed on his own to extract Juozas from where he was holed up.

'Loki,' Danny said. 'I told you he was Loki. Fancy going to ground somewhere we'd never have considered searching. I mean, it's brilliant. The master spy, abandoning all pretence at dignity and going to live in such a place.'

'Perhaps he's frightened,' Chloe suggests. 'We never thought of looking for him there, but nor did they.'

'I wonder what the other residents make of him.'

Chloe is driving skilfully, fully aware of the other cars that are forming a kind of convoy round them. It has been left to them to make the arrest, but they will be guarded all the way. Danny can see the extra lights built into the surrounding vehicles, but only because he knows where to look. Each of the cars contains armed officers. They are there to look out for FSB personnel, to detain them if possible, and if not, to shoot them on sight.

Other armed officers will already be in position at their destination. They will be posing as gardeners and delivery personnel. If Ivor found where Juozas was hiding, it is perfectly possible that the FSB has done the same.

'There must be no mistakes,' Michael told them. 'Your first job is to get hold of the files. Your second is to detain Juozas Žemaitis and prevent the FSB from intervening. We will have an ambulance standing by to take him away. Such places are used to ambulances.'

'Then what?' Danny asks Chloe. 'What happens to him after we snatch him?'

'We hand him over to the interrogators. He'll be debriefed and assessed. If he's as good as I think he is, the files will have been copied. They may even have been cached somewhere else. We need to obtain every copy he made. This won't end today,' Chloe warns.

'But we get to see what he looks like. We get to meet him.'

Danny is feeling good about himself. Chloe's attitude to him has changed. He feels like a trusted member of the team.

'He might be armed,' Chloe warns. 'I would be if I were him. He has never been predictable, and he is still dangerous.'

They've reached the A64. 'About 45 minutes, according to the Sat Nav. Then we'll know.'

'I wouldn't trust that,' Danny tells her. 'The A64 is the Scarborough road. There'll be hold-ups. It'll be stop/start until we are past Sand Hutton. I'd say another hour.'

'You know these parts?'

'It's where I was brought up.'

× × ×

The rotas in the home are changed on a weekly basis. Today Leah is on duty from lunchtime. The moment she goes into the home she feels a sense of suppressed excitement about the place. Helen is in her office. Two gardeners she has never seen working there before are cutting the lawn edges. A third is loading clippings from the trimmed yew into a bag. There's something about them that doesn't fit.

She wonders if Bill has been behaving himself. Or is the sense of excitement because he is leaving, in spite of what Helen promised? She goes through the handover, then her first task is to find Bill. He's not in his bedroom. He's not in the lounge. She checks what they call the music room and then goes outside.

She finds him by the fence, out of sight of the home. He's sitting on a white plastic chair by the hedge. When he sees her, he hails her, signalling with his unnecessary stick to beckon her over.

When she reaches him she pulls up another plastic chair and sits beside him. He seems absorbed in watching the gardeners. There's none of his usual shouting. He whispers, 'Look at that man cutting the yew. I reckon I could do a better job.'

Leah follows where he is pointing. The man is hacking at the yew and pulling lumps out. He doesn't seem to be following a line. Even she can see that the lovely shape of the yew is being butchered.

Bill can stand it no longer. 'Hey,' he shouts, standing up, 'You mate, you're making a fucking mess of that. Let me show you how it's done.'

Before Leah can stop him, Bill is marching towards the new gardener.

The man has stopped cutting and has dropped the shears. Strangely, his hands are hovering around his pockets. He's adopted a semi-crouch position as if this is a long-practised move. Leah is fascinated. Have Bill's sheer bulk and loudness frightened him?

Bill hasn't noticed the oddness of the man's reaction. As far as Bill is concerned, the dropped shears allow him to demonstrate just how the job should be done. He props his stick against the hedge and shouts instructions. 'Stand up,' he tells the gardener. 'Now watch how I do it.'

Leah looks around her. The other gardeners have stopped cutting the lawn edges and are observing the scene intently. 'You need to hold the shears lightly, let them feel the hedge, let them find their own way,' Bill is explaining. 'So first, get the fucking angle right. You're not digging into the hedge, you're caressing it. The blades need to be lined up parallel to the present edge of the yew. Yew grows no more than a few inches each year. You're taking it back to last year's line, so push the shears in about so far. Like this.'

Deftly, Bill begins cutting upwards nearly as far as he can reach. He quickly creates a 20cm wide new line. He's clearly cut hedges before.

Leah can see the man is annoyed, so she gets up and moves closer. Bill sees her coming over. 'He's a fucking dipstick,' Bill tells her, by way of explanation.

Then he turns back to the gardener. 'Now you move sideways, mate. Look where your feet are and keep them that same distance from the base.' Bill demonstrates what he means, then hands the shears back to the gardener.

'You take over now and keep my line going.'

Leah sees faces at the lounge windows. The residents are also watching intently.

The man does as he's told. Bill stands over him and observes, offering a commentary. 'Better,' he says, 'but not good enough. You've not got the feel. You're gripping them too tight. I'll show you.'

To take control of the shears, Bill stands behind the gardener and places his enormous hands on top of the man's fingers. Because of Bill's bulk, the gardener finds himself pressed into the hedge. 'Like this,' Bill says, trapping the gardener's hands as he operates the shears. 'Do you get the feel of it?'

Leah intervenes. 'Bill, leave him alone. It's not your job to train ground staff.'

'But he's hopeless,' Bill shouts. 'This yew is older than I am and he's making a right mess.' Bill turns as he says this and, in doing so, he drags the man sideways and pushes him further into the hedge.

It must have been Bill's sudden turn because, faster than Leah can understand and take in what's happening, the gardener has slipped out from under Bill's hands and Bill is bent double and shouting as if in terrible pain. Then Bill is on his back, lying in the grass, winded. The gardener is standing over him, hands raised. If that was all, Leah could cope, but there's something in the man's hand that Leah doesn't immediately identify. It's not shears. It's not a mobile phone. It's a gun. He's holding a submachine gun and pointing it at Bill's head.

There's a shout from her other side.

'Carl, for Christ's sake, put it away. We are to wait. Those were the orders.'

'Then get this goon away from me,' Carl yells.

As Bill fell, his bag snapped open. Photographs and letters have spilled out and are now spread across the lawn.

Bill hasn't noticed. He's sitting up and clutching his stomach. 'What the fuck did you do that for?' he asks.

Then he lurches to one side, leans over suddenly, and is copiously sick.

Leah, white and trembling at what she's witnessed, comes over to Bill. 'Are you alright?'

'No I'm fu....'

'Say it Bill,' Leah advises. 'Use the word.'

'No, I'm fucking not.' Bill shouts. 'He thumped me in the kidneys. Doesn't he know how old I am?'

The gun has vanished. The man called Carl is standing over Bill. 'I'm sorry, Pal,' he says. 'What I did was instinct, pure instinct. The training kicked in. Can I help you up?'

'Not fucking likely, and don't call me Pal. There'll be a reckoning for this.' He's staring at his assailant. 'If only I was younger....'

Leah places herself between the two men. That's when she looks down at the spilled contents of Bill's bag. It must have always been full of photographs and letters. The photographs are family snaps: Bill as a child at the seaside eating an ice cream; Bill as a Cub; Bill as a Scout; Bill with his mother in the garden. The letters are addressed to William and are clearly from his mum when he was sent to boarding school. Words and phrases spring out at Leah. *Hope you are settling into your new school ... the holidays will soon be here.* Bill must have carried his whole childhood around with him because it was so precious. Leah collects everything together and places it all back in the bag.

'Come on, get up Bill,' she says, when his papers are safely tucked away. 'Let's see what the damage is.'

She tries to lift him but hasn't enough strength. Carl has to assist.

'I'm really sorry, Pal. I never meant to hurt you.'

He seems genuinely crestfallen. An ambulance has pulled up outside the home.

Bill is standing and gasping for breath. Leah clutches him. 'Do you need to go to hospital or are you going to be alright?'

'That's not an ambulance, Pal, even though it looks like one. I can call a real ambulance if you need it.'

Bill is standing unaided. He's still gasping but he no longer feels sick. 'I'll live,' he says. He turns to Carl. 'I don't know who the fuck you are, but you're no gardener.'

'Miss.' It's the other man, the one who told Carl to put the gun away. He's come close to Leah. 'Is there any chance we can forget this happened?'

'That an armed young man rabbit-punched an eighty-year-old who was trying to help him?' She smiles. 'No fucking chance.'

Bill turns towards her and waggles his finger. 'That's my word. It doesn't sound right in your mouth.' Then he turns to the stranger. 'I can forget. But tell me who you are and why you're here.'

The man shakes his head. 'I can't do that. She might tell you. It's her show.'

The man points across to where a car is pulling up next to the ambulance. Two people get out: the driver, who is a woman, and her passenger. Leah ignores the woman. It's the male passenger she's staring at. Her eyesight was always excellent and she can see him clearly, even though he's standing fifty feet away. There's no possibility she can be mistaken. The man who is being introduced to Helen, and whose hand Helen is shaking, is her little brother. It's Danny.

24

'I suggest you ask them,' Carl tells Bill again. 'I reckon this is their party.'

Leah abandons Bill and walks across in a daze. It is Danny, but there's something different about him. Helen is in conversation and pointing towards Bill, then Leah hears Chloe say to Danny, 'Colm, they think it's him.'

'Hello Danny,' Leah says, interrupting what's happening. 'Helen, let me introduce my little brother. This isn't Colm, it's Danny Goulden.'

Danny ignores her completely. He's looking round with intent, his eyes taking in the home and the trees, the drive and the view across the river.

Chloe too brushes Leah to one side. Standing beside Leah is the man who urged her to forget what she saw. 'It's not him,' he says, pointing at Bill. 'He had Carl and let him go. He's no professional.'

Chloe is in conversation with Helen. Leah hears Chloe say, 'The money comes from an account under the name Lowkey.'

Helen is explaining that there's no one of that name in the home. 'How long is he meant to have been here?'

'A couple of years perhaps.'

At last Danny can tear his eyes away from the surroundings. The gardeners are no longer pretending to garden. They are carrying weapons. Other men, also armed, climb out of the cars and deploy. The home is surrounded, and all approaches have been covered. Danny looks across at Bill, who now seems okay and is walking towards him. 'Are you sure this isn't him? He's just how I imagined Juozas to be,' Danny says.

As Leah has been excluded and Danny has not acknowledged her presence, she slips away and goes quickly up to Wendell's room.

Out of habit, she knocks before she walks in. Wendell is kneeling on his bed and looking out of the window. There's a strange smile on his face.

'They've come for you, Mr Lowkey. What do you want me to do?'

'Help me up,' he says. The words are clear and precise, as is his foreign accent. He needs to talk now, just as she did then. She can tell he is out of the habit, but what he says is clear enough. 'Tie my shoelaces first. I need to look my best.'

She looks at him, ties his laces and stands him up.

'Do I look alright?' he asks.

She checks him over, adjusts his tie and his collar.

'Immaculate.'

'Now walk me to the lift.'

She takes his arm and he lets her. They reach the lift and she presses the button. The lift descends.

When the door opens, Wendell takes a quick look

round. She expects him to walk to the lounge, but he heads the other way to the music room. Then he stops. 'I won't make it,' he tells her. 'Please go to the piano stool. Inside the seat is some music. Under the music you'll find two files. I've kept them hidden in different places. I moved them the other night. Please bring them to me. I'll wait here.'

Leah does as she is requested. The files are well concealed. Both are marked *Top Secret*.

When she brings them back, Wendell turns towards the lounge. 'I have to do this on my own,' he tells her. 'Are they still outside?'

'I think so.'

He sets off with his stick. Leah follows him, still carrying the files.

The lounge is full, as if for scheduled entertainment. Every seat is occupied. Those who can stand are looking out of the windows.

Wendell, head up, back straight, walks through the room almost unnoticed because the focus is elsewhere. Leah follows him.

When Wendell reaches the main door he sees the strangers he has come to surrender to, a woman and a man. In his eyes both of them are unbearably young. He's in the last straight. This is all he has to do. He moves his stick forwards. The pressure on his wrist is painful but he carries on. There's a burning spot in his right knee, but Wendell steps outside into the sunlight and walks towards the strangers. They stand aside as if to let him pass.

Then Danny sees that his sister is carrying two files.

Her last introduction was brushed aside; she's determined this one won't be. Following Wendell as he walked so slowly outside, she's had time to look in one of the files.

In it she's found a photograph, unmistakeably of a younger Wendell, but with a different name underneath it.

She faces Helen, her brother Danny and the rude girl who ignored her. They have now been joined by all the new 'gardeners'. One of her hands is on Wendell's shoulder; the other clutches the files.

'May I present Juozas Žemaitis,' she says. 'At least, that's how I think you pronounce it. He's come to give himself up.'

× × ×

The plane lumbers in. Julia, who has a window seat, looks out and notes the parched grass near the Gatwick runway. England has had good weather while she's been away. As the plane comes to a final stop, the inanities of arrival are gone through. Passengers are requested to keep seated with their seat belts fastened until the pilot switches off the seat belt sign. No one takes much notice. In case there is someone who has never flown before, the recording of an inordinately cheerful voice hopes they've had an enjoyable flight and hopes to see them again soon. People who are already vowing not to go near another plane until they absolutely have to, take no notice.

Julia stands up, retrieves her bag from the overhead locker, and makes her way out of the plane and through immigration. All the way across Europe, on the short but crowded flight, she has wondered if she will feel differently once she is back in the UK. She retrieves her case from the carousel and walks towards the car park. Area 4F. She wrote that on the ticket before she left the parking area to catch her flight to Spain. That was when she liked to leave nothing to chance.

Julia drives down the ramps until the car emerges into a dull evening light. England is just as she remembered it, only shabbier. Zakk will be still be in the air. His plane will have followed hers in. What's he feeling?

Now he isn't here she realises she knows hardly anything about him. But what does his history matter? She loves him. At the weekend she'll introduce him to her family. She'll pick him up in London and drive him north to meet the Gouldens. She'll make that introduction and watch their faces. Before that she has to go back to work.

She reaches home, parks, takes her two bags out of the car and unlocks the house. Its smell and its loneliness hit her in stereo. She pushes the door open and steps inside. Will I have to sell this house? Will he sell his? Or should we sell both? Even as she stands in her own hallway, she senses a richer future. She's home and she isn't feeling any differently about Zakk.

× × ×

'He's so small,' Chloe says.

'And old,' Danny adds.

They stare at Juozas. That this mythical figure they have chased through paperwork and to Vilnius and back should turn out to be a little old man who's now rubbing his knee is a source of wonder. They take in his neatness, the shoes and the bright shirt, the carefully tied tie.

Juozas Žemaitis stares back at them. 'You got here before the others,' he says. 'I'm rather glad about that.'

'He needs to sit down,' Leah advises. 'He has to catch his breath.' Someone finds a plastic chair and they seat him, then cluster round as if he's a rare vase or a piece of Jacobean furniture.

Chloe gives an order. Carl and the other 'gardeners' return to guard duty. Two men step out of the ambulance. Both are armed. Faces stare out of the lounge windows. Recently, the entertainment in the home has not been very good, and to have an armed raid staged on their own front lawn, with men waving real guns around, is just too fantastic to miss. When relatives next come to visit, at last the residents will have something to talk about.

Those standing at the window relay what's happening to those sitting down. It's simply thrilling.

That it should be Wendell, not Bill! If it had been Bill they would have understood.

'Can they take Bill too?' Agnes suggests.

Outside, Leah's first duty is to her patient. Still clutching the files, she kneels down beside him. 'What do you want me to do with these, Juozas?'

'Hand them over. The files are what they've really come for.'

'I'll take those, Leah,' Danny says, snapping out of his trance.

Brother and sister face each other. 'Hello Danny. It's so good to see you.' She hands the files over.

Chloe and Danny do a quick check, skimming the pages.

Leah bends low and whispers to Juozas, 'Are those the only copies?'

He shakes his head. It's such a slight movement no one else would catch it. 'The clue is in my room.'

'Did you kill the cat?'

A slight nod. 'I'm sorry about that.'

'How?'

'Laburnum seed ground up in her food.'

He points to the tree. It stretches out from the building, its branches heavy with seed.

'Wherever they take you, Juozas, I'll come and see you.'

'If they let you.'

'Danny will.'

Chloe and Danny have nearly finished.

The residents watch as Wendell walks to the ambulance. Two armed men help him up and climb into the back with him. Before they shut the door Leah waves.

The moment the ambulance leaves, the 'gardeners' climb into another car and follow.

Chloe and Danny disappear to check Wendell's room. They emerge disappointed.

'Danny, are you coming home?' Leah asks.

'His name's Colm,' Chloe insists.

'No, it's not. He's our Danny. He disappeared six months ago. We'd like him back.'

Chloe tries to intimidate. Leah stands her ground. The two face off in front of the watchers at the window. To the watchers' disappointment, neither is armed. The guns have all gone with Wendell.

Helen steps between them. 'Leah, how did you know it was Wendell?' she asks.

'A guess,' Leah admits. 'I knew it wasn't Bill.'

Helen turns and speaks to Chloe. 'Have you got what you came for?'

'I think so. Thanks for your co-operation.'

They shake hands.

Leah has Danny by the hand and won't let him go. Chloe goes over.

'Can I have Colm back?'

Leah keeps hold. 'Only if he gives me his mobile number and you promise to send him home this weekend. Izzy, that's his mother, was distraught when he went missing.'

Danny submits. He raises both hands as if surrendering. 'Okay.'

He recites a number. Leah notes it. As he walks towards the car with Chloe, Leah rings the number. She can hear Danny's mobile. 'Just checking,' she shouts.

Danny waves and blows her a kiss.

Helen and Leah turn towards the lounge. They see the window lined with faces. Helen waves. Those residents who can both stand and wave at the same time wave back.

Before Leah goes home she slips into Wendell's room. At first glance it is as it was two days ago, but then she spots subtle differences. They must have lifted everything when they searched. Leah stands in the middle of the room and rotates slowly, checking each segment.

Danny and the girl were searching for copies of the files. But Wendell didn't say those were in his room; he said the clue was. In which case, it must be hidden where no cleaner cleans and no housekeeper strips; somewhere even trained searchers wouldn't bother to search.

Her first guess is the wastepaper basket. These are rarely moved. When full, the old plastic liner is removed and the new one put in. She pulls out the present liner and turns the basket over. There's nothing taped underneath. Next she tries the radiator. She slips her fingers along the back on the left hand side. There's nothing but dust and dirt. When she does the same on the other side, however, it's clean, which is surprising. She moves her hand downwards carefully. Her fingers touch something which feels like a thin paper package. She pulls, and the package comes away from whatever was used to fix it. It's an envelope, already stamped and addressed to a local solicitor. The cleverness of this arrangement hits her at once. Heat from the radiator will eventually dry the tape, causing the package to fall. The chances are that whoever picks it up will simply post it. That way, even in his absence, Wendell's wishes will be followed.

She takes the envelope and puts it in her tabard pocket. If Danny doesn't come this weekend, she now has a hold over him. She has what he missed.

It's been a long shift and she has news for Izzy. One of her missing children is on his way back. It's time to go home.

25

'Your sister, Col? Your older sister was at the care home where Juozas was hiding and actually looking after him?'

'Yes.'

'And he's such a little old man. We got that wrong.'

'Yes.'

Danny has his face in the Pol Pot file. Chloe is driving or she would lean over and grab it from him. 'That's top secret,' she reminds him.

He continues reading.

'Even from you,' Chloe says forcefully. But this makes no difference. Danny carries on reading. 'And you signed the Official Secrets Act, remember? You can't divulge any of its contents, ever.'

Danny closes the file and puts it in the glove compartment. It's a long drive back to London.

'What will happen to Juozas?'

'He'll be debriefed and released.'

'After the dance he led us?'

Chloe is at her most clinical. 'He didn't spill national secrets. There's nothing we can charge him with. He's an old man; a proud, dapper old man. Even the FSB won't be after him now. That's what we lost sight of. We were so intrigued by his story, so steeped in his legend, that we never thought he might just be an old man who needs help with everything.' She bangs the wheel with the heel of her hand. 'How could I have missed that?'

She takes the M18 rather than the M1 because it's shorter.

'What's in the other file?' she asks.

'I thought you said they were secret, even from us.' Danny makes his point.

'We have a right to read the Balkans file.'

Danny opens it up. 'Some of it is in Lithuanian.' He leafs through it. 'There's no translation.'

Signs to Doncaster fail to entice them to deviate from their route.

Danny flicks through it again. 'It's mostly names and dates.'

'I bet Michael's right, that it's a list of people who are now high up in the Lithuanian government who collaborated with the Soviets.'

'I'd have them shot,' Danny says.

'Ivor was right. You are one of the pure in heart. Are you sure you're in the right job?'

'What do you mean?'

'We deal in percentages. Nothing we ever do is pure and just. For instance, if only Soviet collaborators have learnt how to run a country, who will run the nation if you shoot them all? In Iraq we made them all stand down and look what happened. We're like politicians. We're the artists of the possible.'

'I felt sorry for him,' Danny says.

'Who?'

'Juozas Žemaitis. I think he tried to do the right thing at every point. He tried to be true to his father. When that didn't work out he adopted his father's cause, believing it was Britain's cause too. After the Prague Spring his adopted country let him down, so he fought his own war, first with the partisans, then with pranks and jokes at the Soviet's expense. When Independence came and he'd finally won, he saw that it wasn't a victory. The collaborators had taken over. That's why he never went back. His whole life's work had been tainted. Just imagine how he felt.'

They are now on the M1. Chloe pulls into a service station. 'Comfort break and some drinks. Then we need to talk. Order me a cappuccino and bring the files. They are still dangerous.'

Danny does as he's told. Balancing two drinks with two files isn't easy, but he manages. 'Shouldn't these have gone with the ambulance?' he asks, indicating the files.

'I thought they were safer with us.'

Danny places the files on the table and leans on them as he drinks his coffee. 'Okay, what do you want to say to me?' he asks.

'You've passed, Danny. That's the first thing. I'll be recommending that we take you on as an operative of this Service. Congratulations. The failure rate is surprisingly high.'

'Thanks.'

'And, thanks to your sister, I'll be calling you by your true name from now on, Danny.'

'Yes, I may have to go back to being Danny now.'

He thinks she's finished but she has more to say. 'I've also enjoyed working with you. You've been easy to get along with. We've been forced to spend time together and that hasn't palled.' She sharpens up and adds, 'That's not a proposal. It's a colleague statement. That's all it is.'

Danny smiles. 'Understood and reciprocated.'

'My real question is this: do you really want to join us?'

It's the question he knew he would have to answer sooner or later, so why not now?

'Yes. I need to make something of my life. That's why I disappeared. I was born rich. I never had to work. Dad gave me a generous allowance and I just festered, worked out but never contributed anything. So I disappeared, slept on the streets, met Shaun, put two men in hospital when they tried to attack him, and was picked by Harry to do deep surveillance. That's when I found myself at the heart of things and loved It. So, yes please. It's why I can go back home now.'

'Then there's a trick you have to learn.'

'Which is?'

'This job makes you immoral in the way I suspect most leadership does. It does that insidiously. We have to make decisions. Those decisions affect people's lives. At first we agonise, then we don't. The job gradually chills us inside. We get too used to compromise and it does something to us. I think you'll find that really tough. I suspect you won't want to compromise your principles.'

'Give me an example.'

'You're monitoring a phone call in real time. You hear a blow land and a woman scream. It's an act of domestic abuse. The attacker is the target of phone taps. He is crucial to an investigation. You could send the police round, but then he'll know his phone is tapped. Do you stop the abuse, or stick with what we might call the greater cause?

Danny thinks, shakes his head and says, 'I don't know.'

'You're chasing the leadership of a trafficking group.

You're very close to uncovering the top man. That is a great prize. If you get him, you can unwind the whole operation and send them all to prison. But first you have to stand by while a young girl is trafficked into sex work. Could you do that?'

'Perhaps if I was certain I could nail him, and had some chance of rescuing her.'

'Fate gives you a look into the Pol Pot file, the most disgraceful episode in British diplomacy. The British, just to spite the Russians, insisted that Pol Pot was the true United Nations representative for Cambodia. They did this for years, in spite of the appalling suffering, torture and murder he had inflicted on his people. It's one instance when the Russians were on the moral side and we were not. Could you, can you, keep it secret?'

Danny breathes out. 'You knew I was thinking about that, didn't you? And the honest answer is, I really don't know.'

'Then you have to make your mind up. If you join us you must come into the Service with your eyes open.'

'How long have I got to decide?'

'Take the weekend off. Go home to your family. Think about my questions. We'll need to report to Michael on Monday.'

'I'll let you know.'

When they reach London they deliver the files back to the office they were stolen from and sign them in. Job Done. They can't go for a drink to celebrate a successful operation because of parking the car and driving afterwards, so Chloe drops Danny at Caledonian Road tube station. He doesn't catch the tube. He needs to walk. He has that anticlimactic feeling somewhere deep inside him that success so often brings.

× × ×

Leah reaches home. Usually she walks in quietly. Today, as soon as she is through the door, she shouts, 'Izzy, I've seen Danny.'

Martin and Izzy are in the kitchen. Both rush to meet her.

'Is he okay?' Izzy asks.

'Perfectly, and working for the intelligence services. He came to arrest one of our old men. Danny was with armed men who pretended to be gardeners. One of them drew his gun. They nearly shot Bill but then they arrested Wendell and took him away in an ambulance which wasn't a real ambulance. Danny was with a rather classy girl.'

She has them spellbound. They want detail. She tells them to wait until the weekend, because that's when Danny has promised to come home. 'Wait until he gets here and ask him yourself,' she says, and hurries upstairs to change.

Martin follows her. 'Working for the intelligence services?' he asks.

'I think so. Wendell had two files that he'd cached in the music stool. Both were marked *Top Secret*. I suspect Danny really came for the files. One was in a foreign language. Wendell's foreign too. I think he's been frightened for a long time. He said a rather odd thing when he handed himself in. He said *You got here before the others. I'm rather glad about that.*'

'Said?'

'Yes, he's started talking. I think he stayed silent to hide his foreign accent.'

'Slow down, Leah.'

'I think Wendell, his real name's Juozas, was a spy in a former life. I think Chloe, that's the classy girl, and Danny have been trying to find him. Poor Danny ended up finding me. You should have seen his face. That's the thing about care homes: anyone can end up there. They're like frozen railway stations or static motorway services.'

'Wow,' Martin says, and sits on the bed. 'Was Wendell frightened?'

Leah is slipping into her jeans. 'I'd say he was relieved. He'd seen them outside and knew they were coming for him. He was determined to walk out unaided to give himself up. I carried the files.'

'You said one file was in a foreign language. What was the other one?'

'It was about Cambodia and Pol Pot.'

She sees Martin's eyes widen.

'You read the title page?'

'It was something like *A Report into the British Government's relationship with the Cambodian Government under Pol Pot and the Khmer Rouge*.'

'It was never published,' Martin exclaims, 'and you had it in your hands. I'd have liked to read it.'

'Perhaps you can. Wendell made at least one other copy of each file. He left a letter to a solicitor stuck behind the radiator in his room.' Leah pulls on her T-shirt, smooths her hair, and reaches into the pocket of her discarded tabard. 'I found it and brought it home.' Triumphantly she waves the stamped, addressed envelope in the air. 'Wendell had a backup plan. This is it.'

Martin stretches out a hand. Leah is suddenly reluctant to hand it over. 'Perhaps I should wait and give this to Danny. What do you think?'

Martin wants to read the file but has no right to. 'It

might be too important to leave to the security services,' he suggests. 'And Danny already has a copy.'

Leah hands over the envelope and Martin examines it, weighing it in both hands. 'I would guess from what you tell me that the solicitor is holding copies of the secret files in her safe. I think this must be a set of instructions explaining what she is to do with them.'

Leah is intrigued. 'It's like having another set of Stella's letters and Howard's journal. Last time we got our fingers burnt. We really should give this to Danny.'

'And what will he do with it? Look Leah, it's a nice evening. Why don't we carry out Wendell's intentions? Why don't we walk to the postbox and post his envelope?'

Leah considers this and shakes her head. 'No, I need to think.'

Martin hands the envelope back. 'When you do make up your mind, will you consult me before you take action?'

He's referring to last time. She knows that. 'Of course,' she says.

26

On Saturday morning Izzy's Arts and Crafts house waits for the family. It's a beautiful summer's day. The roof tiles glow. The windows reflect. Hundred-year-old trees are at full stretch in their effort to grab as much light as possible for their leaves. Patches of shade punctuate the prevalent areas of bright sunshine, and the temperature changes deliciously as Izzy moves between them.

It's been three months since Danny was here, since the whole family was together. It was following the death in the sinkhole. Even now they won't be able to welcome Izzy's real son because her search has failed, in spite of all her efforts. She still spends a few hours each week actively searching, and a few moments each day hoping that he will, against all the odds, come looking for her.

The family are gathering reluctantly. James will be there primarily because his mother asked him for help, but also, he admits only to himself, because he has nothing better to do. He'll drive himself and come alone. He's had no further contact with Roz since she cut off his phone call. And after all, he did choose Mindsett over her. He was so close to turning that choice into a political triumph, but his family know that. They must have seen him on the news. If it hadn't been for that *high placed source in the security services* he would have been in Downing Street now and far too busy to go to a family event. But at least he was a nearly man on the national stage; perhaps he can spin it that way with the family. What will they think of his haircut? The sable ringlets are gone, and there are occasional rogue white hairs to be seen on his cropped head.

Danny is only coming home because Leah demanded it and Chloe as good as told him he must. He suspects it's probably time to reappear but, left to himself, he would have put it off for longer. At least he has lived since he last saw them. Will he tell them what really happened to sink Mindsett as Prime Minister and James as his Chief of Staff? He might, but only if he's goaded. He catches the train and is determined to walk from the station as he's always done. If his family become too oppressive he'll ask Leah to take him to the care home. He'd like to search Wendell's room again. He'd like to be absolutely certain that he and Chloe missed nothing.

Julia will pick up Zakk and drive him north. She'd hoped to introduce him to her family in stages, but the gathering of the Goulden tribe gives her the chance to get it over with. She feels strangely vulnerable. She's still dreading the inevitable fuss, but she's made her mind up. She wonders if her mother will approve of her choice. She wonders most of all what James will say. She dreads a shake of those locks of his that have always surrounded his sneering face. Will Zakk stand up to him when James inevitably has a go? She still considers herself head of the family. In that case, Zakk outranks James, and rank has always been important in families, especially to her younger brother.

Leah now has a ring on her finger. Martin put it there. She dreads the reaction, or what might be worse, the utter indifference of the others. She has a problem to solve about Wendell and the envelope. She's seen the look in Martin's eyes. She senses another of his crusades and wants to be on the same side this time. She wonders what Julia's new partner is like, and simply cannot imagine that her sister is in love.

Izzy is pleased. Gary's children will be back together again and with additions. Already Martin hardly seems like an addition. Julia's new man will have to fit in. What will he be like? Julia was what Izzy can only describe as coy on the phone. By saying virtually nothing about him, Julia had forced her to ask if they need separate rooms. 'Oh Mother,' had been Julia's response. 'He's in with me.' It will be nice to have them all together, at least until they start quarrelling. She hopes they behave themselves. She also thinks of her still missing son. Should she put a chair out for him at the dining table on Saturday night?

Beds have been made up and towels provided. Flowers have been brought in from the garden although, if there was ever a house that did not need flowers to brighten it, it's this one. The weather is perfect. No one is expected before mid-afternoon. Leah will be back from her morning shift by then. Martin will not be home until 5pm.

Meanwhile, Izzy walks through the house and the gardens. She decides against putting out an extra chair for her lost child. With Danny returning, she wonders if it's time to accept that she will never find her long lost Patrick. Katherine as much as told her that her son could look after himself, so perhaps no real harm was done. She can satisfy herself with the thought that somewhere in the world is a successful man, to whom she gave the gift of life. The thoroughness of her search has begun to assuage her guilt at having handed him over. It has been a kind of penance and she needs to forgive herself. She looked in the mirror this morning and saw, staring back at her, what had always been her childhood image of an old woman: someone with neat white hair; someone who has weathered what life has thrown at her and reached the serene stage. But she doesn't feel serene. Before they arrive she'll remove the artist's impressions of what Patrick would look like now. They are here to welcome Danny back and welcome Zakk to the family. There shouldn't be a ghost at the feast. It's time to give up her search. When Leah and Martin marry, perhaps she can be a better grandmother than she ever was a mother.

She goes back into the house, picks up the framed picture of her son wearing a hat, and takes it upstairs to her bedroom. She places it next to the photograph of Gary. Then she makes a coffee and carries it outside. She sits in the shade, sips, listens to the birdsong and waits. When her cup is empty she continues to sit there. She's left the front door wide open. Anyone could walk in, but this is North Yorkshire, and no one ever comes to the house except the post girl. She drifts into a reverie and then into sleep.

Danny arrives first. He's powered his way from the railway station with his holdall over one shoulder. He's enjoyed the activity of the walk, putting one foot in front of the other and feeling the earth shift beneath him. Perhaps he's a tad slower than last time he was home, and he might have put on a little weight. Reaching the drive he checks his pace. There is nothing like going back to a family home to make you ask, how far have I come since I was last here? He stands still outside the house. Only his mother's car is parked there, and no one has come out to greet him, so he has time to ask if he feels different. The person who walked out of this house that April morning, he remembers, was confused, obsessed with fitness, and worried about growing older. All that has gone. He feels alright about being back. He has actually done what he set out to do when he disappeared: he has changed.

What surprises him is the way the house has also changed in his absence. When he left it was still his real home, real in the way his London house never was. It isn't that any longer. He's bemused by the thought. He looks at the windows, the roof, the gables and the porch. They are the same but subtly recategorized. The house has gained another title. In his absence it has morphed into his childhood home, somewhere he no longer belongs. The front door is wide open. He would usually walk straight in, but that no longer feels right, so he does what he has never done before: he puts his holdall down on the gravel and rings the bell. Then he steps back and waits.

Nothing happens. No one comes to the door, so he picks up his holdall and walks round the side of the house. He sees his mother almost immediately. She's asleep on the seat, her head thrown back and her mouth open. In the past months the house has shrunk and my mother has grown older, he thinks. He retreats quietly across the lawn and then approaches again by the gravel path, making lots of noise with his feet.

This time his mother wakes and sees him approaching. 'Danny,' she says. He stops short of her, giving her time to come to.

The Gouldens have never been a close family. They don't hug and kiss and say love you to each other. Danny remembers picking his mother up on the muddy path and cutting her wrists free on the day the other Patrick died. That was a moment of closeness. She comes up to him now and kisses him on the cheek. She doesn't look at him or stand back and tell him he's changed. She pats his hand and says she's glad he's home. Then she tells him he must be tired after his journey and asks whether he would like a cup of tea.

He says, 'Yes please,' and follows her into the house.

'Am I in my old room?' he asks.

She tells him he is.

So he picks up his bag and takes it upstairs. He's been back in the family house for no more than a few minutes and already he's disappointed.

He doesn't unpack. He's only staying the one night, so he makes his way back down to the kitchen. He's prepared, if asked, to tell the story of his recent life and explain exactly why he disappeared and what's happened to him since. But Izzy asks nothing except, 'Now, you know who else is coming, don't you?'

Danny shakes his head. 'I know Leah still lives here. I guessed at Martin being around. Who else?'

'James.'

So he might be goaded and he might have to spill his secret. He's signed the Official Secrets Act since then, and he doesn't know if it's retrospective. He'll try to hold his tongue.

'And Julia. Julia's bringing a man with her. I nearly said young man, but I suspect he isn't. At least, I hope he isn't.'

'Wow. So you have a full house to feed.'

'It's lovely,' Izzy says. 'I was so glad that Leah ran into

you. We'll all be here, well nearly all.'

They carry the tea outside and sit on the bench. It's warm, and at least he can soak up the sun.

'Why don't you tell me about Patrick?' Danny asks, when Izzy's lack of curiosity starts to annoy him, and the silence between them threatens to be too long. 'I gather he wasn't our half-brother after all.'

'No,' Izzy says. 'A policeman took my DNA and compared it with the body. There was no match.'

'What did you think when you were told?'

'That my real son wasn't dead. I've been searching for him ever since and failed to find him.'

Danny puts his hand out in sympathy and closes his fingers around her wrist. 'But you were so certain,' he says.

'I was,' she says. 'I've learned since then that the human mind has an amazing capacity to believe what it wants to believe.'

'And if you meet your real son, I mean meet him as a stranger, will you know him immediately?'

'I was fooled once. I won't let myself be fooled again.'

The doorbell rings. Izzy gets up but Danny tells her to stay where she is. He'll go to the door.

Rounding the corner of the house he wonders who this person can be. A rather fat man is standing in the doorway with his back to Danny. He has a large head and a fashionably short haircut. Only when he turns does Danny recognise his brother.

'Hello James.'

'Danny, where did you emerge from? What rock have you been hiding under, you reptile?'

It's said humorously, but it reveals that James is unchanged. Danny will answer the question, because at least his brother has asked him about himself.

'The rock is called London,' Danny says. 'It's where I've spent most of my time. I've also walked nearly all of the West Highland Way and been to Vilnius on professional duties.' He stops there and wonders if James will take the bait, will want to know more. But James is as uncurious about other people as he always was, so Danny asks, 'What happened to your hair? Have you been doing religious penance?'

James frowns but doesn't reply. The brothers shake hands. 'Mum's over at the seat,' Danny tells him.

They walk across in silence.

'James, you came,' Izzy says. She examines his haircut. 'Much more suitable,' she says, stretching out to touch his head. She withdraws her hand quickly as if she's in awe of her older son. Then she scrutinises the rest of him. 'Mind you, it makes you look more overweight.'

'Thanks Mum.' James is wounded. 'You sent for me and I came. You said you wanted help.'

'I did,' she says, and leaves it at that. 'The others will be here soon. As you're on your own this time, I've put you in Julia's room. Julia's bringing her new man with her and I wanted them to have the double bed.'

'According to you I won't fit into Julia's nunnery-sized cot.'

She looks at him quizzically. 'You'll manage,' she tells him. 'You'll have to.' Then she adds, 'I haven't seen you on television much recently. Everything alright?'

Danny's amused.

'It didn't work out,' James tells her. 'It very nearly did, and then Jud messed up and we lost.'

Danny smiles and stays silent as he would have done months ago. But this isn't the same. Then his silence would have been a form of blankness. Now it's knowing and gleeful.

'Never mind,' Izzy says. 'There's always a next time.'

There's a cry from the house and Leah appears, still wearing her uniform and tabard. She bounds across the lawn and hugs them both, James first and then Danny. She holds on to Danny, wrapping one arm round his waist, and says, 'Are you talking to me today? Last time it took me three attempts to get you to notice me.'

'Hello Leah. I'm sorry about that, but I was working,' Danny explains.

Leah looks at him. A searching look, an interested look, Danny thinks.

'Cavorting with armed men and a rather classy girl more like,' Leah says, 'come to kidnap one of my old men.'

'Your old men?' James asks.

Leah turns her attention to her older brother. 'What happened to your hair, James? That cut makes you look…' Leah searches for a suitable word '… rather ordinary, and you were never that.' She pauses. 'For your information, I have quite a few old men and twice as many old women. I'm one of the unskilled and underpaid workforce that keeps this country going. I'm now employed. I work in a care home.'

She sees the sneer on his face before he can hide it.

'And I love the people and the work,' she insists. 'Are you working at the moment, James?'

He shakes his head.

Neither of her brothers has noticed her ring. What did she expect?

× × ×

'Nearly there,' Julia warns Zakk. 'Are you nervous?'

'It's like facing a firing squad. Tell me their names

again. You're the oldest. Next comes James, the one with the long hair. Then comes Leah, your sister, but what's the name of the youngest, the brother who disappeared?'

'His name's Danny. We've heard nothing from him since he walked out of his life months ago. He won't be there. I rather think James will.'

'Danny, that's the name I keep forgetting. What do I call your mother?'

'Izzy. She's really Isabel, but no one ever calls her that. You could call her Mrs Goulden, but that might sound odd.'

'And Leah's partner is called Martin?' Zakk asks.

'Yes, all sensible, common names. Not like Zakk. What were your parents thinking of?'

They've been chatting all the way. Anyone who passed them on the motorway, or was stuck in traffic with them, would have seen an established couple, easy in each other's company. Because the heat is persisting, he is dressed as he was in Spain. On the back seat is his linen jacket, and on top of that his Panama hat. Julia is in a summer dress and her hair is different. The extra quiff has gone. She's conscious that it's probably time to stop wearing her hair long, but first she'll get through this weekend. She's missed Zakk in the two days they've been apart.

'You have to blame David Bowie for my name,' Zakk explains. 'He had an alter ego called Ziggy Stardust. There was a time in my life when I thought I needed another name, so I called myself Zakk. I felt like a Zakk then and I still do now.'

'You'll always be Zakk to me,' Julia tells him. 'But just out of interest, what was your other name?'

The traffic is heavy, so Julia doesn't see Zakk frown. 'That all belongs to another part of my life which I never talk about. One day, perhaps.'

In spite of the traffic she glances across at him. She never asked about his past in Spain because it wasn't going to be that kind of relationship. Then, when it became that kind of relationship, it seemed too late to ask either about his past or about his family. She'll let him tell her in his own good time.

× × ×

Martin is the next to arrive. He shakes hands with James and more warmly with Danny. 'I still owe you,' Danny tells him.

'I was worried about you,' Martin says. 'Leah's filled me in with what happened at the care home and with the work you're doing. It's good to see you again. You look as if you've come through.'

Danny smiles. 'It's a long story.'

'Then save it, but we'd like to know.'

'We?'

Martin suddenly looks coy, even though they are standing slightly apart from the others. James is talking to Izzy and Leah is standing between, listening to both conversations. Now she wanders across and links her arm through Martin's. 'We're getting married,' she tells her little brother, and holds out her hand with the ring.

'Congratulations.' The old Danny would have stopped there. The new Danny has a comment to make. 'He's a good man,' he tells Leah. He shakes Martin's hand again. 'That's great news.'

'Martin's right. I definitely want to hear your story,' Leah assures Danny.

'Later. A wedding in the family. That will take some organising.'

'No it won't,' Martin assures him. 'It will be quiet and planned only by us.'

'Julia may have something to say about that,' Danny jokes.

Leah shakes her head. 'I've got the measure of Julia now. She'll do as we want.' It's firmly said.

James comes over to join them. Izzy is walking into the house.

'Mum's brought me down here on false pretences,' James announces. 'She told me she wanted help finding the real Patrick, but now that you're back, Danny, she's decided to call off the search. From now on, apparently, she'll wait for him to come looking for her. She's gone to fetch the artist's impression to show me.'

'What artist's impression? Danny asks.

'Leah's mum went to a man in London who specialises in creating images of missing people as they might look now,' Martin explains. 'She took the photograph the cult gave her of Patrick when he was sixteen. From that he created three images of what he might look like now.'

'Since the wrong Patrick died, she's spent all her time searching,' Leah comments. 'I suspect she's giving up now because she's tried everything and got nowhere.'

Izzy is coming back across the lawn holding the picture in its frame.

She hands it to James. 'That's what he might look like now.'

James and Danny study the picture. 'He looks just like his dad,' Izzy tells them.

Through the hot air they hear the noise of a car drawing up on the gravel drive. Everyone hears it and they all stiffen. Julia with a man is surprising and interesting. Will he be divorced or still married? Perhaps he's one of those leftover men, James wonders, never for a moment thinking that he belongs in the same category.

'Here they are,' Izzy says. 'Will they find us out here? Should I go and greet them?'

'Let them look for us,' James suggests. 'It shouldn't take them long.'

The family are sticking together. They will meet the new couple like a phalanx.

'I hope he likes us,' Izzy says.

They hear the car door close and then the noise of feet on the gravel. The feet stop at the house and they hear the bell ring. Then silence.

'I should go,' Izzy says, as the silence lengthens.

'No need.' Danny points towards the couple walking round the corner of the house and slowly crossing the lawn.

Zakk has put on his jacket and his Panama hat. He's too far away for the watching group to make out any detail. He's shorter than Julia, but not by much. He has a certain presence. They are holding hands and they lean into each other as they walk. The sun is high in the sky and the hat shields his face, but they can see that he is looking at them,

Julia has counted the reception group and has spotted Danny. That's a real surprise. She whispers this information to Zakk, then adds, 'The whole family are here to greet you.' Have they all been summoned, and why has Danny reappeared, she wonders. 'At least we can get this over with in one go,' she says, sensing that immediate assessments are being made of them as they come closer. It's a long walk under scrutiny.

The reception party holds its ground. The couple have the sun behind them and the others need to shade their eyes if they are to get a clear look at the man who is holding

Julia's hand. It seems to the couple like a strange form of salute: five right hands shading five brows, all lined up.

Julia gets ready to say the line she has been dreading, the line that put her off the idea of having anything but a fling with the man she now wants to marry. They are closing in on the reception party.

At last his face is visible. He's about the same age as Julia, perhaps a little older, not a toy boy. He's handsome and has a lived-in face. He's nervous, but then he's bound to be nervous. There's something else about him...

Zakk and Julia have stopped just in front of her family. It's time for Julia to say the sentence that has so worried her. She does it quickly.

'This is Zakk,' she announces.

She glances sideways at her lover as she says this and feels a real pride in him. This is going to be okay, she thinks. She's back in charge. Now she'll introduce the family to him. She no longer cares what they think.

'Zakk, this is my mother, Izzy.'

Julia is about to identify all her siblings in turn, when she stops. Her mother has taken what looks like a photograph frame from James. She's holding it up in front of her. Her mouth is open. Her expression is a mixture of joy and horror. She's looking from the frame to Zakk and back to the frame, making strange, excited noises. The rest of the family have clustered round her, flicking their eyes backwards and forwards in unison, weighing and assessing. They stand very close together, each reaching for the picture to have a better look.

'Oh glory,' Izzy says. 'He just can't be. Can he?'

27

'What?' Julia asks. 'Why are you all looking at Zakk like that?'

No one speaks. The implications are sinking in. It's Leah who takes the photograph frame from Izzy's hands and walks across to where Julia and Zakk are standing. 'You need to see this,' she says, and hands the artist's impression to Julia.

Julia stares at the picture, not understanding at all.

'What is it?' Zakk asks her.

'It looks like a rather bad picture of you.'

'How come?'

Leah speaks slowly. 'When the Church of the Living Saints gave Izzy a photograph of her real son, taken when he was sixteen, Izzy took the picture to London. She gave it to an expert who does impressions of how people age. This is his best guess as to what my…' she pauses '… and your half-brother might look like now.' She breaks off.

'It could be anyone,' Julia says. 'It's a guess.'

But Zakk is standing very still. His face is white.

Julia turns and stares at him. Zakk stares at the photo, then his legs collapse underneath him and he sinks to the ground. Julia looks down at him. Then, understanding at last what has happened, she kneels beside him and whispers, 'Was your birth name Patrick?'

He closes his eyes and nods. His face is drawn and desperate.

'Were you a member of that appalling cult called the Church of the Living Saints?'

He nods again. He's breathing deeply. Julia, whose face is very close to his, can feel his exhaled breath on her cheek. 'I'm sorry,' he says, between deep gasping breaths. 'I tried to leave it all behind, Julia. I tried to forget. It was the only way I could live a life that was mine.'

She reaches out to hug him. 'Go away,' she yells at her family. 'All of you, just go away.'

The family troop back into the house. When they look back, Julia has her arms round Zakk and is rocking him as if he were the child she never had.

They sit together in the heat of a July day, on warm grass in the lovely garden of a beautiful house. Around them are all the trappings of happiness, but they are bereft. The chill wind of future loneliness is pinching their hearts. Each is thinking that the other will walk away. Julia is wondering if the voracious maw of the Goulden family will swallow up Zakk and jettison her.

Information is like that. Only a few moments ago she didn't know. But now it is too late to deny the truth. Even if her family missed her whispers and the two slight nods, Zakk's reaction told them he is Patrick.

He flung the photograph away as he fell. It skidded on the gravel. No one rushed to pick it up. The glass will be damaged, the frame scratched, but it's done its deadly work.

Julia's mind is suddenly full of practicalities, questions of the here and now. Where will each sleep? What will they do about what they have discovered? How will they get through the next five minutes, the next hour?

Julia feels Zakk calming. Now he uncurls from his semi-foetal position and reaches out to her. They sit on the grass opposite each other, feet towards feet and toe to toe. They reach out and hold each other's wrists as if they are gymnasts about to lift each other up. With long gaps in between, their souls speak to each other.

He says, 'I always felt as if I had known you all my life.'

A wood pigeon is calling across the afternoon. Its cooing is a terrible mockery of what they feel.

She says, 'I'm not prepared to let you go.'

A brown leaf falls through the heavy air. It's curled and crinkled, like something abandoned.

He says, 'I love you, Julia.' Then he adds with heavy emphasis, 'But not with a brother's love.'

Everything has flipped. All the time that so recently stretched in front of them, like a school summer holiday, is already behind them and rushing away at speed.

She says, 'There are places we can go and live where no one knows us, but your mother, our mother, will be longing to hug you.'

He shakes his head. 'I can't do that. I'm not prepared to become someone's son.' Then he adds, 'There's not a single cell in my body which is wishing that we'd never met.'

Time is remorseless, moving forward as it always does.

Leah walks across the lawn towards them. She's carrying a tray. A teapot, cups, saucers, milk jug and scones are balanced on it. She puts it down twenty feet from them and then, without saying anything, immediately turns her back on them and retreats into the house.

It's Julia who recovers first. It's as if all the thinking she's done, and all the doubts she ever had about Zakk, have crystallised under this immense pressure into a single diamond of longing. She gives him an instruction. She says, 'Kiss me, Zakk.' She determines never to call him Patrick. 'I think we need to do this quickly.'

They are two tiny people in a small country in a vast world and she needs to push back against the great forces raged against them.

'Please kiss me.'

They lean forward. Their lips come together. She is like a rider climbing straight back into the saddle after a nasty fall.

He feels her lips against his and waits, hoping to feel that pinprick of desire.

At this moment in time they have never needed each other so much.

Their mouths loosen. He hears Ingrid Bergman's cry to Humphrey Bogart in Casablanca: *Kiss me as if it were the last time.* Soon he is kissing Julia as if it might be the last time, but as their kiss deepens there is no sense of an ending.

That kiss finishes. They smile at each other and kiss again.

They stay outside. They drink the tea but don't touch the scones. The rest of the family leave them alone. Between sips of tea Zakk tells his story.

'Until I was fourteen the cult was just my norm. That's when the man I thought was my father died. I loved him. I had always been less fond of my mother. I never felt I was good enough for her. My story is a common one amongst the vast legions of the adopted. Searching her bedroom after my father's death, I came across my adoption papers and knew I'd been lied to. At the same moment I discovered I had an on/off toggle switch in my brain. I flung the switch, and the truths that the cult had been teaching me all my life up to that point were suddenly untrue.'

'I fought them all then. I'm actually surprised, looking back, that I lasted two more years there. At sixteen I absconded and walked out into an amazing world of girls and music and colour and fun. I walked round Leeds, not understanding much of what I was seeing, but thinking the world owed me for what I'd been through.'

'I ran into trouble almost immediately. I tried to sing to earn money, and a group coming out of a pub turned on me. I was rescued by a big man called Bill who fed me but wanted sexual favours in return. I stole money from him, lots of money, and ran away a second time.'

'That was my lucky day. A woman found me sitting dejected in Roundhay Park. I don't remember her name, but she took me to a charity for the homeless. Slowly, often despairingly, I climbed my way back, learning all the stuff other kids had imbibed with the rhythm of their ordinary lives. I took my lead from Bowie, and from his music which I loved. If he could have another persona, so could I. He was Ziggy, so I called my new self Zakk. I went to college. It was like beginning at zero. I fought my way up to get a job and then I started my own company. I did all that messy stuff with drink and girls and came out the other end.'

'Finally, I felt free. I flicked another switch. I determined to forget what had happened and live a life that was mine. I deliberately forgot about my childhood. I had dreams, nightmares really, in which I found myself back in the cult. Those dreams lasted more than ten years, but eventually they diminished and went away.'

Zakk shrugs.

'Meeting you is the best thing that has happened to me. You don't know how hard I find it to trust people, to believe in them. But I believe in you.'

He kisses her again and it feels natural.

'This afternoon,' he tells her, 'it's as if someone has attempted to flick both switches back.'

Julia shakes her head. When he looks at her he sees determination and a will to win.

'No Zakk,' Julia says. 'No, they won't. No, they mustn't. We live as we are, as we want to be, not as others decide.'

He nods. His teacup is empty.

Without saying anything else they stand up and, hand in hand, they walk towards the house. The rest of the family are clustered in the kitchen. They've been talking but go silent when the couple approach.

Julia takes a deep breath and holds Zakk's hand tightly as she re starts the introductions. 'Hello everyone,' Julia announces, as if this is the first time they've met. 'This is Zakk. It isn't short for Zachariah or for anything else. He's called Zakk, spelled with two ks.'

Izzy, who has been staring at him from the moment they came in, steps forward to meet her real son. Unlike last time she feels no instant connection, only a deep sense of shame, because her choices have led to this moment and its horror. She doesn't attempt to hug him, although she wants to.

The moment has finally come, the moment she's longed for, worked for, lived for, but she's seen the look in Zakk's eyes. They stand apart and shake hands. It's a light touch of the fingers, nothing more. 'Hello Zakk,' she says. 'You are very welcome.'

He hesitates. So much hangs on the choice of the

name he uses for her. He has never forgiven his birth mother for abandoning him to the hated cult. He'll call her by the name Julia told him no one uses. 'Hello Isabel,' he says.

He can see her instant disappointment and he feels cruel. There may come a time when he can talk to her about being his mother, but that time is probably a long way in the future and is definitely not now. He endures the light touch of her hand and gently lets it go. 'Thank you for inviting me,' he says.

That done, he turns to the others, massed on the far side of the kitchen table. 'You must be James,' he says, 'but I was told you had your hair in ringlets. These days there's so much misinformation about.' He shakes James's hand, then easily identifies and shakes hands with Leah. Her response is warmer. Finally, he's left choosing between Danny and Martin. He remembers what he was told. One is shorter than the other and well built. 'Hello Danny,' he says. Then he turns to Martin. 'You and I, Martin, have to be allies against the family.'

Martin is amused. He welcomes Zakk warmly, shaking the proffered hand. 'Their bark is worse than their bite,' he explains.

The important thing now is for Zakk to be alone with Julia.

'This is a wonderful house, Julia,' Zakk says. 'Are you going to show me round?'

She's watched the way he's taken over with amusement and great pride. 'This way, Zakk. It's an Arts and Crafts house built for a rich Leeds merchant and then bought by another…'

Her voice tails off. No one else moves.

'Well really,' James says. 'They can't just carry on, can they?' He looks at his mother, his habit of stating and re-stating the obvious not in the slightest bit diminished by his recent failures. 'If you're his mother, he can't also be Julia's lover.'

'If you hadn't had that artist's impression done, we would never have known,' is Danny's contribution.

'Two Patricks.' James has the floor, and these days this is the only group he can attempt to dominate. 'The false one was all over you and the real one is now called Zakk and, quite frankly, is dismissive.'

Leah has gone to her mother and put her arm round her shoulder. She doesn't say, 'You don't deserve this.' Leah's been in the cult. Perhaps it never felt to Zakk like Uncle Joshua's warm bath. Perhaps Zakk was always the alien because, by the time Izzy gave birth to him, she had already abandoned sainthood. What a mess.

Danny is regretting coming home. Everything about this visit has been a mistake. He was already disappointed by his reception and now this. He wonders when he can ask Leah to take him to the home so he can carry out another search of Juozas's room. He reaches for another scone and hides behind the butter knife and the jam spoon.

Leah peers at her mother. She's stony-faced but she isn't crying. That's a relief.

'Actually, they can just carry on.' It's Martin speaking. 'I think James is wrong. Incest laws vary. In ancient times full brothers and sisters married. In fiction, first cousins often fall in love and marry. First cousins share between 4% and 23% of their DNA. I've looked it up. Half siblings share between 17% and 34%. The amounts can overlap. Incest taboo is there to prevent in-bred children. Perhaps Julia and Zakk can't marry, and they shouldn't risk having children, but what harm are they doing by being in a relationship?'

As with so many of Martin's contributions, this one trails off into silence and no one comments.

The siblings drift away. James goes to Julia's room. Julia and Zakk find him there and are re-directed to James's room. The rest retire to their own spaces.

Leah pulls Martin down onto the bed. 'We can have children,' she says.

'Yet more Gouldens!'

'They wouldn't be Gouldens. I'll take your name. They'll be Stockdales.'

'A rose by any other name ...'

'Do you have to spoil everything with a quotation?'

At dinner that night James drinks too much and becomes voluble again about his favourite subject: himself. He has his opportunity when Julia talks about his haircut.

'Such a shame that you let the ringlets go, James. They made you so easy to spot on television. What actually happened there?'

It's his moment, and James is ready with his explanation. 'The Party suddenly got cold feet about a Mindsett premiership. At the last moment, after we'd won, they involved the security services to prevent it. We came that close.'

Julia sips her wine and winks at Zakk.

'But there was that little matter of your plotting with the Russians, wasn't there?' she goads, slipping back into their ancient rivalry.

'A minor infringement, Julia, the kind of collusion that happens all the time.' James dismisses it. 'There was something fishy about that too. Think of the timing. The very day Jud was due to kiss hands, what they described as a *high placed source in the security services*, I ask you, released the photographs. I mean, I'm not normally a conspiracy theorist, but you have to ask why the photographs weren't made public before the vote. I always suspected that Stella knew and simply bided her time.'

'Why would she do that?' Zakk asks, and is ignored.

'So you were the victim, were you?' Julia asks.

'Something like that. There are dark forces at work, who do their level best to keep outsiders from winning high office. I did some investigating of my own. I think I could even name who was behind it all.' He says this in the all-knowing James way his siblings recognise.

James looks round, daring anyone to challenge his version of events.

'Well, after all, you are my brother,' Danny remarks, seemingly out of the blue and about nothing in particular.

They turn and stare at Danny, then do what they always did in the past: ignore him.

He's come back to the family and nothing has changed. If Juozas had been in any other care home he wouldn't be here. He looks round at his family as if he is seeing them clearly for the first time. He'll stay silent for the moment. Tomorrow he'll make an excuse and slip away.

But James is now enjoying himself. He knows, drunk as he is, that tonight he should lay off Julia, if only because she has reinforcements. But Danny is another matter. Danny is alone and fair game, so he decides to have a go. 'And what do you know about it, little Danny boy? Did you see it on the tele in your gym, just after you'd completed a thousand press-ups?'

Danny doesn't rise to the bait. He really mustn't let James get under his skin.

'Come on, Danny. I've waited thirty years for you to say anything worth saying or anything at all about politics. Now you've re-emerged from your time in the wilderness, give us the benefit of your wisdom.'

Danny smiles at him. 'You don't know as much as you think you do, James. I'd say you've had quite enough to drink. I should go and lie down somewhere in a darkened room and keep taking the tablets.'

James is stung. His needling has failed to work. Danny is unscathed. 'And you do?' he says. 'You do know what happened?'

It's a sneer, almost a snarl of contempt.

'Since when did you know anything about anything?' James pauses. 'Let's put this to the test. This is clearly a day for revelations. Let's hear the wisdom of Danny Goulden. Come on, Danny. Enlighten us.'

He stares across at his brother and notices for the first time that Danny is completely at ease. This spooks James.

Danny has a half smile on his face as he puts down his wine glass. 'Okay,' he says. 'I'll do just that. When I disappeared I lived and slept on the streets. Because beggars are invisible I was recruited to provide deep protection for candidate Mindsett. I was bearded and filthy. I, your little brother Danny, saw Mindsett sneak out of the building after the hustings. I followed him to his meeting with Borstov. I did so in my official capacity. I took the photographs of that meeting between Mindsett and Borstov using a Service camera. Later I observed you handing over to Borstov what I believe was a copy of Stella's letters and Howard's journal. I went to tell Stella Stelling and she declined to take any action, so I eventually went to The Guardian with my story and agreed to be referred to as that *high placed source in the security services*.'

Now, perhaps for the very first time, he has the family's full attention. 'So little Danny shafted you, James. I stopped your immoral nonsense. I did it because I wanted justice for Stella. That campaign you ran was corrupt from start to finish.'

There has been little enough conversation already at dinner, but now the room relapses into silence. James pours himself another glass of wine but doesn't drink it. As soon as it can't be put down to pique, he leaves the room.

The rest of them relax once they are sure he has gone. 'Well done you,' Leah says to Danny as soon as James has closed the door. 'And now you have another name. That classy girl called you Colm. Why's that?'

Danny smiles. He's said more than enough for one night.

28

An hour has passed. Julia and Zakk have made their excuses and gone to bed. James has never come back down. Izzy disappeared as soon as the washing up had been completed.

'Should I go and check on her?' Leah asks Martin.

'No, leave her be.'

Just the three of them, Leah, Martin and Danny, are drinking coffee in the lounge.

'Can you tell us about Wendell?' Leah asks.

Danny shakes his head.

'Because he's always seemed unhappy to me, and I've wondered why.'

'I deal in secrets. I shouldn't have said what I said earlier, but James riled me.'

'You don't need to worry about them,' Leah insists. 'They're proper Gouldens. They're only interested in themselves. Izzy won't tell anyone. James certainly won't.'

'What about Zakk?'

'I think he's only interested in Julia. Good luck to them.'

Leah kicks her shoes off and curls up on the settee. When she's comfortable she tries a new tack. 'I was Wendell's carer. I liked him, even though he poisoned the cat. I was the only one he ever spoke to.'

'He fascinates me too,' Danny says. 'I fear I might be like him.'

They wait for him to go on.

Danny obliges and tells them Juozas's story, ending with, 'So no wonder he seems unhappy.'

'We won't repeat what you've told us.' Leah looks towards Martin, who nods. 'Wendell played jokes in the home too. He turned staff photographs upside down, changed the date on the wooden blocks calendar in the hall, that sort of thing.'

'Can you tell us about the Pol Pot file?' Martin asks.

'No, never.'

'Because if I were Juozas, I would have made a copy. Wouldn't you?'

Danny turns to Leah and becomes business-like. 'I need to search his room. Can you and I go to the home tomorrow and do that?'

Leah looks at Martin again. He nods.

'Of course we can. I don't yet drive, so Martin will have to drive us, but…'

'But what?'

'But I've already searched his room. I did it the day you came and took him away. I think I have what you would be looking for.'

All the time she's saying this she looks in his eyes. She reads hunger and worry there. 'I'll go and fetch it.'

She leaves the room and returns with the envelope, but she doesn't immediately hand it to Danny. 'What I suggest happens,' she says, 'is that you search the room and find nothing. Then you can tell the classy girl that you've done your duty. Meanwhile, I'll keep hold of this. I found it stuck behind the radiator. Wendell was clever. This was his insurance. In a few months' time, when the heating is turned up for the winter, it would have fallen to the floor. Because it's addressed and stamped it might well have been posted.'

She shows it to Danny but doesn't let him hold it.

'It's addressed to a solicitor. I presume the solicitor has a copy of each file and that this letter gives her instructions to make the copies public.'

Both men want the letter, Martin out of his thirst for knowledge, Danny to further his career. Leah holds onto it.

'For the moment, I'll keep it.'

Martin looks disappointed. Danny shakes his head.

'I've signed the Official Secrets Act. The files were marked *Top Secret* as I suspect you know. One is partly in Lithuanian. It probably contains details about the present government's previous collaborations with the Soviets. I suspect it will tarnish for ever the reputations of the so-called Independence heroes. The other is the Pol Pot file, detailing the time when Britain connived to keep a mass murderer in power. As I said, I'm quite like Juozas. I like to see justice. That's what still leaves me uncertain about my new calling. So I suggest you give me the letter. I don't know what use I'll make of it, but I might find it easier than you to manage an anonymous leak to the press.'

'And might you be prepared to let me have a look first?' Martin asks.

Danny shrugs his shoulders. 'I owe you, but either leaking or letting you read the file could cost me my job.'

'Then I'll keep hold of the letter for now,' Leah says.' I

may very well ask Wendell what I should do. After all, this letter is his property. The files weren't, but this is.'

Danny agrees.

'But I have got something for you, Danny. These are rightfully yours.' Leah hands him the new keys to his old house. 'The house in London still belongs to you, although I suspect your utility bills and the rates need paying. Oh, and you owe me for the new locks and the repair to your front door. I'll send you an invoice when you give me your new address.'

She senses his reluctance. 'I won't share it, but the family may need to get in touch. It's either that or I phone MI5 and ask to speak to their *high placed source in the security services*.'

'Text me,' Danny suggests. 'You have my number.'

× × ×

The interrogation of Juozas Žemaitis reveals nothing new. Chloe and Danny take him through the chronology and the facts of his case. In each instance their conclusions are vindicated.

Interviewing him is a surreal experience. Is this little old man really the legendary spy they tracked and chased through the convolutions of his own past, the man who booby-trapped his house before he walked out on his old life? Could he once have been the hero/joker admired by Russian dissidents, the principled patriot with a burning sense of duty?

Talking about his life and what he'd hoped to achieve seems to bore him, as if all he fought for no longer matters, and what he most wants is to be back in the care home and taken into lunch. He only smiles when they tell him that the Russians had also been searching for him. He hadn't stolen the files to publish them, he explains. He'd 'borrowed' them because he wanted something to show for his professional life. He knew his options were running out. He knew he'd reached the stage when he needed looking after. Stealing the files was a final act of defiance on his part. The files guaranteed his continuing importance, his refusal to be nobody. They were a symptom of his rage against the dying of the light.

'And the sword that nearly killed me?' Chloe asks. 'Was that an act of defiance?'

Juozas seems not to remember. Chloe has to explain. 'When I walked into your house, you'd balanced a razor-sharp sword above the door. It was attached to a wire so it would fall point first. The force of it falling turned on maniacal laughter.'

She can see that he remembers because he winces.

'It didn't hit me,' she tells him, and waits for an explanation or an apology.

'I'd forgotten I'd done that. I'm glad you're alright.' He smiles politely.

Is that it? Is that really all he has to say? Apparently not. She sees him wince again.

'The cat wasn't alright,' he adds. 'I was sorry about that. I thought the laburnum would make it sick, not kill it.'

Chloe doesn't understand what he means, but she lets it go. The room fills with the silence of what is unspoken because it no longer seems to matter.

Juozas doesn't mention the envelope stuck behind the radiator. Danny never asks if Juozas made copies of the files. Chloe seems distracted, as if she too is bored with this enquiry and eager to get onto the next case.

'What happens to me now?' is Juozas's only question to them.

They'll look after him for a few days, get him a medical check-up, make sure he's okay, and then they'll probably send him back to the home.

'Is that a promise?' he asks.

They tell him it is.

A nurse comes and collects Juozas soon afterwards, which leaves Chloe and Danny alone.

'Have you an answer for me, Danny?' Chloe asks, when the door has closed. 'It's Monday. Today I have to make a recommendation as to your future employment. Are you in or out?'

She asks this as breezily as possible, but it's no longer just a professional matter for Chloe. Danny senses the undertow beneath the placid surface of her question. She's frowning. His answer matters to her.

And to him. In less than a year, Danny the pampered fitness freak has morphed into a rough sleeper, segued into surveillance work, found himself at the heart of things, and altered political history. He is the mollusc who shook himself free from his Goulden rock and has been pulled by the tide ever since. Chloe is tempting him to find another footing. Is he through with change? He knows himself better now. His body may be less toned, but his brain is sharper.

'In,' he tells her. 'I need the Service. I need its excitement and its variety. I need the pay.' He sees her relax and knows that she wants him to say more. She's looking at him eagerly, and it's a different face altogether from the one he's used to. Now it's as if the frown is only temporarily hitched to her features, like a last patch of snow to a Scottish hillside.

'I went home this weekend, Chloe, and there was nothing there for me. I had a few moments of wicked pleasure in squashing my older brother, James, but I was glad to come back here. I need something to do. I like the work.'

'Good,' she says. 'I hoped you'd say that.' She smiles now and her face changes, melting the frown.

'Something else too,' Danny adds, 'before we leap forward. I think the Service needs me, needs someone who won't automatically follow orders if they shouldn't be obeyed. I disobeyed Harry because he was wrong. I can do that again. You need to know that. You might even want to put that in your report.'

He looks at her closely. 'Does that change your mind about recommending me?'

'No,' she says. 'I knew that about you. I'd factored it in. The Service will gain a good case officer and a man who keeps his word to his friend on the streets and his other friend in the opposition. You're a rarity. If that's your decision, we have another case.'

'We?'

She smiles again. 'I've enjoyed working with you. I have to admit it.'

Then she laughs. It's a sound he hasn't heard before. 'It might even be an advantage to me to have someone who occasionally breaks the rules. There is, for instance, that other rule that operatives of the Service should never become romantically involved with each other. How do you feel about that rule?'

'Are you asking me on a date?'

'I might be.'

'Then ask.'

'Danny, would you like to have dinner with me tonight?'

'Of course.'

Even now, as he leans in for their first kiss, Danny doesn't tell her about the envelope and the possibility of there being copies of the top secret files.

Next morning Danny goes to his old house and unlocks the front door with one of the keys Leah gave him. He pushes his way past another heap of fast-food fliers, picks them up and takes them to the kitchen. In sorting through them he finds the invitation and opens it.

The Prime Minister
requests the honour of the company of
Daniel Goulden
at a reception at 10 Downing Street, Whitehall
on Wednesday 23rd July from 6.30 to 8.00pm.
Dress: Lounge Suit

He has time to reply, but only just. He'll go. He'd like to meet Stella again.

He picks up the lottery ticket. He knows it's still in date. All he has to do is claim it, but he still doesn't want the money for himself.

He wonders if he could help Shaun or Ivor. Shaun is a disappointment. He's been unable to stay off the drink. Danny suspects that Shaun has not yet reached the moment when he wants to change of his own free will. Until he does, he can't be helped. To feed his addiction would almost certainly kill him.

Ivor then?

He could make Ivor his tenant, lend him this house until he gets sorted, but he suspects that Ivor is too much his own man to accept the offer of a permanent roof over his head, let alone a gift of over £2 million.

Who or what charity then?

Unclaimed lottery money goes to good causes. Should he just let them decide? All he has to do is tear the ticket up.

He doesn't do that. So much in life is chance. He's learnt that. He puts the ticket in an envelope and quickly writes down where and when it was bought. He tells whoever finds it that the money is theirs, then adds his own contact details in case the finder has difficulty claiming the money and needs corroboration.

He picks up his documents from the table and wipes the dust off them. He will go back to being Danny Goulden when he isn't working, and his own passport might be useful, even though he already has one under his new identity. He thrusts the documents deep into his pocket. He picks up the envelope with the lottery ticket inside and holds it in his hand. He still loves walking through London, so he counts a thousand steps and then drops the envelope in mid-stride. Looking straight ahead, and without a backward glance, he continues on his way. The envelope might be swept up as rubbish or make someone's decade. That's up to chance.

29

A few days later a queue forms outside the gates that lead into Number 10 Downing Street. Security is tight. When the time comes, the invitees shuffle through airport type scanners and then walk towards the famous front door. Once inside, they are relieved of their mobile phones and directed up the famous staircase, past all the portraits and photographs of previous Prime Ministers.

Martin arrives early. He only told Leah about his invitation two weeks ago when he needed her help to buy a suit. He's wearing it now with a white shirt and a purple tie. He feels unlike himself. As he climbs the stairs he notices that the wall above the bannister is full. Stella's photograph is right at the top. There is no space for anyone else to be Prime Minister. The rooms upstairs are smaller than he imagined. Invitees are moving into one of two rooms. Some go left; he turns right. Now he looks around the room he's in and wonders why he's come. All the people invited seem to be strangers to each other. He accepts a drink and watches the room fill up. People begin talking. Martin notices what he thinks is a late Turner painting on the wall by the fireplace. He walks across to take a closer look. It is, and it's magnificent. He lingers over it, wonders who owns it and whether it shouldn't be on public display. Then he spots Danny and thinks, I know why you've been invited; at least I'll have someone to talk to. Danny does a double-take and comes straight over.

'Of all the people. Why are you here?' Danny asks.

'I did her a service once.'

Martin is about to explain his part in the drama of the election when he is aware that the room has gone silent. The Prime Minister, Stella Stelling herself, has arrived, followed by an enormous cat. She looks older, Martin thinks. She seems strained.

To his astonishment she comes straight across the room towards him. 'So glad you could come, Martin. I try never to forget a kindness. I'll always be grateful for what you did, and particularly for what you said.'

Her warmth and her words are sincere. Then she scrutinises Danny. 'Are you my rough sleeper?' she asks. 'Are you the Danny who came to warn me?'

'Yes.'

'Then I owe so much to you too, although there are times I blame you for everything.'

'Michael told me exactly what you said to him.'

'Did he? Another leak.' She smiles. 'I hate leaks.'

She is a busy woman and they can't detain her; she has a room to work, full of people dying to talk to her. But she seems in no hurry. 'I like to pay my debts, so I thought I should invite you to my prison.'

Martin can't help himself. Hamlet's exchange with

Rosencrantz comes to mind. 'Then is the world one.'

Stella is up for this. 'A goodly one, in which there are many confines, wards and dungeons, Number 10 being one of the worst,' she replies.

They exchange nods. Danny winces.

'I played the Prince at my all-girls school.'

The cat has come across the room. It's rubbing itself against Danny's legs. 'She remembers you,' Stella remarks, 'although I have to say you are looking and smelling a great deal better than when we first met.'

She declines a drink when it is offered to her. There is a short silence. Martin feels he must say something. He says it simply. 'We were so glad you won.'

Danny thinks briefly of all the great and important words that must have been spoken in this building and adds, 'Me too.'

'I wonder if I am,' she tells them. Then, 'Well, enjoy your evening,' and Stella Stelling is gone.

Their glasses are refilled. Silence falls between them. The cat has followed Stella across the room. The two men stand together looking around, wondering who all these people are and why they have been invited. Then Danny feels a tap on his shoulder. He turns round and finds himself face to face with Harry.

Harry, from his own Service. Harry, who used to be his boss. Harry, who ensured that Mindsett was well guarded and Stella Stelling was not.

'I thought you'd been transferred.' Danny says the words before he realises just how they recalibrate their relative positions. He owes Harry. Harry rescued him from the streets and set him on his present path. But Harry was on the wrong side politically. Harry put him in danger. He owes this man but he also has a score to settle.

'You lost,' Danny reminds him.

'Did I?' Harry says. 'Yet here I am.' He sweeps his arm around the room.

'Mindsett lost. Stella won. I used your camera against you,' says Danny.

'Did she win? I seem to remember the vote went the other way. I seem to remember that Mindsett is the one with the democratic mandate from his party.'

'Martin,' Danny suddenly says, turning round to his future brother-in-law. 'I'd like you to meet my old boss, Harry. He rescued me from the streets.'

Martin puts out his hand and Harry takes it, but without enthusiasm.

Then, having brought Martin in as a witness, Danny pursues his theme.

'Surely you're pleased that Stella's Prime Minister? She's doing a great job. Think what a Mindsett premiership would have been like.' Danny's proud of how far he's come, that he can meet Harry under these circumstances as an equal. 'Mindsett lied. Mindsett cheated. Mindsett conspired with an enemy state to influence an election,' he adds, as if these are clinching arguments and he can rest his case.

Harry stares at him and Danny remembers that intimidating look.

'We got decency back,' Danny continues. 'Stella's honest. She actually cares about the people and the country. She's a good democrat.'

Harry is sneering. His contempt is etched on his face.

'I admit that her victory was a setback. We so nearly made it into power,' Harry says.

There is a pause.

'So what will you do now?' Danny asks.

‘Wait,’ Harry says. ‘Nothing lasts forever. Every success has within it the seeds of its own demise. Stella is not to everyone’s taste. We simply wait. The age of decency will pass. Our time will come. All we need is a better candidate.’

Harry turns and walks away. Danny stares after him.

Martin knows Harry’s right.

× × ×

In Yorkshire Leah has the house to herself. Martin is in London. Izzy has taken up a number of activities to keep herself occupied. Tonight she is at the local pilates class. Leah takes the opportunity to do what she hasn’t done for a long time: listen to the house and see what it is telling her. She steps into the hall and walks over to the jardinière with its wreath of oak leaves arranged in a pattern that never repeats. She flicks the rim carefully with her nail and hears the pure sound of the ping as it rises through the stillness of the house.

But it has no echo. She’s surprised. She examines the bowl. It’s the same as it always was. On the sides there are two silver acorns followed by three, then one on its own. Each copper leaf is different. The jardinière has been in the house for over a hundred years. She flicks it again. Once more the pure sound rises to the roof. Leah holds her breath and listens. There’s silence.

She waits and then breathes out. She’s disappointed.

All her life, from being a little girl, she has pinged the bowl and listened to the echo. She has let the house talk to her, has felt a greater affinity with the building than with her family who have lived in it. The building has always told her whether everything is alright or not. Now it’s gone silent on her.

'What's happened?' she asks the building out loud.

The building doesn't reply.

It's gone mute.

× × ×

Wendell is back in the home and back in his old room. Now the Service knows how frail and harmless he is, he has been released to live out his final days in North Yorkshire. His room has extra protection, but the calculation is that even the FSB will not attack a frail old man living in a care home.

These days Wendell has accepted that he must use a walking frame. This doesn't worry him, since his notoriety as some kind of foreign spy has given him added status with the other residents. He's more relaxed and less fearful.

Leah spends time with him when she can. He was, after all, the means of getting her favourite brother back. The spy who originally came from Lithuania has formed a close bond with the care worker from the posh house. He likes to hear her talk. Sometimes he talks back, but mostly he listens.

'There's so much I don't understand about my family,' Leah tells Wendell one day. 'Ever since Dad died we've been on a series of journeys, moving out of our comfort zones, away from the people we used to be, taking chances, chasing dreams. My mother, Izzy, dreamt of finding the son she gave up for adoption. She's found him and lost him again. James dreamt of being important. He came within a whisker of wielding power, then crashed. Julia took a chance with love, only to discover that the man she loves is her half-brother. Danny walked out of his keep-fit life and ended up working for MI5. You met him. He's the one who interrogated you. He's found a job and squashed his older brother, but underneath I think he's still uncertain about his place in the world.'

It's mid July. Outside the leaves are stiff and dark green, the shadows deep. Wendell is sitting on his bed listening. Above his head a swift launches from the nest hidden deep under the eaves. Leah sees the way it falls into flight and powers away.

'And you?' Wendell asks. 'What about you?'

'Me? I've been enamoured, raped and terrified. I've failed to protect my mother from herself. I've had to force myself out from the margins and start talking after years of silence. You know what that's like. Earlier this year I did something that was terribly wrong. But I love my work. I'm engaged to be married to someone I think I love and I know I admire. I'm alright.'

She fixes his tie and ties his shoelaces. She checks him over and tells him, 'You'll do.' Then she adds, 'It doesn't make sense to me. It sometimes seems that the more we've each changed, the more we've actually remained the same. The last few months have been such an upheaval. I look back to the time of Dad's funeral and think how innocent we all were.'

She passes Wendell his frame, and with great effort he hauls himself upright. When he's found his balance she adds, 'What do you think, Wendell? You've lived longer than I have; you must be wiser than I am.'

She doesn't expect an answer, it's just her way of being friendly, but he surprises her.

'Such a thing,' he says, shaking his head. 'I'm not wise,' he tells her. 'I took up the cause my father had bequeathed me, but life is a puzzle without a solution, in my case a set of certainties that each turned out to be false. I did what everyone else does I suppose: I followed his dreams and then my own, picking up the usual accretions of sadness along the way. But I never solved the puzzle. It's as if the moment you think you've cracked it, you discover that the clues have been reset.'

She thinks he's finished, but he hasn't. 'Marry your young man,' he tells her. 'There can't be certainty about the future. That's one of the things I've learned. You have to guess and follow your guesses. But if you think about it, do you want to know what happens next? Would you have life any other way?'

She's touched by what he's confided, with how open he's been about himself. She'd better level with him. 'I found the envelope you left,' she tells him. 'It's in a safe place. My brother wants it. My fiancé wants to read the Pol Pot file. What do you want me to do with it?'

He seems confused at first. 'Behind the radiator,' she explains. 'You made copies of the two files and left them with a solicitor, remember? You stuck an envelope addressed to your solicitor behind the radiator.'

Wendell nods. He understands. 'Knowing the truth about the past, or getting as close to it as we ever can, matters,' he tells her. 'It always did. Wait until I've gone, then do as you think right.'

He straightens his back as much as he still can and heads towards the door.

When he reaches it he stops again. 'Marry your young man. He sounds right for you. I never had anyone like that.' He shakes his head as if to get rid of the thought, then smiles. 'Life is as you describe it, Leah. It really is such a thing.'

Coda

It's 1st March 2020. The weather is glorious. Spring has arrived on cue and stayed. Blue skies dominate the whole of Britain and the daffodils have never been more yellow.

The Goulden family are together again because it's the morning of Leah and Martin's wedding. The couple have got their way and kept everything simple. A slot has been booked at the register office. There will be a reception at a local hotel but no evening party. Little regard has been paid to the normal excesses of a modern wedding. The total number of guests is thirty. It is a wedding in which every expense is being spared except one: Martin has a new van, complete with his shop logo.

Even this is not an extravagance. The old van failed decisively when it was put in for its service and MOT. The floor was revealed to be rotten. Years of carrying heavy books had taken their toll. It was condemned, so the new purchase had to be made. At least it should take them as far as Northumberland on their honeymoon.

In the absence of grandparents, Wendell and Bill have been included. In the care home they have reached an understanding and have grown to tolerate each other. Sarah and Lisa will bring them. This will create a frozen moment, without which no wedding is really complete. Zakk will see Bill and recognise the man who saved and abused him on the day he fled from the cult. There is, after all, not much that you can mistake about Bill. Bill, in turn, will notice Zakk staring at him and wonder if it could possibly be.... But nothing will be said between them because enough time has passed and this is not their day. Bill won't apologise and Zakk will not offer to return the money he stole.

The Goulden family will all be there, but James is the only sibling staying at the family house. Julia and Zakk will be present for the ceremony and reception, but that is all. Danny is basing himself in Leeds, with Chloe as it happens, but he has no intention of introducing her to the family. He will come to the wedding on his own. Chloe doesn't want to dampen the mood and has a day's shopping in mind. She has much to concern her. The Service is already hearing dark things about a new virus from China.

To keep the day simple there was going to be no photographer, but Izzy insisted on one professional photograph just of close family, one proper record of the day.

'That's not us,' Leah argued. 'After all, what are we? A care worker and a bookseller living off Dad's money in your house.'

Martin had to persuade Leah to agree. 'She wants a photo of Zakk, her newfound son,' he explained. 'This is her excuse.'

'Okay.' Leah gave in, but added, 'Just the one.'

So here they are outside the hotel on the front lawn.

Izzy is on Leah's immediate left. Her hair has been given permission to turn white. She's conscious that she's standing in front of her lost son. She can feel his proximity, but she doesn't turn round. She wears on her face an expression that says, I will try to accept what's happened to me. For today at least, I will hide my disappointment.

On her left is James. He's grown his hair long again, but it's as if the hair is still in mourning for his fall from grace. It has refused to regain its old lustre and hangs a little limply to each side of his face. But his head is held high and his features are set in a smile. After all, there is a camera pointing at him and he always was a performer.

Danny is on Martin's right. It's where he would choose to stand. A tiny part of him wishes Chloe was beside him, but most of him doesn't. He always felt a spare part at family events, and this is no different, but he's pleased for Leah and always grateful to Martin. He still shudders when he thinks of the way he threatened the other Patrick with a knife. What would have happened if Martin hadn't intervened? Danny is completely unconscious of the contrast in physique between him and his brother-in-law. His handsome face displays an open smile, but his eyes are somewhere else.

Zakk is standing behind his mother, looking down on the white head of the woman who gave birth to him. He owes her that. He's not wearing his hat, so Julia is clearly taller than he is. He's smartly dressed in a beige suit and is wearing a pink tie.

Julia is to Zakk's right and positioned just behind Leah. She is standing ramrod straight. She knows she can never have a day like this, but she is determined that at some stage she and Zakk will have a ceremony of their own devising. Meanwhile, she stares down at the head of her little sister, somewhat in awe of what Leah has become. She stands very close to her lover. The photographer wants to separate them a little to manage the balance in his composition. Such proximity should be the exclusive preserve of the happy couple, he thinks, but one look at Julia's face tells him not to try.

Leah, wearing a green suit over a white blouse, is standing at the front of the group next to her mother. Her hair has been styled for the first time in her life, and so far it's staying in place. Her face is happy. She's enjoying the day more than she thought she would. It's giving her certainty and she awards it her own stamp of approval with a broad smile.

Martin has his arm round her and she is clasping the hand that neatly circles her waist. He's wearing the same suit he wore to Downing Street. He's had his hair cut so the tufts are under control. He looks down with pride at the head of the young woman who is now his wife. Then, because the photographer is ready, he grins his pleasure at the camera.

Acknowledgements

I am indebted to many people for help with this novel. To Inesa Crayke for providing me with Lithuanian names and phrases. Her help has been invaluable and saved me from having to rely on the vagaries of Google translations. To Paul and Trish who read an early draft and made useful recommendations. To Peter Barnfather for design work. To the real Sarah and Lisa who have looked after my father-in-law so well. But above all to Sheila, who has read the novel several times and told me forcibly what was wrong with early drafts. As always, she has provided her excellent proof-reading service.

But a novelist has other debts. So much of what I write makes use of the stories people have told me and the things they have said. Then there are the other maleficent individuals: Donald J. Trump, Boris Johnson and Vladimir Putin, because hatred of all they stand for is an ever-powerful inspiration

About the Author

Chris was born in Hull in 1947. At the age of nine he was sent to boarding school, where at first he conformed and later he didn't. Escaping from that all-male world he enjoyed his own Prague Spring in Nottingham University, where he studied English and Philosophy spending most weekends and holidays rock climbing. On graduating he went into teaching because he thought this would give him time to write. It didn't, but he enjoyed being an English teacher at Glossop School until one day he read a line from Alan Garner's Red Shift : *Those who will not rule must be content to be ruled by others*. Realising he had never liked being ruled, he went into management and became Headteacher of Brigshaw High School in 1991 and of Huntington School in 1997, retiring in 2007 as a National Leader of Education.

Now, at last, he could concentrate on writing. His first novel *Back Behind Enemy Lines* was published by Sheil Land in 2014 and rose to No7 in the Australian best seller charts. *Girl Without a Voice* followed in 2018 and its story grew into the Long Lost Trilogy with the arrival of *Other Selves* in 2020 and *Such a Thing* in 2021. Chris's poetry collection *Walking Through* was published by Graft Poetry in 2016.

Chris is married and lives in North Yorkshire. On most Wednesdays he is to be found at the Yorkshire Arboretum where he is Tree Team Volunteer, Guide and Trustee.

Printed in Great Britain
by Amazon

68656668R00210